The
GIRL IN RED

Christina Henry

TITAN BOOKS

The Girl in Red
Print edition ISBN: 9781785659775
E-book edition ISBN: 9781785659782

Published by Titan Books
A division of Titan Publishing Group Ltd.
144 Southwark Street, London SE1 0UP

First Titan edition: June 2019
10 9 8 7 6 5 4 3 2 1

www.titanbooks.com

This is a work of fiction. All of the characters, organizations, and events portrayed in
this novel are either products of the author's imagination or are used fictitiously.

A CIP catalogue record for this title is available from the British Library.

Printed and bound by CPI Group (UK) Ltd, Croydon CR0 4YY.

For Rebecca Brewer,
because some heroines have a cupcake stash
instead of wearing a cape

CHAPTER 1

The Taste of Fears

SOMEWHERE IN AN AMERICAN FOREST

The fellow across the fire gave Red the once-over, from the wild corkscrews of her hair peeking out from under her red hood to the small hand axe that rested on the ground beside her. His eyes darted from the dried blood on the blade—just a shadow in the firelight—to the backpack of supplies next to it and back to her face, which she made as bland as rice pudding.

Red knew very well what he was thinking, what he thought he would be able to do to her. Men like him were everywhere, before and after the world fell apart, and it didn't take any great perception to see what was in their eyes. No doubt he'd raped and murdered and thieved plenty since the Crisis (she always thought of it that way, with a capital letter) began. He'd hurt those he thought were weak or that he took by surprise, and he'd survived because of it.

Lots of people thought that because she was a woman with a prosthetic leg it would be easy to take advantage of her—that she would be slow, or incapable. Lots of people found out they were wrong. Someone had found out just a short while before—hence the still-bloody axe that kept drawing the attention of the stranger who'd come to her fire without invitation.

She should have cleaned the blade, though not because she was worried about scaring him. She should have done it because it was her only defense besides her brain, and she ought to take better care of it.

He'd swaggered out of the trees and into the clearing, all "hey-little-lady-don't-you-want-some-company." He had remarked on the cold night and how nice her fire looked. His hair was bristle-brush stiff and close to the scalp, like he'd shaved it to the skin once, but it was growing out now. Had he shaved it because he'd been a soldier? If he had been, he was likely a deserter now. He was skinny in a ropy muscled way, and put her in mind of a coyote. A hungry coyote.

He didn't look sick; that was the main thing. Of course nobody *looked* sick when they first caught it, but pretty soon after they would be coughing and their eyes would be red from all the burst blood vessels and a few days after the Cough started, well . . . it was deceptively mild at first, that cough, just a dry throat that didn't seem to go away and then it suddenly was much more, a mild skirmish that turned into a world war without your noticing.

It didn't escape Red's notice that underneath his raggedy field coat there was a bulge at his hip. She wondered, in a vaguely interested sort of way, if he actually knew how to use the gun or if he just enjoyed pretending he was a man while flashing it around.

She waited. She wasn't under any obligation to be polite to someone who thought she was his next victim. He hadn't introduced himself, although he had put his hands near the fire she'd so painstakingly built.

"Are you . . . ?" he began, his eyes darting over her again. His gaze paused for a moment when he saw the gleam of metal at her left ankle, visible just beneath the roll of her pants.

"Am I what?" she asked. Her tone did not encourage further conversation.

He hesitated, seemingly thinking better of it, then gestured at his face. "Your eyes are light, but your skin is brown. You look like you're half-and-half."

She gave him her blandest glance yet, her face no more expressive than a slice of Wonder Bread.

"Half-and-half?" she said, pretending not to understand.

Red had that indeterminate mixed-race look that made white people nervous, because they didn't know what box to put her in. She might be half African or Middle Eastern. She might be a Latina or maybe she was just a really dark Italian. Her eyes were an inheritance from her father, a kind of greenish blue, and that always caused further confusion.

Their eyes always flicked up to her hair, looking for clues, but she had big fat curls that could have come from anybody. She was used to speculative glances and stupid questions, having dealt with a lifetime of them, but it always surprised her (it shouldn't have, but it did) how many people still cared about that dumb shit when the world was coming to an end.

"I was just wondering what—" he said.

"Where I come from it's not polite to start asking people about their folk before you're even introduced."

"Right," he said. The intruder had lost some of the swagger he'd had coming into the clearing in the first place.

"What are you doing out here on your own? I thought everyone was supposed to go to the nearest quarantine camp," he finally said, choosing not to introduce himself despite her admonishment.

They were not going to be friends, then. Red did not feel sad about this.

"What are *you* doing out here on your own?" she answered.

"Right," he said, shuffling his feet. His eyes darted in all directions, a sure sign that a lie was on offer. "I lost my friends in the dark. There were soldiers and we got separated."

"Soldiers?" she asked, sharper than she intended. "A foot patrol?"

"Yes."

"How many soldiers?"

He shrugged. "I dunno. A bunch. It was dark, and we didn't want to go to the camp. Same as you."

Don't try to act like we have something in common. "Did you come from the highway? Do you know which way they were headed? Did they follow you?"

"No, I got away clean. Didn't hear any of them behind me."

This sounded like something he'd made up to explain the fact that he was alone in the woods with no supplies and no companions and sniffing around her fire looking for something he didn't have.

Red sincerely hoped he was as full of shit as he seemed, because she was not interested in encountering any soldiers. The government wanted everyone rounded up and quarantined ("to safely prevent the further spread of the disease"—Red had snorted when she heard that announcement because the fastest way to spread disease is to put a whole bunch of people in tight quarters and those government doctors ought to know better) and she didn't have time for their quarantine. She had to get to her grandmother, and she still had a very long way to go.

Red had passed near a highway earlier in the day. The experience filled her with anxiety since soldiers (and people generally) were more likely to be near highways and roadways and towns. She hadn't encountered a patrol there, but she'd had a small . . . conflict . . . with a group of three ordinary people about two or three miles into the woods past the road.

Since then she'd tried to make tracks as fast as possible away from anywhere that might be populated. Red wasn't interested in joining up with a group.

She hadn't asked the coyote to sit down and join her, and it was clear he didn't know what to do with himself. Red could see the shape of what he figured would happen on his face.

He'd thought she would be polite, that she would offer to share her space with him. He'd thought she would trust him, because she was alone and he was alone and of course people were pack animals and would naturally want to herd together. Then when her guard was down or maybe when she'd fallen asleep, he'd take what he wanted from her and leave. She was not following his script, and he didn't know how to improvise.

Well, Red's mother hadn't raised a fool, and she wasn't about to invite a coyote to sit down to dinner with her. She stirred the stew over the fire and determined that it was finished heating.

"That smells good," he said hopefully.

"Sure does," Red replied. She pulled the pot off the fire and poured some of the stew into her camp bowl.

"I haven't eaten a darn thing since yesterday," he said.

Red moved the bowl into her lap and spooned a tiny bit of stew, just a mouse bite, into her mouth. It was too soon to eat it and hot, far too hot, and it scorched her tongue. She wasn't going to be able to taste anything for a couple of hours after that, but she didn't show it. She only looked at him, and waited for whatever it was that he was going to do.

He narrowed his eyes then, and she glimpsed the predator he'd tried to disguise under a charm mask.

"Where I come from it's polite to share if you've got food and someone else doesn't," he said.

"You don't say."

She spooned up some more stew, never taking her eyes from him. She was going to lose what was in the pot in a minute when he charged at her, and she was sorry for it, for she was hungry and it wasn't easy to carry those cans of stew around.

He pulled out the gun then, the one he'd been pretending not to finger the whole time.

"Give me what's in your bag, bitch," he snarled, his lips pulling back from his teeth.

Red calmly put the bowl in her lap to one side. "No."

"Give it to me or I'll shoot you," he said, waving the gun in her general direction.

He thought he was being menacing, and it made her snort. He looked like a cartoon villain in a movie, a mangy excuse for a badass—the kind that threaten the hero when he walks through an alley and get thrashed for their trouble. She wasn't dumb enough to think that he couldn't hurt her, though. Even an idiot with a gun was dangerous.

"Are you laughing at me?" His face twisted in fury as he stepped closer.

He was coming around the side where she'd rested the pot, as she'd expected. He was afraid of the axe, though he didn't want to acknowledge it, so he was giving the bloodied blade a wide berth. That was fine by Red.

"What's the matter, bitch? Scared?" he cooed. He mistook her silence for fear, apparently.

She waited, patient as a fisherman on a summer's day, until he was within arm's length. Then she grabbed the pot handle and stood as fast as she could, using her real leg and her free arm for force to push upward and tapping her other leg down only for balance once she was on her feet.

The trouble with the prosthetic was that it didn't *spring*— Red didn't have a fancy blade that could perform feats of athleticism—but she'd figured out how to compensate using her other leg. She needed to prevent the coyote from killing her for her food.

Her sudden movement arrested him, his gaze flying to the axe that he'd expected her to grab. Red could have, she supposed, stayed right where she was on the ground and embedded the blade in his thigh, but that might have resulted in a protracted struggle and she didn't want a struggle.

The goal was *not* to have a fancy movie fistfight that looked good from every angle. She wanted him down. She wanted him done. She wanted him unable to grab her.

Red flung the rest of the boiling stew in his face.

The intruder screamed, dropped his gun, and clawed at

his skin. It blistered and bubbled, and she noticed she'd managed to hit one of his eyes. She didn't want to think about how horrible that felt because it looked like something awful. Red forced down the gorge that threatened at the smell of his burning flesh. She grabbed up the axe then and swung it into his stomach.

All the soft organs under his shirt gave way—she felt them squishing beneath the pressure of the blade, and hot blood spurted over her hands and then there was an even worse smell: the smell of what was supposed to be inside your body coming out, and she did cough then, felt the little mouse bite of her dinner coming back up mixed in with bile. It stopped her throat and made her whole body heave.

But Red wasn't about to let him get up again and come after her and so she pulled the axe straight across his torso before yanking it out. It made a squelching, sucking sound as it emerged. Red wasn't accustomed to that sound yet. No matter how many times she used the axe it made her skin crawl.

The man (for that was all he was after all, just a man, not a coyote, not a hunter) fell toward her and she backed away as quick as she could, no fancy acrobatics involved. Red was not some movie superhero any more than the man was a movie villain. She was just a woman trying not to get killed in a world that didn't look anything like the one she'd grown up in, the one that had been perfectly sane and normal and boring until three months ago.

The man fell to the ground, and the blood seeped from the wound in his stomach. He didn't make any noise or twitch or anything dramatic like that, because he'd likely passed out once his brain was overwhelmed by the pain from his burn and the pain from the axe. *He might live—unlikely*, Red thought, *but he might*. He might die, and she was sorry not that she'd done it but that she had to do it.

Red didn't like to think of herself as a killer, but she wasn't about to let herself get eaten up just because she was a woman alone in the woods.

She gathered all of her things from the site, slung her pack on her back, doused the fire she'd so carefully built. She cleaned her axe as best she could with a cloth, then covered the blade and put the handle in a Velcro loop on her pants.

The gun her attacker had dropped gleamed in the faint starlight, and she reluctantly picked it up. If she left it behind, someone else might find it and that person might cause her trouble later. After all, she hadn't killed all three of the people she'd encountered earlier.

Red didn't know anything about guns except that she didn't like them. Her father had liked to watch crime television shows, and on those programs everyone seemed to know how to click the safety on and off and load the gun even if they'd never touched a weapon before. Red didn't have the faintest idea how to do any of that and she didn't want to fool with a gun in the dark. That seemed like an excellent way to shoot herself in the only organic foot she had remaining. Shoving the weapon (which she assumed was ready to fire, based on the way that fellow had been waving it around) in her pack or waistband seemed just as stupid.

Red despised holding the gun, despised everything about it, hated how cold and hateful it felt in her hand. But she held on to it, the barrel pointed away from her and her finger off the trigger, as she walked away from the place where she'd hoped to camp for the night, the place where she'd wanted to rest for a little while because her half-a-leg was weary from the quick march that morning, and now that she was moving onward again she realized just how much she'd wanted to take off her prosthetic for a while.

She was very good about removing it periodically while she walked, and drying the stump, and putting cream on it so the limb wouldn't chafe, but it was a relief to remove the contraption every night and just let her leg *be*.

The coyote *(the man)* had taken that relief from her, and now she was hungry (for she hadn't eaten her stew) and angry (for she'd had to kill him and she really hadn't wanted to) and resentful (for her leg ached and she was walking when she didn't want to be walking and she was carrying his stupid hateful gun).

Close to dawn she heard the comforting rush of water, and she angled her path toward it. As she got closer to the noise Red's progress slowed—running water attracted all sorts, including bears and other people. For the most part Red liked to avoid both if she could. Her experiences thus far had told her that one was as dangerous as the other.

She came across a handy clump of bushes to hide behind (after carefully examining them for poison ivy—she had quite enough problems without getting a rash all over her face or hands) and waited to see if there was any movement around.

The stream was about six or seven feet wide and running quickly, which meant it would be a good place to refill her water bottle. She knew well enough not to drink from standing water; she didn't know why anyone would want to anyway as it was usually covered in green scum, but probably people got thirsty and desperate and that made them do foolish things. Well, Red had seen plenty of evidence of foolish behavior before the Crisis; it was only logical there would be just as much after.

There was a filter on the bottle that supposedly kept out parasites and other things but that wasn't really what worried her. There was always the chance of a body in water, a bloated infected thing that let its infection ripple out from it, searching for another host to feed its million billion trillion children.

She knew this wasn't an entirely logical fear; the Cough that killed everyone was an airborne disease and airborne diseases didn't usually swim in water, but the virus might have mutated. It was entirely possible that it mutated, and that mutation might mean that whatever had stopped her from catching it before wouldn't protect her now.

This water was running swift, swift enough to reassure her, and she would have to take a chance with a possibly mutated virus. This was not a safe place to stop and build a fire and boil it and let it cool until it was safe to drink.

Red waited and watched for a while, just to be certain that nobody else was on the opposite bank waiting and watching. After a bit she felt her head nod forward and she jerked it back in that panicky way that you do when you realize you're falling asleep and don't want to. She widened her eyes, as if just the act of making them bigger would stave off sleep. She was tired, more tired than she'd realized, and being tired meant that she was vulnerable and that scared her, because nobody was going to keep her alive but her.

I'm being too cautious, she thought. There was nobody about for miles. The only movement she'd heard along her night-walk from the place where she'd killed the coyote *(the man, he was a man, even if he looked like a coyote, even if he looked like something whose eyes shone out of the darkness above sharp teeth)* had been the scattering of little things, chipmunks and squirrels and field mice.

She was the only person near the stream at this exact place. Yes, she needed to be careful but there was such a thing as being too careful—she'd never get anywhere at this rate. Her leg wouldn't let her walk too fast and she knew that she could only make so many miles a day—the brain was willing but at some point her body would say, *Hell, no, not another step*, and that was that. Too much caution only exacerbated her slow crawl. It was safe enough to approach the water.

The bank was steep and anything steep is always awkward when you've only got one whole leg—it didn't matter if she was going up or going down, although up was a little easier. Going down always felt like she might lose control at any second, because she felt the imbalance of her legs more acutely and when she thought too much about walking it seemed to make it more awkward.

Red slid the last couple of feet to the water and her real foot splashed in the stream and she cursed. Her hiking boots were waterproof, but her pants weren't and the water seeped through and ran down her ankle and made the top of her sock wet.

She hated wet socks—ranked them in her top three least favorite things, right after black licorice (just the thought of that anise/fennel/whatever-the-hell-it-was flavor made her nose wrinkle) and people who stopped in the middle of the grocery aisle to fool with their phones when other people wanted to shop. Though she supposed that wasn't really a problem anymore, and it was easy enough to avoid licorice.

The stream was deeper than it had appeared from her perch. Deep enough, she thought, to hide the presence of the hateful thing in her hand that she so badly wanted to be rid of. She tossed it in the center of the running water and heard the satisfying plop as it sank in. Red couldn't see the gun from where she stood, and she hoped that it went straight down for a few feet, and that no one else would find it. Or if someone ever did it would be rusted and unusable.

She crouched in the mud, reaching out with her bottle to fill it from the current, not from the muddy eddies that swirled closer to the bank. Red gulped most of the first bottle straightaway—she hadn't realized quite how thirsty she was until the first cool touch of liquid on her tongue. The scorched bit from the hot stew was still numb.

Red refilled the bottle twice more, guzzling water until it sloshed around in her stomach, and then stood—carefully, as the footing was not very sturdy this close to the water and it would be very tiresome to have to change her clothes since she only had one other pair of pants in her backpack.

Red needed to cross the stream, partly because she needed to continue heading north and partly because *if* that man who came to her fire hadn't been a total liar there might be soldiers somewhere behind her. Soldiers sometimes had dogs with them, dogs to help sniff out the infected and the uninfected alike.

She was sure that a smart, well-trained dog would have no trouble following the smell of blood on her—no matter how careful she was, some of it always splashed on her pants. Dogs could help those soldiers catch up to her a lot faster, but crossing the water would make them lose her trail.

At least that was what always happened in the movies (a good deal of Red's survival knowledge was culled from books and movies)—the hunted would swim across a river and then all the barking, baying hounds following that hunted thing would run up to the edge of the water and bark and turn in circles and the people with them would shake their head and say the dogs had lost the trail at the water.

Red would not be a hunted thing. She didn't want to be scooped up in anyone's butterfly net and pinned to a board. She was going to her grandmother's house, because she was the only person left in her family that could do so. The last time she'd talked to her grandmother (before all the telephone service, wired or unwired, stopped working), the old lady had told Red and the rest of her family to come so they could stay safe in the woods, together.

That was six weeks before, and many things had happened since then. And every day Red imagined Grandma peeking through the curtains of her cabin in the woods, watching for her family to emerge out of the trees and into the clearing.

Whenever Red thought about this her eyes would tear up, because though she *could* go on alone it was very tiring to do so and all she wanted more than anything was to have someone to lean into. Grandma was the nicest person to lean into, because she was soft and round and smelled like whatever she'd just been cooking (and she was almost always cooking).

It was impractical to walk along the bank—the mud

sucked at her shoes and made walking more of a chore than usual. She hated the idea of staying along the higher part of the bank, though, even though the footing was better. There was hardly any tree cover and she would be dangerously exposed. The way the land rose away from the stream hid her from view unless someone got close to the water.

Of course, she reflected that it also meant that any approaching person was also hidden from her. Besides, it would be easier to get away quickly if necessary from the higher part of the bank.

Weren't you just saying not to be overly cautious? She needed to stop weighing and measuring every decision like her life depended on it.

(It might, though)

Well, that was the trouble, Red reflected. Every choice could be the difference between living and dying, and it had been that way for long enough now that she'd almost forgotten what it was like to make silly choices—to watch a horror movie instead of a samurai movie, to have ice cream for dessert instead of a candy bar, to read a book instead of vacuum the floor. She almost wished for a dirty floor to vacuum just then. At least it would mean that nothing had changed.

Red went up on the high part of the bank and tried not to rub the back of her neck. It felt like someone was watching her, but whenever she glanced back there was nobody and she knew damned well that it was her imagination but she couldn't stop it.

Sometimes the more you tried not to think about a thing, the more you did, and Red had a case of what Grandma called "the heebie-jeebies." Once you got the heebie-jeebies it was hard to shake them loose. If you kept thinking there was a spider on your neck you'd keep brushing at your collar even though you damn well knew no arachnid was crawling on your spine. Or you'd keep looking behind you even when there was no evidence that you were being followed.

After she'd walked about half a mile she came to a little footbridge, one of those kinds that swung side-to-side when you walked on them—just rope and some panels tacked on at the bottom. She surveyed it doubtfully. She'd never liked these kinds of bridges even before she lost the bottom half of her left leg. There were always swinging bridges of this sort on playgrounds so certain kids could terrorize most of the others by herding them on and making the bridge shake.

Still, the bridge was the first chance of a dry crossing she'd seen, and she reasoned that at least she would be able to hang on to the ropes if she felt less-than-sturdy. If she crossed on rocks or some such thing there wouldn't be any ropes to grab onto if she felt herself falling.

She slid her real foot onto the bridge and felt the whole thing wobble as soon as her weight pressed in.

"Screw that," she said, her heart pounding as she stepped back. "Besides, what happened to shaking off the dogs? You've got to go in the water if you want to do that."

Red tried not to talk to herself because it reminded her too much that she was alone but sometimes words just fell out of her mouth, like they were trying to remind her that she could still speak.

She shrugged her pack up and down to shift the weight a little bit and decided to go on until she could find a shallow place to cross.

As she walked she started to get the so-tired-she-was-delirious feeling, the feeling that everything ached (but especially her stump, she really did need to rest it for a while) and her eyes were going to wink shut of their own volition.

Soon she would fall down on her face and pass out. It was inevitable—she was pushing herself too hard and too far and she just needed to cross the damned stream and find somewhere she could rest for a while and stop thinking, because the more she thought, the more she worried, the more she drove herself into crazy circles trying to anticipate every possible bad thing that could happen and avoid it.

"Just someplace to put my head down for a while, that's all I need," she said as she sat on the bank and pulled off her sock and shoe from her real foot and rolled up both pant legs, exposing the shiny metal tube on the left side.

The water was cold, really cold, and the shock of it startled her. The stream was deeper than it looked, even though she'd found a place where it seemed shallow. It came up to the middle of her calf instead of just above her ankle as she thought it would. Red slogged across, mindful of rocks that could trip and mud that could trap and any other thing that might go wrong.

When she reached the other side she felt much more awake because that little bit of cold water on her bare skin made her shiver all over. She hurriedly dried her foot and leg with a small towel from her pack, noting that the sun was almost exactly overhead now.

There hadn't been any sight or sound of people or animals since she'd encountered that man the night before, but she hurried away from the stream, grateful for the thicker cover of the woods on this side.

Red did not want to camp so close to the water. She continued on for another half hour or so, keeping a close eye on the shadows around her and listening for the sound of anybody else hiding in the trees.

Then it just appeared before her, almost like a hallucination summoned by her exhausted brain. A cabin. A cabin all by its lonesome, in a clearing in the woods.

For one brief moment she thought she'd somehow gotten to her grandmother's house already, that she'd walked farther than she realized in the night. Then she shook her head and recognized that this building was about a quarter of the size of her grandmother's—Grandma had a two-story with four rooms on the ground floor and a loft bedroom above, built with love and care by Red's grandfather, who always went by Papa.

This was more like a hunting shack, a one-room affair with rough-hewn logs and a small metal chimney. There were beige-colored curtains over the one window she could see, but there didn't appear to be any signs of life.

That doesn't mean anything. Someone could be asleep inside, someone with a shotgun next to his bed who'll blow your stupid head off if you knock on the door. And anyway in the movies people always get stuck in some cabin in the middle of nowhere and it seems like there's nobody around but actually there is a serial killer lurking nearby who can just fade into the trees and wait for someone to walk into his trap.

(Red, don't go thinking stupid thoughts. If there was ever a serial killer here he's probably dead from the Cough just like everyone else.)

That last bit sounded like her mama's voice, her very practical mama.

But there might be someone in there, there really might.

She found her feet moving toward the cabin anyway, even though her brain was saying, *No no no too risky.* Her legs had mutinied, taken the rest of her hostage, because her heart had seen that little cabin—rough and no doubt filthy it would be—and *longed* for it. She longed to sleep somewhere inside, under a roof instead of the open air or the thin nylon of her tiny tent.

She longed for the security of a boundary on all sides, of feeling tucked in and cozy and knowing that nobody could sneak up on her if the door was shut and locked. That was something she'd taken for granted before, before Everything Happened—the feeling of being indoors, of being *safe*.

Red couldn't let go of her caution, though—couldn't just walk right up to the door and act like she belonged there *(because there might be a guy there with a shotgun, there really might, or a killer with a machete)*. She crept toward the one window as quietly as she could, which was not very quietly because there were dry dead leaves all around the clearing that seemed as loud as firecrackers in the still air.

She peered into the interior through the little crack in the curtains but couldn't see anything except the handle of an old-fashioned metal percolator sitting on a table under the window. The rest of the cabin was too dark. So she looked closer at that percolator handle, because it was the only clue she had.

The dust was thick on the top curve of the handle, too thick to have been used by anyone recently. Which meant there probably wasn't anyone inside. Probably.

She walked all around the cabin, looking for footprints *(like you're some kind of tracker, ha, what do you even think you're looking for?)* because even if she wasn't some kind of tracker she could recognize a fresh print in the dirt if she saw one and she didn't see any around the cabin or by the door.

Having done the only safety check she could do, Red

approached the front door and tried the handle.

It was locked.

She laughed out loud then, and the laugh sounded a little crazy because she was exhausted and hungry and she'd been so concerned about a maniac with a gun that she hadn't thought of the possibility of the owner locking the door when he left his cabin at the end of last season.

And then she cried a little too, and when she heard herself doing that loony laugh-cry thing she knew she was getting hysterical and she said, "Enough."

Work the problem, Red.

That was her dad's voice, not hers—it was the thing he always said when she was stuck and frustrated. For a long time it annoyed her until she realized that he was telling her to take a breath, to step back, to consider all the options one by one. It was a marvel of brevity, actually, to say all of that with just four words.

The window was far too small to climb through, even if she could break the glass—and she didn't want to, for if she managed to get inside she wanted the window closed.

She peered all around the door, because sometimes folk kept emergency keys around in hidden places just in case. She got up on her tiptoes (and nearly fell over for her trouble, because she was balancing on just one leg) and felt around the frame at the top of the door and found nothing except a big old splinter that embedded itself in the middle knuckle of her ring finger and made her shout.

The splinter would have been nothing in the Old Days (she'd come to think of the time before everything changed this way, and just like the Crisis it was always capitalized in her head)—she would have yanked it out and maybe slapped a bandage on the wound and that would have been that. But now an infection was so much more than an infection. Not only was every open wound a potential pathway for the murderous, possibly morphing disease that had killed so many people, but without antibiotics any cut or scrape might be a killer.

Red did, as a matter of fact, have some antibiotics in her bag—a fortuitous discovery made early on in her journey—but she didn't want to use them unless she needed them. Those pills were more valuable than diamonds.

So she sat down in the dead leaves in front of the door and pulled her first-aid kit out of her pack. She carefully scrubbed her hands with an antibacterial wipe and then did the same for the tips of the plastic tweezers in the kit. The splinter came out easily, and she cleaned and bandaged the bloody hole that remained and then stuffed her kit back in her pack.

Red sighed then, not wanting to stand up. She was just so tired. She'd never known a person could be so tired before everything had happened but it was like a cloak on her all the time now, a cloak made of tired that pressed down on her shoulders and made her neck droop.

And because she was sitting down in the dead leaves she saw something she hadn't seen before—the little knot in one of the logs, just about a foot off the ground. Red took out her flashlight (solar plus a hand crank, so she wouldn't have to hunt for batteries, and one of her better ideas) and peeked inside the knot.

Four or five inches back, far enough that someone couldn't find it by accident, something bronze gleamed.

Red grabbed the key and heaved herself to her feet. As she unlocked the door she felt a surge of joy.

Inside. I can sleep inside.

The dust was thick enough to get stirred up by her feet and make her cough. She fought the impulse to slam the door shut behind her *(safe, she could be safe at least for this one night)* and instead found a broom hanging from the back of the door and swept out all the dust and opened the curtains to let in some light.

There were two cots folded in the corner and a small wooden table with two chairs and the percolator she'd seen from the window.

The chairs had metal frames and yellow vinyl seats and looked like something the owner had found in someone's garbage, but they were sturdy enough and Red supposed that anything would do if you just needed someplace to sit and eat before heading out into the woods for the day.

Next to the window were three wooden shelves, and on

the bottom one were plates and cups and bowls made of metal and painted blue with white speckles. There was an open mason jar with utensils sticking out of it and next to it a cast-iron frying pan and a big pot. There was even a camp stove and some cans of propane, which meant that she wouldn't have to go outside to build a fire.

But the shelves above were full of real treasure. Canned soups—lots of them, in lots of varieties, and just-add-water meals that were vacuum-sealed. There were packages of dried pasta and two jars of tomato sauce and even a sealed package of crunchy bread sticks, though Red figured these were probably stale. On the floor below the shelves was the best find of all—several sealed gallon bottles of water.

The first thing that disappears from stores when there's anything resembling an emergency is bottled water. People in America live in terror of going without water, a resource that is—or was—ridiculously abundant in that country. As soon as it became clear that the disease was spreading faster than anyone realized and that folks were going to have to dig in or evacuate or whatever, the cases of bottled water flew out of grocery stores like they'd sprouted wings.

On the news there had been the inevitable footage of people fighting like animals over the last few cases of water in a grocery store. Whenever Red saw this kind of thing she always wondered why the person filming hadn't tried to help or intervene instead of taking video of his fellow man at his worst.

Red could pack the dried meals in her bag when she left the next day and they wouldn't add too much weight, and while she was here she could eat pasta with tomato sauce. It seemed like an unbelievable luxury, the idea of spaghetti and tomato sauce from a jar. There was even a table to sit at, instead of crouching over a plate on the ground.

But first she unfolded one of the cots. It smelled a little musty, but what was that if she could sleep raised above the ground—the ground that seemed to seep through the bottom of a tent and into the warm lining of a sleeping bag and make everything sort of damp no matter what precautions she'd taken against it?

She closed the door and locked it—there was a lock on the knob and a bolt lock just above her eye level and the sound of the bolt clicking home was beautiful music. All around her she felt the comforting press of the walls keeping her in, and she heard no noises of little animals scuttling along or birds twittering or wind in the trees. It was silent, and she was safe.

But what if someone comes along while you're sleeping?

No, she was not going to do that again, not going to go around in circles and make herself completely insane. She was going to take off her leg—and she did, clicking the button at her ankle and pulling the artificial joint out of the socket with a happy sigh.

Red unrolled the sock that she wore over her stump and

cleaned and dried it and examined her skin for blisters or redness. The fear, always the fear with a stump was that you would Do Something that would result in having to take more of the leg off.

This was the constant threat that had hung over her in the early days after they'd amputated, and she never lost the free-floating anxiety that somehow the remaining part of the leg would get infected, that the infection would get into the bone, that there would be gangrene or necrosis and then the saw would come out and she'd lose a little bit more, and then a little bit more until there was nothing left of her leg at all.

Of course she could go on if that happened—she'd only been eight when her leg was amputated, and had now spent more of her life with a prosthetic than without. There was very little she couldn't do, and she didn't really think about it as a limitation (even if a lot of other people who looked at her with sympathetic gazes did).

But you never *really* got over that loss, she thought dreamily as she snuggled into her sleeping bag. You never stopped feeling the lack of the thing that was gone. Just like all the days she'd walked alone in the woods, and every time she'd turned to say something to her brother or her father or her mother, and found that they weren't there, even if she felt they were, that they ought to be.

CHAPTER 2

All Our Yesterdays

BEFORE

They had to get to Grandma's house. It had been decided, and Red was ready to leave, but no one else seemed to be and it was certain that she was the only one who felt any sense of urgency about it.

Adam had dithered around all morning, trying to fit everything he couldn't bear to leave behind in his pack, and their parents weren't doing a very good job of hurrying him along.

Red's brother was only home at all because his university term hadn't begun when the outbreak started and as a precaution they'd told all the students to stay home until the danger passed, thinking (correctly in Red's opinion) that a dormitory was the perfect petri dish for spreading disease—all those not-very-hygienic students crammed together in a rabbit warren of shared spaces.

But the danger never had passed. It had only gotten worse, despite quarantines and precautions and the supposed late-night efforts of desperate doctors to find and manufacture a vaccine to stop the nightmare that was rolling across the country.

Her parents, too, kept sighing over the things they had to leave behind—the photographs and the books and her mother's wedding dress and the bronzed baby shoes and other things Red kept telling them didn't matter, it was their lives that mattered, but nobody would listen to her. That's what happens when you're the baby of the family, even if you're a twenty-year-old baby.

Red's mother was already sick then, had started coughing the night before. That cough started off sounding oh-so-innocuous, like something was just stuck in her throat that she needed to get out, and she drank several cups of tea with honey and exchanged a thousand worried glances with Red's father, because they both knew what it meant and didn't want to say it out loud.

Parents, no matter what age they were or what age their children were, would always try to shield, to pretend nothing was wrong. But Red was no dummy and she knew what that cough meant, knew it meant they'd all been exposed and now they just had to wait and see if they would all catch it. Not everyone did. Some people seemed to be naturally immune.

It was a stretch to call those people lucky, as it usually meant they were the sole survivors of their family group, and it couldn't feel lucky to be the last person left to mourn your loved ones.

The strange thing, to Red's mind, was the way immunity *didn't* seem to run in families. Like if Mom survived it didn't necessarily mean her kids would, though you'd think whatever special sauce she had would get passed to the next generation. Or if there were three kids, who presumably all had similar quantities of their parents' DNA, then why did only one child survive but not the other two?

It was almost, Red thought, as if the virus were picking and choosing, like it was sentient, like it *knew* that things would be better for its long-term survival if all the hosts weren't killed off in the initial wave.

Then she would dismiss this as crazy-thinking, the product of too many apocalyptic science fiction novels and late-night horror movies.

She'd spent many nights huddled under her blankets reading far too long, unable to stop even when she needed to go to sleep. Red was paranoid about diseases, about wars, about the world coming to an end because all those books and movies told her all the ways it was possible and she knew sooner or later one of them would be right.

Her mother, who'd never read anything published later than 1900 and definitely did not think much of horror movies, had said genre fiction would rot her brain. Red could at least acknowledge that this wild theory about sentient viruses was evidence that genre fiction had multiplied her natural imagination tenfold.

Mama was an English lit professor who taught classes on Shakespeare at the little (little, which meant "prestigious and ridiculously expensive" and mostly populated by white kids from rich families) college on the other side of town. Her mother said she sometimes got sideways looks from those white kids who didn't expect a black woman teaching their Shakespeare class.

"One boy asked me in front of the class if I liked Shakespeare because it was like rap music, the rhythm of the verses," Mama said, sighing in that way that made Red know she was tired inside, in her heart rather than her body.

"What did you say?" Red asked. She wasn't surprised by the boy's remark, although she felt she ought to be. People didn't often surprise her because she always expected the worst of them. Mostly she was curious about her mother's response.

"I asked him if all white people liked country music and NASCAR," Mama said. "I shouldn't have, because he got embarrassed and squirmed around in his seat. I just lost my temper a little. There I was standing in front of the class with four degrees and this undergrad wanted to know if I fit in some mold he'd already cast for me. But he apologized to me after class, so it was all right in the end."

Mama's school didn't open up for the fall term either, for the same reason that Adam's didn't, and she never saw that boy again. Red always wondered if the boy learned anything that day—learned about making assumptions about people you didn't know based on the way they looked. Or maybe he just realized that it wasn't smart to insult the person who graded your papers.

All through late August and early September they had watched in horror as town after town and city after city was decimated by this sickness, this mysterious terror that had sprung up in several places at once without any warning. In each town just a few people were left behind, people who wandered about looking lost until they were scooped up and sent to quarantine camps.

Red and her family knew that was what happened because it was on the news—at least, until the news stopped broadcasting and every channel was nothing but those colored bars and the long continuous tone that accompanied it.

"That used to mean the end of the broadcast day, at least on some channels. Other channels just went to static after the national anthem," Dad told Red, the first time they saw it. "This was before every channel ran continuously."

"When dinosaurs roamed the earth, you mean?" she said, giving him a sideways smirk.

"Not quite as far back as the dinosaurs. Maybe cavemen," Dad said, tugging on one of her curls. "And then you had to wait for programming to start again in the morning."

"I don't think it's going to start again tomorrow," Red said, pointing the remote at the TV and clicking through channel after channel playing the same thing.

Dad sighed, and she turned the television off. Adam threw his head back and huffed at the ceiling. "I bet the electricity will go out soon, too," he said morosely.

"Well, we have the generator," Dad said.

"What good is the generator if there's no TV and no radio and no Internet?"

"Oh, I don't know," Red said. "Refrigeration, maybe? Unless you enjoy eating meat that's been contaminated with bacteria."

This comment earned her a dirty look before he left the room, which was his default response when he didn't know what to say back to her.

Red was one year younger than her brother, who'd just turned twenty-one and thought that qualified him to know everything about everything but from what she could tell just meant he understood less than ever. Hormones were probably involved in this stupidity. Red kept hoping he'd outgrow it.

Adam said from the first that there was nothing to worry about, that the government would take care of everybody, that it wasn't as bad as it seemed. It was like he was deliberately misunderstanding the way diseases spread, thinking that a few quarantines would magically make it all stop.

But the truth about quarantines was that you could never catch everyone in your net, not even if you tagged and tracked every person who'd come in contact with the Typhoid Mary. And in this case, there didn't seem to be a Typhoid Mary. Instead, pockets of sickness had just bloomed up like hideous flowers in several places at once, and then spread so fast that tracing the vectors was something like impossible.

And "the government"—well, Red had zero confidence that the government would be able to do anything. Not because it was full of bad people or there was a giant conspiracy or anything like that.

Her belief came from the fact that she could read and think and knew that the departments that address pandemics were underfunded and unprepared for the scope of the problem. She also knew that while the wheels of governing ground exceedingly fine, they were also slow as hell. By the time funding was authorized it would be too late. And it was.

So Red made her own preparations. She had been ready for hours, days, weeks before her family started to even consider leaving their home. Ever since people started falling down dying, ever since she saw the first reports of towns being quarantined and serious CDC officials making serious statements every night on the news.

The possibility of evacuation was a certainty, to her mind— whether by government intervention or by simple necessity.

Sooner or later, she'd been sure, they would have to leave.

Their home was somewhat isolated—five miles outside a small town, and bordering a stretch of wooded state land that kept their surroundings quiet and protected from the sound of the highway a few miles distant. They had no close neighbors, which was not wonderful if you needed a last-minute cup of sugar but a definite advantage when proximity meant infection.

While that isolation might have saved Red and her family from the first ravages of the disease that rolled over the country like a tornado, she expected that an army truck full of survivors would show up any day to take them to a camp, just like in those movies about the end of the world. Everyone always ended up at a government camp, ragged refugees surrounded by gun-toting soldiers in gas masks.

She had treated the memory of those movies and books she loved just like an instruction manual. Red had always liked camping, though her mother was inclined to fuss whenever they hiked. Mama seemed to think Red didn't know her own body well enough to stop if she needed to, and so Red was pleased when Mama decided Red and Adam were old enough to go backpacking without her or their father. Adam was an okay brother in at least one respect—he never asked Red one million times a day if her leg was sore or if she needed to sit down.

As soon as Red knew the End of the World was nigh she

started packing. She sorted and discarded things in her pack until it was down to just the necessities—clothes (breathable layers that could be rolled up small), food with a long shelf life, a portable water bottle with a purifier, some of those space blankets that volunteers wrapped around marathoners at the end of a race (they were lightweight and packed into a rectangle the size of a playing card box and were good for extra insulation if need be), soap (because she was not going to stink all day and all the time, and if you could only pack four pair of underwear you were going to need to wash them sometime), baby powder and skin cream (because when you have a prosthetic leg your stump gets sweaty and chafes if you walk a lot and powder and cream help and she was not getting through the apocalypse without those things, that's for damn sure) and antibacterial gel and a first-aid kit and other gear deemed vital for living.

It is astounding how much crap humans need to survive, Red thought as she packed all these things. And this was just the survival gear—she wasn't carrying photo albums or books (*okay, just two books*—the apocalypse would be a lot more pleasant with Robin McKinley along) or any of the other random junk people took with them when they didn't need it.

Red liked Godzilla movies and in the old movies there was inevitably a scene in which Godzilla would be destroying some prefecture and a person would be fleeing with literally every single thing they owned on a little cart. There would be furniture and dishes and all this other random crap, and of course a baby perched in a basket at the top of the pile like an afterthought, like, "Oh, we've got Mother's tea set packed, maybe we should bring the baby, too. We have space."

Red knew that if she was fleeing from a giant monster with nuclear breath she would not be poking along pulling a cart of furniture. She would be running like hell to the shelter farthest from the rampaging creature, which was what sensible people did when being chased by monsters.

She also would not be fleeing directly in Godzilla's path, which was another thing that always made her nuts when watching those movies. Didn't anyone ever move at a perpendicular angle away from the monster's feet? She just wanted to see one person dart to the side and wait for the creature to pass.

Red tested her go-pack until she was certain she could carry it for a long time without its weight dragging her down. When you have a prosthesis even the slightest change in weight can affect the way it fits. She knew the stump would swell a little, especially at first, and she wanted to get used to both walking and carrying. This wasn't going to be a weekend backpacking trip. She was positive this was going to be a leave-home-possibly-forever trip, even if nobody else in her family agreed with her.

Adam wondered where she was going off to on all her long walks through the woods that bordered their house, but she was going to be more prepared than prepared. She would be fit and ready to leave. Everybody knew that the highways were always jammed up when there's trouble and anyone who tried to drive was just going to have to abandon their car and walk anyway. *She* wouldn't be the one complaining that her legs hurt and her feet were sore, and she only had one foot and one and a half legs to complain about.

And besides, she didn't want to be a burden. She didn't want to slow her family down or keep them from being safe.

She decided to take one of the chef's knives from the kitchen and wrap it in newspaper, but her father caught her stuffing it inside her pack and made her put it back.

"We might well need it for that purpose in the future," he conceded when she explained why she wanted it. He didn't even roll his eyes when she said that it was for protection from thieves and murderers when they had to leave the house. She loved him a lot for that. Her dad never made her feel like a fool, even when she acted like one. "But in the meantime we are staying in the house and I need it to slice onions."

Still, Red wanted to be prepared to leave at a moment's notice, and a moment's notice meant she needed something sharp in her pack. She spent a few hours sorting through all the *stuff* that accumulated in the shed—*it seemed sometimes like the stuff was having babies or something, where did it all even come from?*—and came across a small hand axe with a snap cover for the blade. And that was even more perfect because an axe was good for more than just protecting herself from those who would try to hurt her. She could chop wood for a fire or use the blunt end as a hammer if she needed.

Once everything was arranged just the way she wanted it, she put the pack on her back and refused to so much as step into the bathroom without it. Wherever she went it was with her. When she sat down in the dining room to eat she slung it to the floor beside her chair (ignoring Adam's rolled eyes and her parents' exchange of glances—Red knew what they thought but she didn't care).

She was ready for anything and she wasn't going to be the one caught unawares, and damn Adam if he thought he was going to share the food in her pack just because he couldn't be bothered to get ready for the world ending.

Red hated it, absolutely hated it, when she was reading a story or watching a movie and the thing a character needed the most was left behind. Like when the protagonist was in danger and he always carried a gun with him but at just the wrong moment he put the gun down on the edge of the counter and turned his back.

At that point she would start screaming the house down that the bad guy was RIGHT BEHIND HIM PICKING UP THE GUN and sure enough the camera would show the barrel rising behind the character's head and she would pound the armrest in frustration while all the people around her said "shush."

That was why she never went anywhere without the pack. She knew if she left it downstairs while she went up to her bedroom then Something Would Happen (a bomb, a fire, a sudden invasion of zombies) that would require her to leap from her bedroom and escape into the forest and her pack would be left behind in the living room and she would die starving in the woods.

Folk in town gave her funny looks when she went to the pharmacy or the grocery store with a huge pack and sleeping bag on her back, but then they gave her funny looks anyway because of the color of her skin and because of her leg so that wasn't anything new and exciting.

If someone she knew and liked asked about it she just said she was getting ready to do a thru-hike, like when people got it in their heads to walk the whole Appalachian Trail, and then they would exclaim about how exciting it was and that they hoped she had a good trip.

The Cough hadn't come to their little town yet at that point, and those first few weeks when panic was springing up in every urban area it seemed the virus might pass them by. Life just went on like nothing exceptional was really happening in the world, even though a big city about a hundred miles south of them had been hit hard already. Most people seemed to think that it was perfectly normal that Red would be planning a camping vacation.

Really, Red thought, *it's like they don't know what's*

happening outside town. Do they think anyone will be going on vacation any time soon?

But every time she would smile and say thank you and go about her business, secure in the knowledge that if she had to run for her life at that very moment she would not die of exposure in the wilderness.

Red thought she had everything all figured out. But she'd forgotten one thing, the most important factor in all those apocalypse books and movies that she loved so much; it was never the Event—illness, asteroid, nuclear war, whatever—that was the problem. It was what people did after. And people always reduced to their least human denominators when things went bad.

CHAPTER 3

Toil and Trouble

Her name wasn't really Red, of course. Christened Cordelia by her Shakespeare-loving mother, she only answered to Red. Her dad gave her that nickname, and once she heard it no one would get a response if they called her Delia.

Her very first babysitting-money purchase was a bright red hooded sweatshirt with a zip up the front, and she earned that sweatshirt because the deLuccis had four boys between the ages of two and eight and that job was as awful as it sounds.

Once her dad saw her in it he said she looked just like Red Riding Hood. She'd been looking for an excuse to ditch her name for at least a year (it's not easy being a Cordelia in a classroom full of Ashleys and Jessicas and Madisons—she always lamented that if Mama wanted to give her a Shakespearean name, why couldn't her mother have named her something beautiful, like Juliet?), and she'd never been without a red sweatshirt since. Cordelia was her name, but Red was who she was.

Mama always wrinkled her nose when anyone called her Red (the same way she wrinkled her nose at Red's reading material and scary movies). She tried for a long time to get Red to acknowledge the name she had chosen, but there is no one more stubborn than a teenage girl, so after a while her mother decided it wasn't her hill to die on.

If Mama was talking to someone else—like, say, her father—she would always refer to her as Delia, though. This was her mother's way of showing Red that she hadn't one hundred percent won the battle. Red was sure Mama hoped she would grow out of it. But she never did. At least, not before her mother died.

Grandma—Dad's mother—lived about three-hundred-odd miles away. Those were road miles, miles on smooth pavement with rest stops, and the only conflict was what they would listen to on the radio (NPR, always, which was probably inevitable when your parents were college professors, and that made Red eternally grateful for the existence of personal headphones). When it was pretty clear that a lot of people were dead or dying, and that if they didn't move along they were going to get scooped up in a government net and sent to one of the quarantine camps, they had a family conference.

"Let's go to Grandma's house," Red said. "She's alone in

the woods, her cabin is far away from everything, and we can go through state or federal land for a good part of the trip, which means we can avoid the roads."

"I've never seen anyone so paranoid about roads," Adam said. "What do you think is going to happen if we go on the roads? We'll get chased by Ringwraiths?"

Adam hadn't actually read *The Lord of the Rings*, just watched the movies, so this reference irritated Red because she hated it when he pretended to know things he didn't know anything about.

"Ever heard of roadblocks? If you want everyone in a certain area to go to a central location like oh, say, a *camp*, then you set up personnel on all the roads and catch people when they drive up to you," Red said. "Or how about traffic jams? Have you ever watched the news when there's a hurricane or something and a bunch of people are trying to leave a city? The roads get backed up. There are accidents."

"We don't live in a city," Adam pointed out. "We live in a backwater college town where seventy-five percent of the population is only present during the school year, and the school year never started. Last time we were in town half the stores were closed, which means most people have either left or they're sick already. I doubt the roads are going to be backed up."

"Right, because no road we travel on will ever cross with another road or meet up with a large population center," Red said, rolling her eyes.

"That's enough," Dad said, rapping his knuckles on the table.

Dad was tall and thin all over, from his long bony legs to the blond hair slowly disappearing from the top of his head. He had greenish-blue eyes, just like Red, and he didn't seem like the authoritative type, but when he said stop, Red and Adam stopped, and it didn't matter that they weren't little kids anymore. "We are going to have to walk. I think that's pretty clear."

Adam huffed. "Really? You're going to believe all the nonsense she reads in her books?"

"No," Dad said. "I'm going to believe the evidence of my own eyes. We've already seen those traffic jams on the news. And lots of people probably abandoned their cars when they got sick. If anything, we want to stay as far away as possible from people—dead or alive—who might be infected. There won't be a lot of folks heading into the woods, and Red's right about one thing—there is a lot of state land between here and Mom's cabin. If we plan carefully enough we can stay well away from roads and populated areas."

"But that will take forever!" Adam said.

"Quit whining," Red said. Adam acted younger than she did most of the time. She had read somewhere that it took longer for boys' brains to mature than girls' brains, which explained a lot. Still, knowing why he acted that way didn't mean it was any easier to tolerate him.

"But, Frank," Mama said. "What about Delia's leg? How long can she really walk? It's hundreds of miles."

"Don't talk about me like I'm not in the room, Mama," Red said. "Anyway, I can make the walk better than you can, probably. I've been training."

"But perhaps we should take the car part of the way—don't interrupt me, Delia—so that you don't have to go as far on your leg. Yes, I know you've been training and walking around with that crazy backpack for weeks, but you just don't know what kind of effect all that exertion will have on you."

"It's my leg," Red said. "It's attached to my body and I know better than you what I'm capable of."

"Don't be rude to your mother," Dad said.

Red wasn't trying to be rude, but this was the worst part of being an amputee. She could deal with the fatigue and the swelling and the stares and the unbelievably rude questions from strangers. What she couldn't deal with was people who were not amputees acting like they knew what was best for her, and yes, that included her family.

Even though she'd lost part of her leg years and years ago, her mother would still sometimes look at the prosthetic leg with big welling eyes and wipe away a tear.

Red didn't cry over her lost leg. What was the point? But Mama did, like crying might magically make her daughter whole.

The second worst thing was when people said dumb shit

like, "You're so brave." Red didn't think getting hit by an idiot who was looking at his cell phone instead of the road while he was driving made her more brave than anyone else.

Besides, what else was she supposed to do? Refuse her fake leg?

She'd chosen the leg because she thought (even at the age of eight) it gave her the most mobility, and the lowest possibility of sympathetic glances (when she wore pants the prosthesis was covered, and only her limp gave her away). Sympathy made her back teeth grind.

"I'm not trying to be rude to Mama. I am telling you that I am just as capable as you are," Red said. "And after all these years you should know that."

"I am not saying that you're not capable, just that you might get tired. I don't think you should dismiss my concerns just because they don't fit your view of yourself," Mama said, her eyes narrowed.

"Stop treating me like half a person," Red said. "I am missing my leg below the knee. My brain is still functioning. I know what I can do and what I can't."

"I said, don't talk to your mother that way," Dad said, but it was like he wasn't in the room because Red and Mama were in the Death Stare Zone and nothing and nobody came between them in that place.

"Delia, you persist in thinking you are normal—" Mama began.

"I *am* normal," Red said.

"I don't think reading that much science fiction makes you normal," Adam said.

"Stay out of it, Adam," Red said.

"Yes, Adam, stay out of it," Mama said. "Delia knows everything already, so why should adults who care about her try to tell her anything?"

"I'm an adult, too."

"Then act like one. What if your stump gets blisters from all that walking? What if you get an infection? I'm not talking about this terrible disease," she said, gesturing toward the window and the nebulous millions. "I'm talking about a regular bacterial infection. The kind that can get in your body through an open wound and kill you. There won't be any ambulances or emergency rooms out there."

"You can get an infection, too, you know," Red said. "You could trip over a rock and cut your hand open and get just as infected as your poor crippled daughter."

Mama sucked in her breath between her teeth, because Red had used the C-word—the word that had been forbidden since the day she came home from the hospital.

"You are not a cripple," Mama said.

"You say that, but you don't act like it," Red said.

She hated the way her mother could make her feel like a little child, the way only Mama could make tears clog up her throat and her hands form helpless little fists.

Red shouldn't have stayed home and attended her parents' college. She knew that—she'd been accepted at better universities than Adam (much better, actually, and she'd been very mature about not rubbing it in his face, no easy task when she'd been seventeen) because her grades had been outstanding—but she'd been worried about them being alone.

Her parents were older than most of her peers' parents—Red's mother hadn't had Adam until she was thirty-eight—and while they were hardly feeble they were approaching the age when little things started going wrong and getting more difficult. Red's father took pills for his blood pressure, and Mama seemed to tire more easily. It was just part of aging, nothing especially unique about it, but Red had worried about the two of them in that house so far out of town, especially when winter came and their quarter-mile driveway would need to be plowed before anyone could even run to the grocery store for milk.

It had been easy for Red to say she would take her degree at the place where they were both on the faculty, and let them think it was because she still needed them to take care of her when it was actually the other way around.

Unfortunately, that meant that she'd never outgrown her childish relationship with them, never established herself as an independent adult. And so Mama persisted in thinking Red was, well . . . if not helpless, then certainly not entirely capable. Never mind that Red did most everything around the house and ran almost all the errands, too, and all while maintaining a 3.8 GPA. Not that her GPA would ever mean anything again, she realized. Nobody needed a good GPA when the world was ending—or if not ending, then at least changing beyond all recognition.

So the two of them narrowed their eyes at each other across the table because one of them believed Red was still a baby and the other knew she wasn't.

"Enough with the deep freeze, you two," Dad said, frowning. "Whether or not Red can make the journey is irrelevant."

"I can—" Red began, but Dad held up his hand.

"It doesn't matter if you *can*, because you'll have to. And so will I, and your mother, and Adam. And one thing Delia's right about, Shirley—she's in better shape than any of us for a long walk."

Mama cut her eyes away from Red and to her father in a way that made Red think there would be more Words later on the subject in the privacy of their bedroom. And sure enough, late that night, Red heard the rolling music of their argument from the room down the hall, the way their voices rose in frustration and then hushed again when they realized they were getting too loud.

So it was decided that they would walk, but nobody was as prepared as Red was to leave, and so it was also decided (over

Red's strenuous objections, because she wanted to *go* now that going had been decided upon) that they would depart three days from that first family meeting. In the meantime, Mama started coughing.

Red knew exactly when it happened, when her mama got sick, almost down to the minute. There was plenty of food— mostly in cans, but other shelf-stable things like granola bars and whatnot—in the pantry. Living outside of town instead of in it meant that they kept their house better-stocked than most—you never knew when a snowstorm might keep you from the grocery store for a few days.

They also had plenty of that most precious of emergency resources, bottled water, for the same reason. But what they—meaning Red's mother and father—did not have was appropriate footwear or clothing for such a long hike.

When Red and Adam were young, Mama had occasionally gone camping with them, but she'd given it up by the time Red was ten. And while Dad still enjoyed a walk in the woods, he usually wore sneakers while doing it and it had been quite a while since he'd carried a pack full of gear. They both needed sturdy waterproof boots and rain shells and sleeping bags. There was a sporting goods store in town that carried all of those things, and so it was proposed that they take a trip to acquire them.

"No way," Red said, when Dad announced that they were all piling into the car for this purpose.

Dad just looked at her with that patient way that he had, and waited for the explanation.

"As Adam pointed out yesterday, more than half the stores were closed last time he was in town—what, two weeks ago?" Red said. "That means there's been an outbreak here too—we've just been lucky enough to avoid it. I don't think it's a good idea to go into population centers unless we absolutely have to."

"I can't hike in my sensible three-inch heels, Delia," Mama said.

"Well, you shouldn't start such a long walk wearing shoes you haven't broken in, either," Red said. "You were worried about me getting blisters. If you try to hike three hundred miles in new hiking boots you will *definitely* get blisters."

"Okay, fair point," Dad said. "But we still need sleeping bags and rain gear and packs to carry it all in."

"What about your old stuff?" Red asked. "Isn't it in the attic?"

"We sold all that on Craigslist a few years ago," Mama said. "It was just taking up space in there."

Red refrained from asking why they had sold useful things, like camping gear, but left so much random crap (like her little red wagon from childhood and three different models of lawn mowers, only one of which actually worked) in the shed outside. That wasn't the point, really. The point was to keep them away from town. If they went into town they might be infected.

"The whole point and purpose of this plan is to avoid large groups of people and places where there might be infection," Red said.

"I understand what you're saying, Red, but we're not remotely prepared for this. We aren't like you," Dad said. "We aren't even like Adam, who at least has camping gear."

"What if there are government soldiers there?" Red said. "Sweeping the area for survivors to take to one of their quarantine points?"

"So what?" Adam said. "Then we go to the quarantine. I'd rather go to a camp than on this loony trip through the woods to Grandma's house, anyway."

"You'd rather be imprisoned by the government in a place that is a breeding ground for illness instead of walking free and healthy?" Red asked.

"We're not going to make it, anyway," Adam said. "We'll get about twenty or thirty miles or so and then one of us won't be able to walk anymore, and when we stop for the night some platoon will see our fire and pick us up anyway. Let's just skip the long hike and go straight to camp."

"We already decided, Adam," Dad said, frowning at him. He held up his hands to Red. "And it's already been decided that we're going to town to get the gear we need, Red. If you and Adam want to stay here and avoid possible infection you can do that, but Mama and I must go."

"I don't think we should be separated," Red said

immediately. That was another thing that always happened in stories. People were always like, "You wait here while I go check out some meaningless thing two miles away," and guess what? They never came back and then their party would have to go on a foolish search that would endanger everyone.

Red knew that if Mama and Dad went into town alone, they wouldn't return. Something Would Happen. But if they all stayed together, then everyone would be perfectly fine. Those were the Apocalypse Rules, and Red was going to abide by them until they were all delivered safely to Grandma's doorstep.

It never occurred to Red that Grandma wouldn't be there when they arrived. Even though hundreds, maybe thousands, of people were dying every day, it seemed impossible to contemplate Grandma dying from the thing that was killing everyone.

Grandmas didn't die from stuff like that. Grandmas went on and on, enduring year after year, shriveled and worn but somehow ageless. Grandmas outlived grandfathers and after they grieved they just rolled up their sleeves and got on with it. Grandmas knew how to do everything (except maybe with their smartphones—they would need a little help there but in this new world smartphones were just garbage anyway, so that meant grandmas were now without flaw) and get through any crisis. So of course Grandma would be there at the end of the road.

And Red was going to do her damnedest to make sure all four of them got there, too, whatever the odds might say.

But her father insisted that they drive into town. And of course town was where Mama got sick.

One of the many things Red had managed to acquire early on in the Crisis was a pack of surgical masks and another of vinyl gloves. She'd ordered them online and had them shipped to the house long before the local pharmacy ran out of them. Before they climbed into the car for that ill-advised trip into what Red thought of as the Contagion Zone, she handed one of each item to her family members with all the solemnity of a priest handing out the host.

"Don't roll your eyes at me, Adam," Red said. "You are an idiot, but I don't want you to die. So put the damn mask on."

"You really think this flimsy thing is going to help?" Adam asked, giving the mask a doubtful glare as he held it in front of his face.

"It's an airborne disease, isn't it?" Red said. "At least, the CDC sounded pretty sure that it is. I suppose it's possible that it mutated."

"Into the *Thing from Another World*!" Adam said in his best horror-movie-announcer voice.

"The mask can't hurt," Dad said, in that deceptively mild tone that meant Adam ought to listen.

Adam put the mask on.

Mama also gave her mask an uncertain look but she put it on without complaint, carefully arranging her hair around the elastic band. Red was very tempted to make a remark about no one caring what her mother's hair looked like, but she bit her tongue because there was still a little frost in the air between them and she wanted things to thaw instead of escalating to polar vortex.

Besides, Mama had always been sensitive about her hair. She always stroked Red's smooth fat curls with longing, repeating a thing that Red hated to hear—that she had "good hair." Mama's hair was kinky—if she let it grow out like Red's she would have a proper Pam Grier Afro, and Red thought it was gorgeous.

But Mama, she didn't like it. She wanted it straight and smooth, the exact opposite of everything that she was born with. So she subjected herself to chemical treatments and salves and oils and smoothers and watched vigilantly for a hint of frizz. She took great pride in her appearance generally, and a little thing like a worldwide pandemic wasn't going to result in lowered standards.

Despite the fact that the whole family was together as they should be, Red couldn't shake her trepidation as the car coursed slowly along the winding back roads. Her father always obeyed the speed limit, even when her mother sat gnashing her teeth beside him (Mama was well known by the local police as a lead-foot driver), even now when there was no one around to enforce that speed limit.

Red peered out the window at the other houses sprinkled along their route. Most of them were set far back from the road as her own home was, and so it was hard to tell if there was anyone left alive inside them. She was genuinely surprised to see no abandoned cars along the side of the road. Yes, they lived in a fairly isolated area but she'd expected some sick people to try to leave town and have to stop because they were unable to drive. But there was no evidence of that.

As they got closer to town she noticed that more of the houses had no cars in their driveways, and a few of them had broken windows. Red assumed that survivors were looting for whatever was available—food, medicine, blankets. It was understandable, because people just wanted to survive. But it was also sad, sad to see someone's castle broken open and violated, sad to see doors hanging drunkenly from their hinges or possessions strewn on the lawn. Photographs might not be useful if you were looking for food, but there was no reason to throw them around and break them, in Red's opinion. There were plenty of ways to get what you needed without being a destructive jerk.

The number of houses increased, signaling the approach of the town proper, and with that increase came more signs of destruction, of chaos, of panic. It had been a couple of weeks since any of them had come this far, and it was difficult not to be surprised by just how much had changed.

At that time many of the businesses were closed up and several houses had appeared empty, but there was no sense of end-of-the-world-type panic—just an unusual hush that came from lack of cars and folks moving around the same space. The grocery store had still been open then, and while things were pretty picked over a general sense of decency had reigned—nobody taking the last ten gallons of milk for themselves, nobody punching anyone out for a case of water. This was a small town, after all, and in small towns everybody knew everybody. No one wanted to behave badly and be reported for this behavior to a neighbor.

So it was startling to see furniture dragged into the street where it had been set on fire, and clothing tossed all along the sidewalk. It was a shock to see broken bottles everywhere, and rusty stains along pavement that could only be blood.

Then they saw it.

In point of fact they smelled it before they saw it—a deep, gut-wrenching reek that seeped through the closed car windows and the masks they wore over their mouth and nose. It smelled like gasoline and burnt fat, like the flare-ups on a barbecue when the meat was dripping.

Mama pointed and said, "What in the name of heaven is that?"

They could see a large pile of . . . something . . . blocking the center of the street. With the sun behind it the pile was just a big black shadow, not a uniform hill but a messily stacked pyramid, one with trailing edges and uneven sides. It was tall, though, for all of that—if not a story high then close to it. Dad slowed the car down and came to a stop maybe forty or fifty feet away from it.

"Should we get out and see what it is?" Adam asked.

He sounded scared, a thing Red rarely heard from him. Adam was all bravado all the time, had been like that since he was twelve or thirteen, and he had been very unconcerned about almost everything that had happened since the Crisis began. In fact, the only thing that had resulted in something like panic from him had been the lack of reception bars on his smartphone.

"I suppose we ought to," Dad said, his voice full of the reluctance that he clearly felt. "We have to get around it to get to Hawk's in any case."

"We don't have to keep going forward," Red said. "We can turn around and head home and figure out your supplies from what we have there. I'm sure we can pull something together."

Mama and Dad looked at each other. Dad's mouth twisted. "I wish it were so, Red, but our reasons for coming here are still valid."

"What if the sporting goods store has been looted?" Red said, with a trace of desperation.

She didn't want her mother to get out and see what was out there, not up close. She didn't know why it was so important that Mama not see this, but it was. Her mother was sensitive, though she pretended not to be. Even though they'd all sat together watching people be terrible to each other on television (until the TV had gone off forever) this was somehow different. It was close-up. It was real, not separated from them by the glass of the television and the glare of the camera. And it wouldn't be good for Mama to see it. It just wouldn't.

"I guess I'll leave the car here," Dad said.

He sounded uncertain, which was not like him at all, and Red didn't like that this one little jaunt into town had already made two of her family members act in ways not like themselves.

"Turn the car around before we get out," Red said.

Dad looked over his shoulder at where she sat in the backseat just as she always had since she was a child. All four of them were in their prearranged positions—Dad driving, Mama beside him, Red behind Mama, Adam behind Dad. Boys on one side and girls on the other, because Adam had wanted it that way when he was five and they'd never gotten out of the habit.

Her father looked like he wanted to ask why, then changed his mind. Instead he did a quick three-point turn so the nose of their SUV faced the way they'd just come.

For one wild moment Red wondered if she told Dad to keep driving back to the house if he would just do what she said. The sight of the thing in the street had clearly shaken him. But she didn't think she could get away with two direct orders in a row. He was still Dad, and in a minute he would remember that.

He pulled the key out of the ignition and they all climbed out of the car at the same time, like they were following the steps of a dance. Red slung her pack over her shoulders and closed the car door behind her. Now they all faced the obstacle in the street and the smell outside the car was far worse than that inside and the masks might keep out free-floating disease but they didn't keep out the stench.

They walked forward, again without speaking, because they all knew that they had to get past the Thing in front of them and there was no point in dawdling when an unpleasant task had to be done.

Red had a feeling they all also knew just what it was that they were looking at, but no one wanted to say it out loud.

After about twenty feet of walking it was clear what it was anyhow, and there was no more pretending that it wasn't awful.

Someone—or several someones, probably—had dragged a bunch of people into the street just inside the town line and piled them on one another and set them on fire. There were charred skeletons in the middle, where the fire had been hottest or burned longest, but the bodies around the bottom and outside still appeared mostly like people, people who'd been singed around the edges, their eyes wide and staring.

(Red thought: *I hope they were dead first, I really do. I hope they died quietly in their homes and were not subjected to the terror of a fire just because they were coughing and someone was trying to do a half-assed cleanup by burning all the sick people. Because that would mean that things were much worse here than even I thought, and I can always imagine the worst.*)

It made her worry, and made her wonder. Wonder and worry about just who had done the stacking and burning, and where those people were now. Her eyes darted all around, searching for suspicious movement in upper stories. It couldn't be possible that everyone was gone from the town.

Somebody would be lingering—maybe because they were sick, or because they were afraid to leave. Somebody would have witnessed whatever terrible event happened here.

Then Mama made a choking sound, that sound that you make when you're about to throw up and you don't want to but it's going to happen anyway. She bent double, and it was just the stink getting to her, Red knew that, but then Mama did the thing she *absolutely should not* have done. She reached behind her and pulled at the elastic binding around her hair and took off the mask.

"No!" Red said, but it was too late. Mama dropped the mask to the ground beside her as she fell to her knees.

Dad reached for her, holding her shoulders as she retched. "It's okay, Shirley, it's okay."

Red raced to her mother's side and picked up the mask. *It might not be too late*, she thought. If Mama put the mask back on right away she might not get sick. Of course Mama didn't want to throw up inside it, that made perfect sense (the thought of puking inside a medical mask was really too horrible to contemplate, in Red's opinion), but why hadn't she at least kept it over her nose?

"It's all right," Dad said, rubbing between Mama's shoulder blades. "Just take deep breaths."

"No, no," Red moaned. "Don't take deep breaths."

But nobody was listening to her then, and she sat watching helplessly as her mama—her brilliant and beautiful and difficult mama, they didn't always see eye to eye but they loved each other for all of that—took deep breaths in an attempt to stop the vomiting.

And with every rise and fall of her mother's chest Red could practically see the plague that had killed so many people rushing into her mother's mouth and nose, cheering with delight at having found a new victim.

But maybe not, Red thought. Maybe there was no sickness in the air, because everyone who was sick had been burned in the fire and all their little microbes had been burned with them.

But Red knew better, she really knew better, she might not be a doctor but she was so paranoid about germs that she knew you could never get rid of all of them. There were always a few that survived, the hardiest of them all, and they would reproduce and make hardier children.

Or maybe the germs were invading her mother's lungs (throwing a party on the way down, infecting every bronchus and bronchiole they passed) but it wouldn't matter because Mama would be one of those people who were immune to the disease.

(But if Mama carried it then Daddy might get sick)

This was a very little-girl thought, and she recognized it as such, because she hadn't called him Daddy for ten years or more.

(Or Adam)

She didn't want her brother to get sick, either, even if he was a pain in the ass. But available statistics promised that if one member of a family carried the germ, then most of them would catch the sickness and die.

Which was why Red wanted them to stay home in the first place. Which was why she wanted them to wear the masks. Which was why she sat there feeling free-form panic as she watched her mother breathing in the diseased air that would eventually kill her.

It didn't make her feel any better later, when they were home, and the next day her mother started coughing. It didn't make Red feel any better because she'd been right about the risks and nobody listened to her.

Mama did stop retching, and she did put the mask back on, but Red knew it was just a sop to make her feel better.

They carefully skirted the pile of bodies and went on to the sporting goods store.

Their town had a proper, old-fashioned main street, though it seemed more of the local businesses were replaced with national franchises every year. The students who attended the college seemed to prefer it that way, having a Subway and a Starbucks and a Chipotle at hand, although they also kept the local vegan restaurant in the black with their (in Red's opinion, strange) enthusiasm for farro and wheat berries and homemade veggie soups.

Every shop that Red's family passed had been broken into and picked over. It looked, Red thought, like the concerted action of a gang rather than the disparate efforts of a few. And she was feeling worried about this, feeling troubled that there might be a pack of wolves about waiting to gobble them up. She felt her eyes move unconsciously again, darting all around and searching for the people that she knew must still be lingering, but there was nothing.

There was nothing and no one and no noise and *that* was the thing she realized was bothering her—the lack of noise. It wasn't just the obvious—no people bustling around, no cell phones ringing, no cars rumbling in the road. It was the loss of that background buzz that most people never noticed when it was there, the omnipresent hum of lights and electric wires. Without it the air seemed too big, too empty. And all of that empty space might be filled by floating death, tiny little germs in search of a new host.

The condition of Hawk's Sporting Goods was no surprise to them after seeing the rest of the town. Of course the windows were broken, the contents (normally kept so precise and orderly by the owner, Andy "Hawk" Hocholowski) spilled all over the floor in a seeming orgy of unnecessary destruction.

They could have climbed in through the broken display windows, but Adam opened the front door anyway. The lock was pried open but the bell above the door rang cheerfully as they pushed inside.

Red automatically looked for Hawk behind the counter, expecting to see him there with his familiar blue flannel shirt (he only wore blue ones, in various patterns and combinations but there was always blue) and his half-smile, half-frown. He was a curmudgeon by nature, not naturally friendly, but he was loaded with knowledge and wanted to share it, so he'd opened the store so he could do that.

"And also," he told Red once, "because I spent enough time in the military to like the idea of nobody giving me orders."

Of course Hawk wasn't there, and Red wondered if he was one of the charred skeletons piled helter-skelter in the center of town, or if he'd died quietly in his upstairs apartment, or if he'd managed to escape and was off camping in the woods somewhere, waiting for it all to pass.

She hoped it was the latter, and that they would see him on the way. Red wasn't a natural joiner, but she liked the idea of bumping into Hawk and having him in their little band.

When she'd first gotten her prosthetic leg she'd felt like an alien, like the whole world had put a spotlight on her. She went into the ice cream shop with her mother to get a cone after the first fitting and Mary Jane, the two-thousand-year-old proprietress (she wasn't really two thousand, of course, but she seemed that way when Red was eight—just kind of infinitely old the way some old people are, like they'd always been that old even when they were young) had given Red a giant sundae instead of the small cone she ordered, with whipped cream and chocolate sauce and a cherry on top and firmly told her mother, "No charge."

Red knew that sundae was a kind gesture, that it was supposed to make her feel good, but all it did was make her feel worse knowing that Mary Jane felt sorry for her. She felt nauseated the whole time she was eating that sundae, choking it down over the bile that rose every time she thought of the too-kind gaze Mary Jane gave her. She didn't taste a bite of that ice cream, but she ate it all the same and said thank you and smiled as she was supposed to when it was done, and when Mary Jane asked if she enjoyed it Red lied and said, "It was the best sundae I've ever had."

After that they went in the sporting goods store to get Red a new pair of sneakers (her right foot had grown, even if her left foot never would again) and when they went into the store Hawk looked up from the counter with that familiar half-smile, half-frown like his face didn't know what it wanted to do with itself.

He limped around the counter to meet them and he stopped in front of Red and without another word rolled up his right pant leg and she saw the shiny gleam of metal there. Her eyes snapped up to his bright blue ones and he winked at her. Then he rolled his pant leg down and said, "What can I do for you ladies?"

She hadn't known until that day that he had an above-the-knee prosthesis, the product of an IED he'd encountered in a sandy country overseas, because he always wore cargo pants that covered him from hip to ankle. But when he'd rolled up those pants to show her his false leg, he made her feel better than a dozen ice cream sundaes could have.

The store register had been smashed repeatedly, probably with a big hammer, and all the cash removed. Red thought this was dumb, because what good was money in a world like this? It was just bits of green paper.

The vandals had left behind things that were useful, and so the family collected up sleeping bags for Frank and Shirley and new raincoats and backpacks and flashlights and other things that Red pointed out that they needed.

"I don't know if I can carry all of this, Delia," Shirley said, looking doubtfully at the large pack that Red handed her.

There were a lot of things Red felt she could say at that moment, things like *You're going to have to if you want to survive* or *How do you expect to get to Grandma's house without proper gear?* or *Maybe you won't have to if you got sick when you took your mask off,* but she didn't say any of those things.

She only patted her mother on the shoulder and said, "You can, Mama."

And her mother dropped the pack and hugged her then, hugged her so tight, and Red held on to her because she knew Mama was sick and she wasn't going to make it.

CHAPTER 4

Hide Your Fires

AFTER

Red dreamed, though not of the coyote. She'd expected to see his eyes gleaming at her across the fire, to feel the wet slickness of his blood on the blade of her axe. When she settled into the cabin for the night she wasn't so foolish as to believe that four walls could protect her from bad dreams. Bad dreams were a given.

But there was no coyote lurking in the darkness. Instead, she remembered the crossroads—the reason her axe had dried blood on it when the coyote came to her fire.

It was a place she'd dreaded for several days. The very fact of it had loomed in her mind as she approached it. There was no way around it, which sucked, because it was on her top five list of Places to Avoid in an Apocalyptic Situation.

It was an interstate highway.

Before three quarters of the population started dying

from a disease that no one had ever seen before, highways were a modern marvel, though most people didn't think of them that way. Flat straight roads that crossed state lines, with restaurants and toilets and hotels at prescribed intervals? Miraculous. Without them interstate shipping would never have been possible, nor even the concept of the cross-country road trip. Sure, they were also the source of accidents and miles-long traffic jams, but interstate highways connected America in a way that nothing else could.

But Red knew that, since the advent of the Crisis, a highway could only mean DANGER. And that was the way she thought of it, too, in all capital letters.

Most people would prefer to stay on highways, whether they were walking or in cars, because they were nice clear demarcated lines that could take them from point A to point B. There was no bushwhacking or messing about trying to use a compass. That meant that any living people around would be on or near the highways, and Red was trying very hard to avoid people.

Highways would also be littered with abandoned cars, and abandoned cars meant not only the presence of infected bodies but also obstacles that predators could use to hide and then scoop up prey. If you were the kind of person who wanted to steal and rape and murder, then a highway was nothing more than a feeder tube for man's worst instincts.

Even if there weren't any creepy killers around, the

possibility of a military roadblock was very strong. And since the military often had dogs, just approaching their vicinity was risky.

Red did not want to cross the highway. There were so many strong reasons not to do it.

But it was a highway, which meant that it ran straight across her path. There was no avoiding it without walking hundreds of miles out of her way.

It wasn't even that easy to approach the highway without revealing her presence. The trees that hid her from sight ended about forty feet before the road began.

Red hovered in the shade of those trees, wishing they would get up and move with her like a herd of Ents. Ahead of her there was a stretch of scrubby yellow grass, not tall enough to hide her but high enough to carry ticks. Red hated ticks, and with all the woods-walking she'd been doing, each day ended in a thoroughly paranoid tick check all over her body. She did not want to survive the Cough only to end up with Lyme disease.

After the scrubby grass was a deep ditch that ran along the side of the highway, so that rainwater would drain and prevent the road from flooding. It looked, from where Red stood, to be very steep. Between the pack and her leg any kind of extreme angle was a struggle for her and she did not relish the thought of climbing down and up again. And she would be vulnerable there, just a little fluttering moth trying to get out of a jar.

There was one thing to be grateful for—no military roadblocks. From where Red stood she could see cars—several of them had that domino-fender-bender look, wherein one driver slams on their brakes suddenly and the vehicles behind do the same but not soon enough. She could also tell, even from that distance, that there were people still inside some of them.

Of course, these people were not moving.

Nothing was moving. There were no living humans around that she could see, no birds, no rabbits, no deer. Nothing. The breeze was so faint that it barely ruffled her hair.

"This is about as safe as it's going to get, Red," she said to herself, but very softly, so no one else could hear.

She set off across the yellow grass, her pants rustling against the dry stalks. They seemed inordinately loud in the still air.

When she reached the culvert she spent a few moments determining the best plan of action. She thought the ditch was thin enough that she could step across it if she climbed only partway down. What she did not want was to end up in a tangle of limbs and/or with a broken prosthesis at the bottom because she'd underestimated the space, so if she got halfway and thought she couldn't make the step safely, then she would laboriously climb all the way to the bottom and back out again. The bottom of the ditch ran with brackish water that smelled like someone's cow field and she did not want her boots in that if she could avoid it.

Red managed to make the step—only just. She nearly tipped over backward and had to dig her fingers into the soil on the opposite bank so she wouldn't end up in an undignified heap at the bottom, like a turtle with its legs waving in the air.

She was out of breath when she reached the actual road. She carefully climbed over the metal barrier and then huffed out an annoyed breath. The domino-fender-bender meant that she couldn't walk straight ahead unless she climbed over the cars. Red could do it, in a pinch, but it would be a lot of effort for little gain. Better to walk east for a bit and see if there was an opening between bumpers.

Red studiously avoided peering into the cars. She wasn't squeamish but there was no reason to stare at rotting bodies. Besides, looking into the cars felt strangely invasive.

She finally found a space where she could crab-walk sideways between a gigantic blue SUV and a tiny silver Honda. Since she was walking sideways she couldn't help looking straight into the Honda, and that one glance showed her a long-haired woman, openmouthed and wide-eyed (though not really wide-eyed, since her sockets were mostly empty, the tender jelly eaten away), with her hands still clutching the wheel. The skin of her face seemed like it was moving, and Red realized that insects were doing their decaying work on her flesh.

That wasn't what bothered Red, though. It was the car seat in the back, the one with a desiccated little mummy strapped safely inside.

Red closed her eyes tight until she cleared the bumper of the car and staggered away, not opening them until she faced the other side of the highway. She hurried across the other two lanes, crossed the barrier in the middle, and made for the field on the other side. The ditch wasn't quite so steep there, and she was down and up again and feeling pretty secure about her chances as she crossed the patch of yellow grass that was a mirror of the one on the opposite side.

She'd had her ears open, listening hard for anyone's approach, but the sight of the woods made her a little giddy and she was still trying to shake off the scene in the Honda.

Which was why when the blond woman stepped out of the trees Red was shocked that she hadn't heard her coming. She ground to a halt, her hand going automatically to her hip, where her axe hung.

"Hello!" the woman said, waving in a friendly fashion.

They were about ten feet apart, close enough for Red to see that the woman had the kind of blandly open face preferred for physician's office receptionists. She looked like she would be helpful and cheerful and laugh at your stupid jokes while she took your insurance card.

She wore a pair of denim cutoffs and a gray hooded sweatshirt, absurd clothing given the increasingly cold weather. Her legs were covered in scratches and bug bites, and so were her hands.

"Hello!" she said again, and took a step closer to Red.

She wore black Converse low-tops with no socks.

Her smile was toothy and pinned on her face like a mask.

I know you, Red thought.

Everything about the woman was suspicious. She was dressed inappropriately, she had no bag or pack, and she conveniently popped out of the woods close to a place where people might cross.

The only question is how many more are there, Red thought, and carefully unbuttoned the plastic cover around the axe blade.

The woman didn't seem to notice Red's careful movement, so intent was she on maintaining eye contact and her toothpaste-model grin.

"Hello!" she said for the third time, and Red heard an undercurrent of annoyance this time. "Are you alone?"

Red didn't say anything, only carefully eased her pack off her back and dropped it at her feet.

The blond bait *(for that was what she was, she was bait for lonely travelers, and soon she would ask Red to come and sit by her fire and she and her friends would put Red on a spit and eat her all up)* took another step and Red pulled the axe off her belt and held it up.

"That's far enough."

"Whoa!" the woman said, and theatrically held her hands in the air.

Her tone was so fake, so clearly unconcerned, that Red

knew there was at least one more person lurking nearby.

"There's no need for that," the woman continued. "I'm all by myself, just like you. I was hoping maybe we could be friends."

"I don't need any new friends. My Facebook profile is full up," Red said. "And stay where you are."

The smile finally dropped. "You're not very polite, are you? Is this how you always greet someone you've never met before?"

Only someone who's trying to jump me, Red thought, but she only said, "Yes."

"Look, you're a woman alone. I'm a woman alone. I just thought it might be safer for us to travel together."

"It might be," Red said. "Except you're not alone."

The woman's eyes—brown, Red noted idly, and it was unusual to see blond hair with brown eyes—slid to one side and then quickly back at Red.

At least one, coming from my right side. He would have hidden somewhere in the maze of cars, and signaled his partner from the road once Red's back was to him.

"What do you mean? Of course I'm alone. I've been alone ever since my family died." Her voice was suddenly choked by tears.

"Does that work? The fake plea for sympathy?" Red was playing it cool, keeping her voice very even, but her heart was doing a jittery stutter-step and she could taste her own blood in her mouth. There was no guarantee that she would get out of this alive, even if she did everything right.

"What do you mean, fake?" the woman said, and her voice was edged with anger.

It was the first time Red had heard a sincere emotion from her, the first time the mask fell away completely.

"My whole family did die. My husband, my daughter, my two sons, my sister and her whole family. I have no one now. No one."

"And what would your family think of you if they could see you now? Do you think they'd be proud of you, trying to take from someone you don't even know?"

The woman looked stricken, like Red had physically hit her. And because she was shocked and not on her cue her eyes slid right again and so Red had ample time to turn and see the man running toward her.

He was tall and thin and had long greasy-looking black hair that stuck to the side of his face. He held a hunting knife in his right hand, and the fact that he was tall put Red at a massive disadvantage because he had a longer reach. She'd have to get inside his reach, away from the blade, and fast.

She'd taken a basic self-defense class once, one of those offered at the college. Self-defense was not about long drawn-out battles. It was about disabling your attacker long enough for you to run away.

So she didn't square off like she was going to have a fight

with him. She held the axe close to her body, waited for him to get close, then dropped to her right knee and swung the axe into his thigh.

Blood spurted into her face but she couldn't think about it, couldn't think about the fact that he might be infected and that his blood had gone into her nose and mouth. He screamed and dropped the knife and when he did she swung again, taking out his other leg.

He crumpled to the ground, crying and screaming and cursing her.

Red stood up as fast as she could and turned back toward the blond woman, who she felt sure would be running at her already. But the woman just stood there with her mouth open, like she was watching a movie that was supposed to be predictable and had taken an unexpected turn.

The man was still cursing, still calling Red every name a man calls a woman when he's angry. But his voice was fading out very quickly, a song coming to its end.

Red had hit an artery. She knew this because the blood was spraying out in time with his fading heartbeats.

"Daaaad!"

A voice from the trees, and Red saw a teenage boy—a gangly, more youthful mirror of the man dying in front of her—run past the stunned blonde and fall to the ground next to the man.

"Daaaad!" he wailed.

For a moment Red was sorry, sorry she'd killed the man who'd clearly intended to kill her. The boy looked about fifteen or sixteen, old enough to harm her if he wanted, but he only threw himself on his father's chest and wept.

Red felt sick then, sick at what she'd become, but she couldn't really be sorry. She couldn't be sorry that she'd killed that man before he killed her.

The adrenaline still pushed through her and made her hands shake but she picked up her pack and slung it on, all the while keeping the axe trained toward the weeping boy.

The blonde moved then, in little slow mouse steps, toward the boy and the man. Her face was the color of ash after a fire has burned out.

Red walked past her, close enough to touch, but the woman drifted by like she couldn't see Red at all.

CHAPTER 5

Daggers in Men's Smiles

BEFORE

Before they left town Red insisted on going into the pharmacy to see if there were any antibiotics available. Of course they were useless against the Cough, which was viral and tricky, but as Red had pointed out there were still plenty of bacteria that could kill you if they crawled inside an open wound.

She didn't expect there to be any left because the first thing folks asked for when they got sick was antibiotics (whether they needed them or not). She had a feeling that any smart people around or people who'd passed through would have snatched them up, or that the pharmacist at least would have snagged them and taken them home.

They stared around at the scattered packages all over the pharmacy floor.

"I can't believe there's so much medicine in the world," Mama said. "I never really thought about it when it was all lined up in packages on the shelf. But look at all of this. Something for every discomfort you might possibly feel— there's a pill for it, a cream for it, a spoonful of something to swallow."

"Wonder how effective most of this would be over the long term," Dad said idly, shifting the piles of boxes with his toe. "All these boxes have expiration dates on them."

"That's because they want you to buy more even if you don't need it," Adam said. "Throw out the old stuff and buy something new."

"It's because the efficacy of medicine declines over time, especially if you keep it in a humid environment like the bathroom, which most people do," Red said.

"Well, there is that place in every bathroom called a 'medicine cabinet,'" Adam said. "You can't really blame folks for that."

He reached down and picked up one of the packages. "I can't believe there's any cold medicine left. Remember that story we saw on the news? All those people knocking each other out for Nyquil and Robitussin?"

"They thought treatment meant a cure," Red said. "There's not enough science education in this country. Just because the medicine makes you feel better doesn't mean you're not still sick. You're just not showing symptoms. But the bugs are still building their little colonies inside you, even if you don't know it."

"What everybody got wasn't responding to Robitussin anyway," Adam said.

There wasn't much to say to that, so they all just peered around again.

"What is it we're supposed to be looking for here, Red?" Dad asked. "Amoxicillin?"

"Yes, and any other kind of antibiotics you can find," she said. "They won't be up here with the over-the-counter things. They'll be in the back where the pharmacist was. But keep your eyes peeled, because it looks like someone made a mess of this store for no damned reason and they might have tossed the good stuff up here."

"I thought the good stuff was something that made you feel good," Adam said. "Like opium."

Red was so intent on checking labels that she didn't rise to the bait. "Nope. The good stuff is a Z-Pak. They're like the superheroes of antibiotics. It's what they give you when you've got pneumonia, or when you've got strep throat or something that won't go away with just amoxicillin. But any kind of antibiotics would be good, if we can find them."

"I didn't know you knew so much about medication, Delia," Mama said.

"She's paranoid about infections," Adam said. "Of course she knows how to treat them."

Red picked up a tube of hydrocortisone cream that caught her eye and stuffed it in her pack. It might come in handy.

She also grabbed some ibuprofen and a jar of Vicks VapoRub. If she got a regular old cold (not the virus that was killing everybody), the menthol smell always made her feel better, even though she knew that it was all in her head. She associated it with childhood and snuggly sheets and chicken noodle soup and even as an adult when she got a cold she'd rub her chest with Vicks.

Everyone else had moved into the back pharmacy area—Behind the Counter, as Red thought of it. It was a land of mystical geography, normally navigated only by those who knew just what all those multisyllabic words on the jars meant and how they interacted with one another.

"Hey, I found some!" Adam said excitedly, his voice muffled as he bent over to pick something up. He held up a bottle. "Amoxicillin."

"I think most pharmacies group their medications by type, so look around and see if there is anything else," Red said, slowly making her way to the back area.

It wasn't as easy for her to just step on the piles of medicine boxes like everyone else. She always had to be careful of her balance, so she kicked the detritus out of her way as she went, clearing a path until she reached Adam.

Their parents wandered away to another side of the store. She saw them in the mirror that ran all around the ceiling perimeter. They were looking at (and apparently debating the merits of) a mangled display of gel insoles for shoes. It wasn't a bad idea, really, since Mama wasn't much of a walker, but it probably wouldn't matter anyway. Because Mama was going to get sick. Red's mind turned away from that thought, put it in a closet and shut the door.

Red carefully went to one knee and rummaged in the piles of medicine. "More amoxicillin," she said. "And . . . yes! Azithromycin."

"Is that your superhero drug?" Adam said. "When are you getting your medical degree, by the way?"

"Maybe if you cracked a book open at college now and then you might learn some things besides how to do keg stands," Red said.

"Only white guys do keg stands," Adam scoffed. "I am a connoisseur of craft beer."

"You're half white," Red said.

Adam glared at her. "Okay, only all-white guys trying to prove something about their masculinity to other all-white guys do keg stands. Better?"

"I think that's one of the most perceptive things I've ever heard you say. Of course, there is the problem of antibiotic resistance," Red said, frowning at the boxes.

She was the kind of person who actually read the fact sheets that the WHO put on their website. She'd lost about half a day once scrolling through all of them. "It's possible these won't do a thing. And I do wish I knew more about how long you're supposed to take them, depending on your condition. I know that a lot of times people feel better right away but they're supposed to keep taking medicine a few days longer to make sure everything bad is snuffed out."

"So we *won't* be saved by antibiotics? Make up your mind, Red," Adam said.

"Just take these," Red said, handing him several boxes. Better safe, she supposed. If one of them contracted an antibiotic-resistant strain of strep or pneumonia, there wasn't a lot you could do about that anyhow. Red was sure that doctors in hospitals would know what to do about it, but there would be no hospital staff handy. She put a half-dozen boxes in her bag, along with three bottles of amoxicillin.

There were still several containers left, and Red debated whether to take them all. If something happened, if one of them got sick . . . there was no telling what they might need. But then she thought of someone like her, maybe someone alone and sick, maybe hoping like hell that there were a few packages of antibiotics left in the abandoned pharmacy. So she didn't take everything, and hoped that a person who needed the drugs would find them.

Adam stood up. "I'm going to get some candy."

Red shrugged. "It's not the most nutrient-dense choice for a long walk, but whatever."

"I'm not getting it for the walk. I'm getting it because I want Twizzlers and there are a shitload of them in a pile over there."

Red didn't like to waste her sweet tooth on most candy,

which was filled with scary-sounding chemicals and fillers and thickeners that made her disease-paranoia antennae go *twang*. She didn't want to catch a virus, and she for damned certain did not want cancer. Artificial colors *might* be perfectly safe, but then everyone thought it was okay to put arsenic in wallpaper once upon a time and she didn't think that had worked out too well.

She followed her brother anyway, because there might be some other useful thing lying about. "Did the folks who trashed this store take *anything*? Or did they just pull it all off the shelves?"

"They took the money and the beer," Adam said. He pointed to the tall refrigerators along the wall that were normally filled with six-packs.

"Huh, you're right," Red said. "I didn't notice that."

"The great and powerful Red *didn't notice something*?" Adam said, grabbing his chest and pretending to have a heart attack.

"You're so funny, har har," Red said.

Then there was a sound that made them both jump, and they turned toward the front of the store. A woman stood just outside the glass door (which was still intact—the vandals had used a crowbar to pry open the door rather than smash the glass as they had done at Hawk's).

She was leaning against the door with both hands splayed against it, and the impact of her hands had made the sound that startled Adam and Red. But the woman didn't appear to have the strength to push the door open. She looked like a plastic bag drifting along in a current of wind, like her bones weren't functional anymore and her muscles were just holding on because that was what they'd always done.

The woman didn't seem like she knew where she was, or what she was doing. Her eyes were wide but Red didn't think she could see anything. She was wearing black leggings and a green sweatshirt and her brown hair hung oily and lank against her very white face. Her feet were bare.

And she had blood running out of her nose and mouth.

Not a little blood, not a slow rusty trickle. This was a horrific red gush, impossible in its flow. *Where was the blood coming from?* Red thought. *How could she be hemorrhaging like that? And why had none of those sober-faced anchors on the news ever mentioned this?*

All they had talked about was a cough, a cough that eventually killed the sufferers. Red had imagined something like a deadlier whooping cough, a mutation that defied the existing vaccinations. She hadn't imagined this, hadn't imagined free-flowing blood and zombie eyes.

"That's some Ebola shit right there," Adam said, moving closer to his sister.

"No, Ebola isn't airborne," Red said.

"Come on, I remember you reading that book about Ebola and the author was talking about how blood came out of every orifice. You read me so many gory bits I couldn't eat my lunch," Adam said, and pointed at the woman whose fresh blood was running down her face. "You're telling me that's not it?"

"Ebola isn't airborne," Red repeated. Her brain was clinging to this fact, clinging to the reports about a killer cough. Ebola had a longer incubation period, and it first presented flu-like symptoms, not a cough.

But nobody had talked about the blood. If everyone who got sick was bleeding like this, then how was it that the doctors hadn't warned about it? And if the major news networks decided this information was too much for their viewers then it should have been on YouTube, or Facebook, or something. Red couldn't believe nobody had filmed this with their phone.

Unless it's a recent mutation. Unless this didn't start happening until all the lights went out and the Internet went black and the phone networks were down.

Or unless there really was a vast conspiracy and the government had made sure nobody spoke about this, but really how could they do that? You couldn't silence millions of people, and millions of people all over the world had been impacted. Don't get any more paranoid than you already are, Red.

The woman coughed against the door, and Adam and Red automatically flinched away even though the glass and their masks were between them and the infected woman. Blood flew out of her mouth, splattering all over the glass in huge clots. Once she started coughing it was like she couldn't stop. The Cough started in her stomach, deep in her diaphragm, and it seized her whole body. She convulsed with the Cough, her spine curving back at the start and then arching forward, and with every breath more blood was expelled.

"It's like a morbid modern art painting," Adam said.

"I didn't know you knew anything about art," Red said, but the response was automatic. She wasn't really thinking about Adam or art. She was thinking about whooping cough and Ebola and reports about symptoms that didn't line up with what she saw at that moment.

The woman's face was slowly being obscured from their sight by the volume of effluvia coating the glass.

Mama and Dad came up to join them and they all stared like the woman was doing some kind of performance.

Red shook her head, shaking off the trance that had come over her at the sight of the blood running down the woman's white, white face. Her mind wanted to solve the problem, wanted to know why this particular symptom hadn't been generally known, and she'd gotten caught on a track thinking about it. That was stupid, because the longer they stayed the more likely it was that one of them would get infected, mask or no mask.

(One of you is already infected)

But you don't know that for sure, Red thought.

"We can't stay here. And we can't go out that way," she said, pointing at the front door.

"What if there are more like her in the back?" Adam said. "A big crowd of infected people waiting to get us?"

"First of all, they aren't zombies, even if they kind of seem like it," Red said. "I don't think people are gathering in swaying hordes to eat our faces."

"She looks like she might eat someone's face," Adam said doubtfully.

"She looks like she's going to fall over any second now," Mama said. "I think that's Kathy Nolan—it's hard to tell— she's the one who had twins a few years ago? I wonder what happened to her girls."

The thought of those two little girls dying coughing and covered in their own blood was too terrible, so Red put that aside too, in the closet where she knew Mama was sick and soon this would happen to her.

Mama was going to end up like this, coughing gouts of blood out of her mouth and her eyes would be dead like this woman's and if Red looked into them then Mama wouldn't be there anymore, wouldn't be there to argue with her and call her Delia instead of Red.

(don't think about it)

"Even with the masks on we don't want to go out right past an infected person," Red said. "So let's peek out the back door and see if it's safe to go that way."

"Won't the emergency alarm go off?" Adam said.

"The electricity isn't on," Red pointed out, but she didn't

add *you dolt*, though it was so tempting. Really, what did the boy go to college for? "And it wouldn't matter anyway. Nobody is going to arrest us for stealing Twizzlers."

Adam looked down at the packages of candy in his hand, the bright artificial red the same hue as the blood emitting from the woman who was probably Kathy Nolan. His mouth twisted and he dropped them to the floor.

Red waved her arms to indicate that they should all start moving toward the back of the store. She didn't know how she'd gotten to be in charge, but everyone else seemed paralyzed by their first close-up sight of an infected person.

It was hard, somehow, to turn her back on the woman who was literally coughing her life onto the glass of Swann's Pharmacy. Red knew she couldn't do anything to help her, and that contact would only increase the risk of infection, but it didn't feel right. People ought to help each other, especially when the world was ending.

They made it back to the car without encountering anyone else. The town was so small and so quiet that they could hear the wet expulsions that Probably Kathy Nolan made all the way back to their vehicle. Even after they climbed into the car and sped away, Red thought she still heard that woman coughing, coughing, coughing.

And the next evening Mama was coughing, too, just like Red knew she would be.

* * *

Mama's cough had gotten worse by the day they were supposed to leave, though it hadn't reached the convulsive body-shaking stage that Probably Kathy Nolan had exhibited outside the pharmacy. And there was no sign of the hemorrhaging, either, so Red hoped that was just an anomaly (and that would explain why nobody had reported it—Red liked to have things understood and filed and cataloged with full details).

Red knew that one of the reasons Dad was delaying their start was Mama's cough. He hadn't felt confident that she could manage the trip to begin with (he hadn't said it, there was just something Red noticed in the way he looked at Mama), and now that she was coughing he definitely didn't feel confident.

They were supposed to start at sunup so they could get a good amount of walking completed on the first day, but it was nine thirty a.m. and there was no indication that they were going to leave soon. Red wondered if they were going to leave at all.

So far no one else had shown signs of infection, though Red suspected her father would soon. Maybe Adam would get it, too. In all her calculations, though, she never considered the possibility that *she* might be the one to get sick. She laughed at herself a little, because it was beyond arrogant, but she just *felt* she wouldn't get sick now that the killer was inside their home. Red was going to be the final girl, the sole survivor of a massacre, just like in horror movies.

She had to think this way, to make it something outside herself, because if she truly considered the reality of her whole family dying before her eyes and leaving her alone she would curl up into a ball inside her closet and stay there. And that wasn't her. Red had never hidden from anything in her life. When life punched her in the face she stuck her chin out. She didn't fall down.

But it was easy to stick your chin out when you had a team in your corner waiting for you when the bell rang at the end of the round.

Dad and Mama were in the kitchen, murmuring quietly about things that they didn't want Red or Adam to hear. Adam was upstairs, and Red could hear him squeaking around on the hardwood floor as he found one more thing he couldn't live without and had to figure out how to squeeze it into his already overstuffed pack. She was certain that at some point in their journey he would realize he needed to shed unnecessary things and they would drop from his backpack one by one, like the bread crumbs that were supposed to lead you home.

Except these bread crumbs would lead people *to* them, Red was certain of that. She loved her family but she did not love the way they were so unprepared for the reality of the Crisis.

Adam seemed to think everything would be fine if only they would join up with all the other lemmings in government camps. Even after seeing Probably Kathy Nolan expelling blood from her lungs all over the window of Swann's Pharmacy, he still thought it would be a great idea to live in close quarters with lots of people and let someone else worry about food and shelter. Adam wasn't interested in surviving on his own, and so he dillydallied around upstairs hoping another answer would present itself and he wouldn't have to carry his pack across the "goddamned country" (his words, and he'd gotten a raised eyebrow from Mama for the blasphemy) to Grandma's house.

Red pulled her pack over her shoulders. More than ever she felt the urgency of not leaving it behind, even to go from the living room to the kitchen. She was not going to be the dumbass heroine in the movie who put her Very Important Object on the ground and ended up losing it in a perfectly predictable plot twist. Her neck had been prickling all morning, and she didn't know if it was because she had some premonition of Bad Things Happening or simply because she was eager to leave.

Mama and Dad stood close together by the dining set, their heads resting against each other, like each was drawing strength from the other to keep on standing. Dad's pack was there, filled and zipped up, but Mama's was overflowing with all kinds of useless things while use*ful* things were scattered on the table. When Red entered they pulled apart, looking guilty, like she was a hall monitor who'd caught them necking behind the lockers.

She looked at them and tapped her wrist. "We've got to go."

Mama made a helpless little gesture at her pack. "I'm not ready."

Her voice was scratchy because she'd been coughing. No blood yet, though. Maybe not at all, Red hoped. Maybe Probably Kathy Nolan had a unique reaction to the virus, one that not every victim would develop.

It was possible.

Red sighed and went to the table, looking at the mess of her mother's pack. "First thing is, you don't need all these clothes. Two sweaters? No. One sweater, and you wear it, either on your person or around your waist. See?"

She gestured at her own clothes—a lightweight wicking T-shirt with long sleeves, a gray-and-red striped sweater (also lightweight and wicking), and her customary red hooded sweatshirt over both. On the bottom she wore synthetic cargo pants that would shed water easily if it rained and wicking socks (for her real foot, since her fake foot did not get sweaty) and her well-worn hiking boots.

Mama wore her "Saturday pants"—cheap cotton sweats that she threw on when she wanted to relax. They weren't very practical for walking a long way, but Mama wasn't crazy about exercise and so she didn't even have yoga pants or leggings like all the white women in town. It was sweats or jeans and Mama's jeans were all the neat, dressy type. On top she wore a cotton T-shirt with the name of her college printed on it. This was about as exercise-ready as Mama got.

Mama's face was gray and there were lines of strain around her eyes and Red didn't want to see them there. She didn't want to acknowledge that Mama was sick because maybe if she pretended it wasn't there it wouldn't be true.

(That's more little-girl thinking, Red, and no wishing and pretending is going to make it so)

Red started unpacking everything in Mama's pack and sorting it into "keep" and "leave" piles. "Mama, you can't carry all this. And you haven't got any food in here, either."

"Red, about this walk—" Dad started.

"Don't say we're not going," Red said, not looking up at him but continuing with her task. "Don't say that we're going to stay here or wait until a patrol comes by because we all talked about it, we decided, and we're going."

"Cordelia," Mama said.

Red had to look up then, because Mama never ever called her Cordelia unless she was really serious.

"Cordelia," Mama said again, but softer now. "I'm not going anywhere. I've got the sickness. You know it, even if you've been trying to pretend that it's not true."

"We don't know for sure," Red said.

"Yes, we do," Mama said. "I'm not going to make it to Grandma's house. I'm not going to make it more than a night or two, if the reports are true. And the longer you all stay here with me the more likely it is that you'll catch it, too."

"Don't tell me to go without you," Red said, and she was surprised by the fierceness of her voice. "Don't even try to tell me that."

"Cordelia," Mama said for the third time, and three times for anything makes it a spell, a curse, a whisper of magic that can't be undone.

Red felt her Mama saying her real name deep in her heart, felt all the love and longing of it, the promise that a name was when a parent gave it to her child.

"I know you always hated that name," Mama said, and she smiled a little. She was speaking slowly so she wouldn't cough, and Red saw the lines of effort in between her eyes. "You wanted a pretty name, like the girls in your class, and Cordelia was fussy and old-fashioned. But I named you that because Cordelia was strong. She held fast, even when her father banished her for refusing to lie to him. She stayed true, and came to liberate Lear from her sisters even though he'd cast her out. She's not around much in the play, but she made an impression. Just like you. Even when you were a newborn you made an impression."

"She dies at the end," Red said.

"We all die at the end," Mama said. "What we do before the end is what counts. And you are strong, my Cordelia. You're a fighter, and I know you'll get where you want to go because you won't have it any other way. But I won't get there just because you want it to be so. I'm going to die right here in my house, Delia, in the place where I loved your father and raised you and Adam and built my life. My happy, happy life."

Red's fingers stopped moving over the objects on the table, clenched into fists. "I knew we shouldn't have gone into town. I knew it."

"Red, if your mother was going to get sick it could have happened anywhere," Dad said.

"Don't give me that hand-of-God bullshit," Red said angrily. Mama winced, because she didn't like swearing and she definitely didn't like anything close to taking the Lord's name in vain. "I don't believe in any God guiding all this. We could have avoided this. We could have kept her safe."

"Red, I know how you feel . . ." Dad said.

"No, you don't," Red said. "She's your wife but she's my mother, do you understand that? She's my mother. I'm not going to get another mother. And I could have kept her safe if I'd insisted we stay here. We should have stayed here but nobody ever listens to me. It's just paranoid Delia talking crazy talk about the government and killer bacteria."

"Delia," Mama said. "You have to let me go. You and Adam, you have to take your things and go because I am not going to make it. But you still can."

"And you'll stay here, too. Is that how it is? The two of you stay here and die while Adam and I go skipping into the woods like in some fairy tale, hand in hand with our bread crumbs," Red said to her father, and she hated the way she sounded, so accusing.

If this was the last time she saw her parents, this should not be how they spoke to each other, but she couldn't help it. It felt like they were giving up and that made her so angry, because they had a plan and they weren't supposed to give up. Giving up was something for other families, not hers.

"How can I leave her?" Dad said, his face long and tired. "I don't want to live without her."

"I don't want to either," Red said. "But you're telling me to do what you won't do. You're telling me and Adam to go on living and abandon you."

"Do as I say, not as I do," Dad said, with a little half-smile. "Isn't that what parents always say? And I'm probably going to be sick soon, too."

Red gave him a long, steady stare. "And what if you're not? Are you just going to stay here by yourself and desiccate slowly? Or are you going to follow us?"

"No," Dad said.

"No to which?" Red said.

"No to both."

The unspoken hung there in between all of them, binding Dad and Red and Mama together. After Mama died, if Dad wasn't sick, he would kill himself.

"This was not supposed to be how it would go," Red said. "I knew the rules. I knew, and we were going to avoid all the stupidity that kills people in a story. We were not going to be like those people. We were all going to get to Grandma's house safely. We were all going to live."

"You can't write this like a story, Red. This is life, and it doesn't follow your rules."

"'Life's but a walking shadow, a poor player that struts and frets his hour upon the stage. And then is heard no more: it is a tale told by an idiot, full of sound and fury, signifying nothing,'" Red said.

It just came out, a thing she had unconsciously memorized. She'd always liked *Macbeth* the best. She liked horror movies, and *Macbeth* was a proper horror story, with ghosts and witches and blood.

"I didn't know you read Shakespeare, Delia," Mama said, a little wonder in her voice. "But I would be hurt if that's what you really believed—that life is worth nothing. Just because I'm sick doesn't mean my life is worth nothing. I had you and Adam, didn't I? You're the piece of me that goes on."

"Of course I read Shakespeare," Red said, ignoring the rest of Mama's statement. She didn't want to be the one to go on. She wanted her mama to live. "My mother is a distinguished Shakespeare professor. How could I not?"

She'd read several plays in secret, because she wanted to understand her mother, but she didn't want Mama the Professor quizzing her about it.

Mama put her arms around Red, crying now. "I always

thought there was so much space between us, and as you got older it seemed the gulf got wider and wider. But you were always trying to close the gap, weren't you? I see that now. I wish I'd seen it sooner."

Red didn't say anything, couldn't, because all her tears were choking her and she didn't want to weep, not now. And she realized that Mama must have been just as certain as Red that Red wouldn't get sick, or else Mama wouldn't have put her arms around Red's neck like that and breathed so close to her face. Red was going to live, and instead of triumphant victory it suddenly felt like a horse she'd have to drag with her all the rest of her days. The only consolation in being a survivor was that you'd survived.

Adam came into the kitchen then, carrying his too-heavy pack and looking clueless, Red thought. It annoyed her that he didn't know what had just happened, the decisions that had been made, and it annoyed her that the thought was unreasonable. How could he know if he wasn't there when they were all talking about Red and Adam leaving Mama and Dad behind to die? But there he was, with his stupid face not knowing anything and rubbing her raw because he was giving them all that put-upon look he did so well.

"I am ready for the unreasonable trek," Adam said, sighing. "I still think this is dumb."

"Well, I don't want to hear about how dumb you think it is because it's just going to be you and me until we get to

Grandma's house and I'm not listening to you whine for that long," Red snapped.

Adam glanced from Dad to Mama to Red. "What's going on?"

Red was going to say there was no time for a recap, and she didn't want to drag it out anyway. Wasn't everything terrible enough without running over the same ground again? But then there was a sound, a very unexpected sound, and they all froze.

"Truck," Red said. "It's a truck, it's one of those patrols coming to see if there are any survivors. It just turned in at the bottom of the drive. We've got to go now."

But Adam was doing the Adam thing—the opposite of what she wanted him to do, always—and moving out of the kitchen and into the living room and toward the front windows when she wanted to slip out the back door and across the expanse of their lawn and into the woods before anyone noticed them.

"Don't go up there, you idiot!" Red hissed, and then Dad and Mama followed him and she threw her hands up in the air.

They apparently all *wanted* to be caught, but Red wasn't going to be caught by anyone. Her pack was prepped and on and she was leaving. She would like it better if Adam came with her because it was nice to have someone with you in the woods, in case you got lost or hurt. But she would go without him. She *would*.

And she would go without saying a proper good-bye to her parents if she had to because they all knew how they felt and love was in their heart and all of that bullshit (*it's not really bullshit, though, it's true but I can't think about it now because it hurts, it hurts so much to leave them*, Red thought) and nobody would blame her if she just went because they all knew how Red felt about the soldiers, about the camps, about being trapped inside somebody's jar.

Still, she stood there, hesitating, because it was really easy to make grand declarations in your mind but not so easy to follow through on them. It didn't feel right to leave without saying good-bye, or without Adam.

Then Mama and Adam were back in the kitchen, looking frantic, and Red heard a very unfamiliar sound from the living room. It was the sound of ammunition going into a rifle.

Dad had a hunting rifle—Red didn't know what sort it was; she did not like the guns that he kept in the hall closet and he practically never used. Dad had hunted with Papa when he was younger—just deer because deer were everywhere—but he confided to Red that he never liked the killing part so much as he liked the walks in the woods, and when he got older he stopped doing the hunting and stuck with the walks. But he never got rid of his hunting rifle, never sold it off or gave it away, and Red wondered why.

"I might need it someday," Dad had said.

"There's a pickup truck full of guys out there with guns,"

Adam said, grabbing Red's arm and pulling her toward the back door like she hadn't wanted to go just there a minute ago. "About six or seven of them, and one of them is Martin Kaye and he's yelling for Mama and Dad to come out. It doesn't seem like he's here to offer assistance in our time of need, either. Seems like it's a truckload of racists that want to eliminate miscegenation, and since you and me are the result of said miscegenation this doesn't mean anything good for us, either."

"What?" Red said, shaking him off. "For real? Everybody's dying and they've got nothing better to do than go around trying to earn their white supremacy badge?"

"For real, Delia," Mama said. "You and Adam have to go now."

"You and Daddy can't stay here, either," Red said, panic rising up. "Those motherfuckers will torture you. Or worse. Mama . . . you don't know what they'll do to you."

"Watch your language, Delia," Mama said. "I know very well what they want to do. I know better than you. When I married your father it was not exactly a common thing for a black woman and a white man to walk hand in hand. I got spit on enough times to know there were people in the world who thought we were doing wrong. Although I never thought Martin Kaye was one of them. He was always polite to us."

"He had to be," Red said. "And now he doesn't feel he has to be, so he's going to hurt you and Daddy because of it."

"I do not want to be burned alive, Red, let's go," Adam said.

Adam had much darker skin than Red did, and he was clearly thinking of that and how those motherfuckers (she could think that even if Mama didn't like her saying it) would see him as a black guy. He was not even considering their parents—his brain was all about Adam.

"We can't leave Mama and Dad, you dummy," Red said, looking from one to the other.

She heard then the slow slide of the front window coming up, and the barrel of Dad's rifle scraping against the sill. The open window made it easier to hear the voice outside—Martin Kaye, their neighbor from just about a mile up the road. The same man who always said, "Hey Shirley," to Mama when they passed in the grocery store and asked after her health. That man. That man that Red and Adam had known all their lives was outside now with a bunch of his friends and all those friends were holding weapons and they had come to kill Red's whole family.

"Mama and Dad already decided to stay, you said so," Adam said, his teeth gritted. "Come on, come on, you're the one who's been so goddamned eager to leave."

She had been the one so eager to leave, but that was when they were all leaving together. That was before the leaving meant men who would do Dad and Mama harm while Red and Adam scampered away.

"We can't," Red said.

"Don't you get it?" Adam said, grabbing her arm again and pulling her, but she dug in and wouldn't let him move her so he had to let go. "You're the one who's always watching those movies and reading those books and talking about rules and stupid behavior. They're *giving us a chance to get away*. They are trying to save their children and by standing here arguing you're not letting them do that."

Red heard a click from the living room, and then a boom, and then Martin Kaye was outside screaming instead of yelling epithets at her parents.

"We love you, Cordelia," Mama said. "And you, Adam."

"I love you, Mama," Adam said, and darted back long enough to kiss her cheek.

"Mama," Red said, and she wasn't ready. She wasn't ready at all for it to end like this.

"Now, Red!" Adam said, and he opened the back door and he was out in a flash.

"You stay with your brother, Cordelia," Mama said, and she decided for Red by turning away and entering the living room.

In half a second she was out of sight and Red stood there looking at the afterimage of where Mama used to be.

A second later she heard the report of Dad's rifle again, and then the responding fire from the men who'd come to kill them all.

She had to leave. She had to leave them or stay and be killed with them. In stories someone would always valiantly sacrifice herself so someone else could live, and that was what Mama and Dad were doing now.

Somehow Red had always thought if there was valiant sacrificing to be done she would be the one to do it. After all, she was the one who knew everything about these kinds of stories.

If this were a movie I would be yelling at the heroine to move before she got killed too.

Red couldn't really run fast—her prosthetic leg wasn't one of those made for athletics so the best she could manage was an awkward jog, especially with the heavy pack. She eased out the back door so it wouldn't slam shut and give her position away, but it didn't really matter because it sounded like a movie Western out in front of the house and so much louder than she expected.

There was about a quarter mile or so between the back door and the thick stand of trees that would hide her from anyone who came around the house with a gun.

She didn't see Adam anywhere, and she hoped like hell that he hadn't just run all out and abandoned her. The last thing Mama told her to do was stay with her brother and Red was going to listen to her mother.

(For a change)

You'll never have a chance to not listen to her again because she's gone, Dad's gone, they're gone forever, if those men don't kill them and they surely will there's still the sickness, the Cough, they are gone gone gone

She felt the toe of her right boot catch in a little rut in the grass and stumbled forward, but she didn't fall down.

That would be the biggest damn cliché, falling down and flailing helplessly when trying to escape. All those movie heroines twisting their ankle and then turning helplessly to see some Thing bearing down on them instead of just getting the hell up and running some more and I am not going to fall, I am not going to get caught, I am going to make it into the woods and when I find Adam I am going to strangle him for leaving me behind.

She heard the guns and heard someone yelling again but she couldn't tell what they were saying and she didn't care. Adam was right (and she was *never* going to admit to him that she'd thought that for even a half second); their parents were trying to save them and she wasn't going to waste their sacrifice and she only hoped like hell that Dad would kill as many of those motherfuckers as he could and if he couldn't kill them then he would kill Mama before those men did something horrible to her. Red didn't want to think such a thought, that her own father might have to kill her mother out of some kind of mercy but Red would rather that a million times over than any one of those men getting their hands on Mama and making her suffer.

The stand of trees looked like it was a thousand miles away, but that was only because her heart beat so hard she thought it would come out her eyeballs and her eyeballs bulged and her lids felt peeled back and everything had narrowed to just that last twenty feet, fifteen feet, ten feet and then suddenly she was just there like magic, like teleportation but she heard the harsh rasp of her own breath and felt the burn of adrenaline in her veins.

Red knew that just because the trees were overhead, that didn't mean she was safe, so she kept moving as fast as she could. There was no sign of Adam and she wondered just how damn far he'd gotten without her and then all of a sudden he just emerged from behind a tree trunk.

She halted and then she did fall, because his appearance was too abrupt and she lost her balance but she didn't face-plant, just came down hard on her right knee and both elbows.

"Goddammit, Adam," Red said, picking herself up and dusting pine needles from her sleeves.

He didn't say anything, which was unusual, because he rarely missed an opportunity to take a dig at her. She looked at him and saw he was just standing there with tears running out of his big brown eyes.

"I didn't mean to," he said.

"Didn't mean to what?" she said.

"I didn't mean to leave them. I didn't mean to leave you."

She didn't say anything, which was unusual, because she rarely missed a chance to tell him he'd been a dolt. But there was nothing she could say this time, so she walked into his arms and they held each other tight because they were all that was left of their family, just Red and Adam in the woods.

CHAPTER 6

What's Done Is Done

AFTER

Red woke in the cabin with that heavy slept-too-long feeling. She couldn't see the position of the sun outside the window, but it was bright, which meant it was long past sunrise. It had been quite a while since she'd slept through sunrise, or had gotten more than a few hours of rest at a stretch. Instead of feeling refreshed she felt thick and sluggish, like she could go back to sleep despite having snoozed for twelve hours or more.

She blinked and then the sun was much less bright than it had been before she blinked and she realized she must have dozed off for a few more hours. Red probably could have slept for a while longer but nature was urgently telling her to get the hell out of her sleeping bag, so she put her prosthetic leg back on and pulled her boots on without tying them.

She shuffled to the door in her long underwear, rubbing

her arms when she opened the door and felt the blast of cold from outside. All the dead leaves outside the door were dusted with frost and it felt noticeably colder than it had the day before. Red hurriedly dealt with her business, not for the first time contemplating how much easier this would be with male equipment. At least her butt wouldn't be flapping in the cold breeze.

Once inside she put all of her layers back on except her rain jacket and then set up the camp stove and propane that the owner had left behind. Soon the little cabin was filled with the smell of tomato sauce bubbling in the pan. Red's insides twisted with hunger—she hadn't been able to eat the stew that she'd made before the coyote came to her fire—and she had to force herself not to jam a whole package of pasta into her mouth.

It was only off-brand tomato sauce and cheap dried pasta but she couldn't remember the last time she'd eaten something that tasted so good, so *luxurious*. Eating spaghetti felt downright decadent after weeks of canned stews and trail mix and dehydrated meals mixed with water.

It would cost her something in weight in her pack, but she was definitely going to take that other jar of sauce and a couple of packages of pasta when she left the cabin. Red gave the camp stove a regretful look. She would like to bring it with her—it would be a boon to have hot food without lighting a fire and sending out a signal to anyone who might be nearby. But it was far too big and bulky to carry, and it needed propane cans and those were bulky too. If Adam were with her then maybe they could have split the weight . . .

Don't think about Adam.

Adam wasn't with her. There was no value in going down that road again.

Red had a packable down jacket (red, of course) and she reckoned she was going to need it from here on out. She'd hoped to get to Grandma's before it started freezing at night, because while she didn't mind camping she didn't care to do it in subzero temperatures. And she knew very well that the snow would follow quickly once the temperature dropped. Snow would make her trek more difficult and she was already walking slowly.

On the other hand, she considered, *cold might slow both the spread of the virus and the constant patrols.* They had to stop trying to round up everybody sooner or later. She was frankly surprised at the determination to do so even in the face of decreasing numbers—both the general population and the military. Just because they were enlisted didn't mean that soldiers didn't get sick.

And this motivation for catching *everybody*? If Red was inclined to think the government had sinister motives, she might think there was a sinister motive behind all this. If the point of quarantine and containment was to limit the spread of disease, then a few people walking solo through unpopulated areas would hardly be a factor. But the patrols didn't seem to want to let anyone go, and they were wasting (in Red's opinion) valuable resources trying to find every single person.

It's about more than just the virus. But she didn't want to think about the virus, or the government, or sinister patrols circling the cabin while she slept.

Given that the best part of daylight was already gone, Red decided to spend another night in the cabin. She knew this was partly a desire to sleep indoors again, and she forced herself to acknowledge this and also to acknowledge that she would leave in the morning no matter what the weather.

It would be too easy to get bogged down there and stay for several nights, snug under a roof and with plenty of food that she wouldn't have to carry. But the longer she stayed the more difficult it would be to start again. Her legs would get weak and she wouldn't be able to carry her pack, and any hardiness she'd built up sleeping outdoors would disappear. So she promised herself

(pinky promise Red just like you and Adam used to do when you were little)

(don't think about Adam)

that she would prep everything for departure before she went to bed again, and as soon as she was up in the morning she would leave.

Her belly felt stretched out, overstuffed from her gorging,

so she took out one of the two books she'd packed and read for a while by the light of her clip-on booklight. Outside the doors of the cabin all the little night creatures of the forest scampered through the dead leaves.

She imagined there were also bigger creatures out there, deer and foxes and coyotes (real ones, not the human kind) and maybe even some bears. But the larger animals drifted silently between the trees, and Red fell asleep with her book on her chest, just as she had so many times at home back when the world was normal.

The next morning she kept her promise to herself and was off just after sunrise. She couldn't resist a chance for a hot breakfast, so she mixed up some of the oatmeal she found on the shelf before starting off. Breakfast and lunch were usually eaten cold and on the trail and it was an indulgence to have oatmeal (which she'd never been crazy about before but it was another thing that suddenly seemed gourmet).

Before she started she checked her map and tried to get a rough idea of where she was. She was right in the thick of the forest now—it had been two walking days since she'd come close to that highway but she wasn't sure how far she'd walked in the night after that man came to her fire. Whenever she crossed a road or a town she marked the place on the map and then adjusted her path accordingly. It had been some time too since she'd encountered a marked or blazed trail, but she figured she had about a hundred miles or so to go to Grandma's.

Red expected to cross one of those marked trails soon—maybe in the next day or so. That trail would lead her about nine fairly straight miles until she encountered a state road. There was no way around this road—it cut right through the forest from east to west in a sidewinding slither. She dreaded crossing the road, because a crossing always came with the risk of an encounter, and because she'd just crossed that highway recently with bad results.

There was also a town very close to the crossing, which increased the possibility of meeting someone she did not want to meet.

Since there wasn't any way to avoid the road, she decided that following the trail would be better than continuing to blaze through the forest. It was much easier, much less tiring, to walk on a path, even if it wasn't perfectly groomed.

Crossing the country through the woods meant a lot of bad footing and slow going. Mama had insisted that Red's half-leg would tire over the course of the journey, and she was right. Despite all of Red's preparations the truth was that her amputated leg did tire faster than the other one, and at the end of some days she limped until she couldn't go any farther. She'd started out with a grand notion of hiking eight or ten miles a day but the truth was that most days it was more like five or six—especially if there were any hills to climb—depending on how energetic she felt and how difficult the ground.

The two nights' rest in the cabin had helped, though. It had been a relief to be off her feet, real and prosthetic, and to sleep for as long as she needed.

She wasn't making terrible time, she considered as she folded up the map, but it could be better. If she'd been really fit and two-footed she might have made that ten or twelve miles a day. But Red had to take her body as it was, not as she'd like it to be. She'd prepared for the walk, but it was harder than she'd thought it would be (this was easier to admit to herself than it would be to admit to anyone else).

But the snow would come soon. Snow meant not only cold but poor footing, and heavy snow would probably stop her in her tracks for a day or more.

Red set off that morning without the nagging sense of being watched that she'd had before she found the cabin. *That's because nobody* was *watching you before. You were just paranoid because of that man at your fire. But you made sure he wasn't getting up again to come after you and there was no one else and you need to stop thinking enemies are lurking behind every leaf, Delia.*

She only called herself Delia when she was thinking a thought that sounded like something Mama would say, or if she was trying to be especially firm with herself.

The exercise soon warmed her muscles but a brisk wind made her nose and cheeks cold and she wished she'd thought to pack something like a balaclava.

Can't think of everything, Red. Though she had tried, she really had. Her packing list had been refined with surgical precision. She pulled her scarf up over her nose and her hat down low over her eyebrows and kept on, because that was what she had to do.

Around midday she stopped to eat a cold lunch of a protein bar and raisins and tried not to think about the pile of spaghetti that she'd eaten the night before. She'd lost a day sleeping in the cabin and she couldn't afford a long, leisurely lunch hour.

A couple of hours after lunch she came upon the trail she'd expected to find. It surprised her a little, because she hadn't realized she was so close to it, and that meant that she'd walked farther than she realized the night before she found the cabin. No wonder she'd been so tired when she got there. Adrenaline and fear (because she could admit to herself now that it was in the past that she had been afraid; she never acknowledged her fear unless she had to) had pushed her harder than she would have if she'd been in her right mind.

There hadn't been any sign of people all day—not a crumpled candy wrapper or discarded water bottle or any kind of sound. Still, she listened carefully before stepping onto the trail and made sure to scout all around for potential hiding places in the event that she did hear someone coming.

The trees were quite thick on either side of the path— oaks and evergreens, mostly—and it would be easy to disappear from view just ten or fifteen feet away from the trail. The key was not to be seen first, not to attract any interest or attention. Since most people made so much noise (unless they were trying to be quiet, and that made them suspicious in Red's eyes) she would have a chance to dart away before anyone caught a glimpse of her. She hoped.

Red had no doubt that there were still good and ordinary people left in the world, people who were just trying to get by since everything had gone crazy, people who were probably a lot like her. And those people might make reliable companions, might make this long lonely walk more bearable. Especially since she'd had to leave Adam behind.

(don't think about Adam)

People were herding animals, and of course there was safety to be found in a herd. But there was also danger. Herds were easier to track and find than one lone person.

And Red didn't trust other people—didn't trust that they wouldn't try to hurt her or steal her supplies, or even that they wouldn't try to force her into staying with them instead of continuing on to Grandma's. She didn't want to be answerable to anybody or to have to share what she had so painstakingly acquired. You couldn't always tell if someone was good just by looking at them, and Red was taking no chances.

Her hand axe was hooked through a loop at her belt so that she could grab it easily if necessary. It was not a necessity she was fond of, and she shook her head to clear it of the memory of the man-coyote's flesh ripping apart under her blade. She'd much rather slip into the cover of the trees and wait for any stranger to pass than have another homicidal encounter. There was already too much death weighing on her heart. Red didn't want any more weight.

The sun was going down earlier and earlier every day, and the tall trees made it seem like dusk well before sunset. The thick cover, however, made it difficult to find a good place to pitch her little tent. Red had a hammock, though she didn't love the idea of sleeping out when it was so cold. The rapidly falling dark made her decision for her since she wasn't able to find a suitable spot. The lack of clearings also meant that there was no safe place for a fire, and that meant another cold dinner.

Two nights in that cabin made you soft, Red, she thought. So what if she wasn't able to have a hot dinner? She'd find a good place to pitch her tent the next day, and then she'd build a fire and have one of the cans of soup knocking around in her pack.

The surprise find of the cabin in the woods meant that Red could put off a little longer something she'd been dreading beyond all measure—going into a residence or a town to find more food. She'd started off with lots of lightweight backpacker food, the kind of stuff that came in pouches or plastic containers. These were things that she'd ordered online early on in the Crisis, when she could see which way the wind was blowing even if nobody else could.

But as time had gone on she'd run out of that food, and she and Adam

(don't think about Adam)

had been forced to scavenge in abandoned houses or shops. Red didn't have a ton of survival skills—she could light a fire without matches and she knew how to find running water and things like that, but she couldn't hunt or fish and even if she could kill something she wasn't sure how to clean the carcass and make it safe to eat.

And the way she figured it was that there was plenty of packaged food in the world—there was probably more packaged food than everyone in America could eat even before the Crisis decimated the population. One grocery store that she and Adam happened upon had been hardly touched at all, the shelves lined with every kind of good imaginable—except for milk and bottled water. When there was a panic people always came for milk and bottled water.

Most of the bread had been injected with preservatives so it was still good to eat, and she smiled at the memory of the two of them delightedly toasting slices of bread over a fire and spreading them with peanut butter. The peanut butter had been in Adam's bag

(don't think about Adam, don't think about him unless you want to work yourself up again)

and Red thought that if she found another grocery store she would grab some more of it because even without bread, peanut butter was one of life's greatest joys and she could eat it straight from the jar with a spoon.

Thinking about peanut butter wouldn't solve the problem at hand, though. She was going to have to use her hammock, and that meant a cold exposed night. There was no point in walking any more when she could see the thickness of the trees far ahead of her on either side of the path. And it would not be fun to try to attach the hammock in the dark.

She turned off the path, looking for trees that were set the correct distance apart. After ten or fifteen minutes of searching she found what she wanted and got her hammock in place.

There wasn't really a good place to build a fire, and anyhow she was still fairly close to the trail because she didn't want to lose track of it and have to waste time getting back. Ever since she woke up in the cold that morning she'd felt a low-level anxiety building up about her pace, even though she'd told herself to accept the fact that she was going as fast as she could. Trouble was, going as fast as she could still felt too damned slow.

She thought she wouldn't sleep that well in her hammock, especially after the coziness of the cabin. In the hammock she didn't even have the psychological comfort of her tent fly. But she dropped off almost immediately. It was a good thing, too, because she woke a couple of hours before dawn when the snow started to fall.

CHAPTER 7

The Grief That Does Not Speak

BEFORE

Adam and Red walked in silence for a while. Red didn't know about Adam but she couldn't get past the grief in her throat to say anything. Every time she felt her voice rising up it would meet that clump of tears stuck behind her tongue and whatever she was about to say would just fade back into her lungs.

There was no sound except the clomp of their boots in the dirt, the wind in the branches, the chatter of birds in the trees.

The birds didn't know that Dad and Mama were dead. The birds didn't care that everyone was dying and those who weren't dying had gone crazy. The birds just went about their bird business, finding worms and building nests and shouting at other birds that came and perched on branches in trees they'd staked as their own.

Adam abruptly came to a stop, peeling off the trail and sitting down on one of the boulders scattered all over the woods. Red knew that these were the fragmented remains of glacier deposits but as a child she'd thought they were dropped here and there by fairies, and never lost the habit of calling them "fairy rocks."

"This is bullshit," he said, taking a long swig of water from his bottle.

"We can't stop here," Red said. "We're still too close to home."

"You think those rednecks are going to chase us into the woods?" Adam snorted. "They were out looking for easy pickings. They're not going to leave their truck to follow us."

"I can't believe so many people have died and a whole truckload of motherfuckers like that lived," Red said, unable to keep the fury out of her voice. "Why is it that assholes just go on and on, even when the world would be a better place if they just dropped dead?"

"Because their assholery protects them. They're so full of bile that the virus can't get a toehold," Adam said.

"I hope like hell Daddy shot as many of them as he could before . . ." Red said, then faded away.

"Before he died?" Adam said.

There was a strange kind of challenge in his tone, and Red wondered why it felt like his hostility was directed at her.

"Something bothering you, Adam?" Red asked. She'd never been able to back down when he challenged her. Even the merest hint would get her hackles up.

"Yeah, something's bothering me, *Cordelia*," Adam said. "It's bothering me that none of this would have happened if not for you and your stupid ideas."

"Are you trying to say it's my fault that a carload of racists showed up at our house to kill us all?" Red said.

"I'm saying that if it wasn't for you and your insistence that we go on a three-hundred-mile hike across country we wouldn't have even been there. We would have gone to a quarantine facility like everyone else with sense and we would all still be alive there."

"You don't know that," Red said. "Mama was sick. She could have gotten sick in the facility, too, or anywhere."

"She got sick when we went into town to pick up supplies for this godforsaken hike," Adam said, and he was edging closer to a yell, his voice rising with each word. "We didn't need to go there in the first place except for *you*."

He spit out the last word, and it seemed to Red that he was spitting out years of resentment with it.

"Let me explain something to you, because you don't seem to understand," Red said. "This virus is everywhere, you understand? *Everywhere.* That means if you don't have the magic immunity, you're going to get it. I didn't want to go into town at all, because I was afraid that one of us might get sick, because anywhere that people are is where this damned virus is too. If we'd stuck to the plan, if we'd left from the house three days ago, if we'd avoided any place where people might be, then we might have made it to Grandma's. Yes, all four of us. But we didn't. We can't undo the choices that were made, and yelling at me won't fix it."

Their voices seemed so loud, even though neither of them was quite at shouting level. The tweeting birds had flown away, startled by the evidence that humans were stalking through their woods. She felt exhausted all of a sudden, too tired to argue with Adam anymore. Red waved her hand at him.

"I'm not taking the blame for this, even if you want to give it to me," she said. "What I am going to do is keep walking, because I think we're too close to the house and anyone even vaguely nearby can hear our voices. I want to live, so if you want to live too you can come with me."

His face contorted in a spasm of anger, but she fixed her eyes on the trail in front of her and pretended she didn't see. Her heart beat fast in her chest and she wondered if he would follow. They were supposed to stay together. That was the last thing their mother had told Red. But at the moment she felt she would not have minded if Adam stomped off on his own. Let him get picked up by a patrol if that was what he really wanted. Red was going to Grandma's house, with or without him.

She was ten or fifteen feet away when she heard him exhale loudly, and then the sound of his heavy footsteps as he jogged after her.

* * *

They never talked about that argument. Adam seemed to want to pretend it never happened and Red went along, though secretly she dug a trench in her heart for the day when the war started again.

That kind of feeling that Adam had didn't just go away, and if she was completely honest with herself (and she tried to be) it hurt like all that was holy to have her brother blame her for their parents' deaths.

But Red took that great big blossoming pain at Adam's words and put it in a closet, a closet that held her grief for her dead parents and her fury at the people who'd killed them and her anger at the incompetence of those who should have seen this sickness coming and done something to stop it.

If she opened that door she'd find she was mad at everything and sad too and Red didn't need to feel all her feelings just then. She needed to keep on so that she and Adam got to Grandma's house intact.

They walked for a couple of hours—nothing too brisk, and Red thought of it as less of a mosey through the woods than a careful pace. She couldn't help feeling that someone might be ahead of or behind them, and if they went too fast it was harder to hear every sound all around them.

And Red wanted to hear if they (what "they" she didn't know—could be her parents' killers or government soldiers or just a pack of strangers out to take what they could get) were coming for her and Adam. Even if Adam thought it was her fault that Dad and Mama were dead, she wanted to keep his dumb ass alive. He was all she had and she was all he had and Mama told her to stay with her brother and she was going to do that.

Unless he insisted on going to the quarantine camp. That she could not abide. If he really wanted to clump up with the other sheep then he could do that by himself.

Sorry, Mama, Red thought. *I can't let him take me to one of those places.*

The stretch of state land behind their house was about twenty or twenty-five square miles. It was broken up by another small town nearby—a one-road village with a gas station and a few storefronts even smaller than their own hometown—and then the forest started again. In that part of the woods there was a campground about seven or eight miles from the border.

A dirt track led straight to that campground from the main road. There was nothing much to the campground—just tent sites with picnic tables and fire pits and a lime-reeking outhouse—but Red thought it would be a good place to aim for. The site wasn't especially popular since it wasn't near a lake like the other camp-ground in the area. Mostly it was a place for day hikers to stop and eat lunch and use the facilities, such as they were.

"How far from the road do you think we are?" Red asked over her shoulder, trying to calculate in her head. She didn't think they could make that campground before nightfall. That would be a lot of hiking, and it was already midday.

Adam shrugged. "Maybe three or four more miles."

"Right, that's what I was thinking," Red said. "We should find someplace to stop before we get there and set up camp for the night."

"Whatever," Adam said. "I'm hungry. You got any food?"

Red came to a full and abrupt stop. She turned around with all the slow drama of a stage actor and stared at Adam.

"What?" he said.

He'd stopped when she had, and he seemed totally unaware of the reason for the fury building on her face, though not totally unaware of the fury's existence. He took a half step back.

"Why don't *you* have any food?" Red said through her bottom teeth. "What the *hell* is in your pack if you don't have any food?"

"Hey, it's not my fault," Adam said. "I thought we were all going to divvy up stuff in the kitchen but then . . ."

He trailed off.

"Adam," Red said. "You spent half the morning putting shit in your pack. And it's completely filled to the top. Where were you going to put any food even if the plan was to divvy up supplies?"

Adam shrugged. He looked like a little kid all of a sudden, a little kid who'd done something senseless and impulsive and didn't really have a reason why except "because."

"Adam!" Red said, and she heard the yell and tried to dial it back because the forest was so quiet and yelling could attract attention and she was trying so damned hard *not* to attract attention. "For crying out loud, you've gone backpacking before. You know how important weight is and about leaving enough room for essentials. This is not new information for you. For Mama, yes. For you, no. So just what the hell is in your bag?"

"Stuff I didn't want to leave behind," Adam said, his mouth flattening. "Do you have any goddamned food or not? Because I am starving and I am not walking another step unless I eat."

"I am not walking another step until you open your bag and show me what nonsense you have in there," Red said. "And then you're going to throw out anything useless and make room for things you actually need to survive."

Her mind was racing ahead. They would have to go into someone's house, or into a town. She had enough food for herself for two weeks—she'd calculated it very carefully, every meal and snack. Red had known that at some point they would have to scavenge, but she hadn't expected it on the first day. That town they would pass through wasn't much of a town, though she supposed the gas station would at least have snack food.

Assuming it hasn't been raided or destroyed.

"You are not taking a damned thing out of my pack," Adam said, breaking into her thoughts.

"Yes I am, if you want to eat," Red said. "I've got the food, so I make the rules."

"You think I can't take that pack off you?" Adam said. "I could take it and run away and you'd never catch me."

He didn't say, *Because you can't really run with that leg*, but it was definitely implied.

Red felt that trench she'd dug in her heart earlier, felt all the barbed wire going up around it, started mentally stockpiling grenades. But she didn't throw them at Adam, the way she longed to do. They'd always had a squabbling relationship, always quick to point out the fault of the other. It would be incredibly easy to fall into that again, but this time there was an undercurrent of anger that had never been present before.

Adam blamed Red for their parents' deaths. He'd said that, right to her face. And it lay there between them, a dirty thing neither of them wanted to touch but couldn't fully ignore.

So she could make another angry remark, and this could escalate, and each would probably end up trying to wrestle the backpack away from the other and likely they would separate. Red didn't *want* to separate. Adam was her brother, like it or not. And Mama said they should stay together. She hung on to that. *Mama said we should stay together.*

Red bit her tongue and silently pulled her pack off and

dug around until she'd found a protein bar. She held it out to Adam but it didn't feel like a white flag somehow. It felt like unexploded ordnance.

He looked from the protein bar to her face and then looked away, something like shame in his eyes. "Thanks," he muttered.

"You're welcome," she said, and started hiking again.

She didn't repeat that they were going to have to find supplies soon because he'd been an idiot who hadn't packed any food. Once Adam had eaten the bar and his brain stopped badgering him for food he would realize that himself. She just tried to think about what was before them—what she knew was ahead, and what complications might be in the way.

Even though the next town was nothing much to write home about, it was still a space where there might be people— infected people, dangerous people. That was why she wanted to camp for the night before they reached the road, and then cross it in the morning—preferably before dawn, under cover of darkness. She knew that if she even suggested such a thing at that moment, Adam would at best laugh at her paranoia. At worst it would start another argument and she wasn't in the mood for an argument.

But all the same she fortified for the future, because Adam wasn't going to magically change his mind. They shared that quality—once an opinion was formed it was very, very difficult to dislodge it. Adam couldn't shout at the men who'd come to their house, or destroy all evidence of the virus that infected their mother, so he'd fixed on Red as the source of all his woe. It was up to her to be the better person, to control her temper, to wait for him to conclude that his anger was misplaced.

Mama, give me strength, she thought, because it was probably going to take some kind of divine intervention to stop her from snapping Adam's head off if he picked another fight. Red thought she was pretty good at self-reflecting. She knew her faults.

Adam didn't complain when Red suggested they pitch their tents in a clearing she found about a quarter mile before the road. He didn't speak as she boiled water over the small fire she built and handed him a meal from her bag. He added water to the meal, ate it with a spoon from his own pack. Red figured she ought to be grateful he at least had utensils, because she only had one set and she did not know what kind of fight would ensue if they had to share a fork. After dinner he went into his tent and didn't come out again, leaving his sister alone by the fire.

CHAPTER 8

The Serpent under It

BEFORE

The next day they packed up their gear and continued on. Adam hadn't objected to Red's plan of trying to reach the campground. She didn't know if this was because he agreed with her or he just didn't care anymore. Whatever the answer Red was always happy to have her own way, so they moved quietly through the last bit of the trail before they came upon the road.

All night Red had slept lightly, imagining she heard noises (usually trucks with large engines filled with armed men) that weren't there.

The trail ended at a small dirt turnout—a place for hikers to park their cars before they set off into the woods. The path picked up again across the road with a matching turnout on that side. Down the street to their left was the gas station and the little village.

She'd half expected to find a roadblock, or that the one-road town would be bustling with soldiers and people on their way to quarantine camps. But of course there was nothing.

"We'd better go to the gas station and see if we can find some more food," Adam said.

Red knew they would have to do this, but she felt the same strong sense of reluctance that she had before their family had gone on their ill-fated quest to Hawk's Sporting Goods.

"They won't have anything nutritious," Red said. "We'd be better off waiting until we can find a bigger town. It seems like a big risk for little reward."

"Bigger town means more people," Adam said. "And there's nobody around here, just like at home."

He started walking along the side of the road without consulting her again.

"Adam, wait!" Red said. "At least stay in the trees."

"Why?" he said. "Red, you'll be able to hear the sound of an engine long before it gets here, and when you do you can scurry into the forest like a little mouse and hide."

She could tell he wasn't going to listen, that he'd decided and that was that. So she didn't argue anymore though it was so hard not to say anything, not to tug him into the safe cover of the trees that lined either side of the road.

Red felt the back of her neck prickling, felt like someone was watching her from afar, someone who would swoop in and scoop them up and throw them in the back of a van.

She found herself holding her breath so she could hear better, hear any silent enemies that might try to sneak up on them, and then she gave herself a little shake because it made absolutely no sense to deprive herself of oxygen.

The gas station was empty, as expected, and the few shops that lined the road all had their *CLOSED* signs turned out. There was no evidence of the damage that had occurred in their hometown—no rampaging destruction, no broken windows.

This little village never seemed populated at the best of times and the postapocalyptic look wasn't that much different, Red reflected. It was like everyone was still inside having breakfast and none of the stores had opened up yet.

The gas station door was locked. Red and Adam peered inside the windows, an untouched array of chips and snack cakes and cigarettes and lottery tickets on display.

"We'll have to break the door glass," Adam said.

Red wrinkled her nose. She was reluctant to do that for a number of reasons—chief among them that breaking the glass seemed too much like theft. Of course it was ridiculous to think that way—the owner was unlikely to come back, and even if he did, would he really begrudge some hungry kids the food they needed?

She also didn't want to break the front door glass because it faced the road, and Red couldn't shake that prickly someone's-watching-me feeling. How could they hear someone coming along if they were making a bunch of noise breaking the glass? And there was nowhere to hide.

"Why don't we see if there's a back entrance?" Red said. She tried to make her suggestion sound casual, like it wasn't fueled by vague suspicions of lurking enemies.

And right after she did that she got annoyed with herself, because she was tiptoeing around Adam's feelings and it pissed her off that she had to do that. It wasn't natural. *He* didn't seem especially concerned about *her* feelings.

Mama said you should stay together.

Red knew that underneath that excuse *(yes, it was an excuse, really)* was a lurking fear that Adam might leave her. She wasn't usually afraid of being alone—she was a fairly solitary person by nature—but she was afraid of her brother unknotting that last family tie, of loosing her into the world to drift without anyone else who would remember the last moment their mother said good-bye.

But it was hard, really damned hard, not to speak her mind when she wanted to tell him that it was stupid as hell to stand out in front of the gas station, visible to anyone who might look out from a window or drive by.

Just thinking about the possibility of a spy in a window made Red glance behind her and squint at all the residences for a twitching curtain. It was not impossible that someone had survived in this little town and that they'd refused to go to a camp and that they were watching Red and Adam right now and they had a rifle ready if it looked like the two of them would get up to any mischief.

The trouble is, Red, that you can imagine too many possibilities. And imagining all the possibilities can get you in hot water just as easy as not thinking things through.

Too much consideration and she could end up lost in the weeds, paralyzed by the vast permutations of potential outcomes.

"Who cares if there's a back door?" Adam said. "It's probably locked, too."

Red shrugged. "It might not be. Isn't it worth checking? We could at least save ourselves the trouble of breaking glass."

Adam opened his lips, his ready-to-argue face on. Then abruptly he closed his mouth, turned, and went around the right side of the building.

Red hurried after him, surprised by his lack of response but also relieved. She didn't know how much longer she could avoid arguing with him. Being so considerate went against the grain of her personality. She felt her stiff shoulders relaxing as both she and Adam cleared the corner of the building. She couldn't see the road from there nor the second-story windows of the few buildings that had them (it was not only a one-horse town, but a one-story town for the most part) and that meant they couldn't see her either.

A weedy field, littered with crumpled cigarette packs and dirty soda bottles, bordered the small parking area. Past the field the trees stretched up again into the forest.

There was a car parked behind the station that hadn't been visible from the road—a modest-looking blue Ford sedan. Red wondered if it was the owner's car.

Adam reached the back door first—he had a head start, and Red was distracted looking around for possible spies. The door was a solid gray and the keyhole was part of the silver knob.

Red thought it strange that there wasn't a deadbolt as well—those little door locks seemed like they would be easy to pick. Not that she really knew anything about picking locks other than what she'd seen in movies, where someone with a bobby pin or a paper clip always seemed to be able to get around a securely locked door. She supposed that the owner didn't see the need for extra security. There wasn't even a camera over the back door, and she thought every gas station had video cameras these days.

Adam paused in front of the door, his hand hovering over the knob. Red wondered why he was hesitating. He looked up at her and smirked.

"Bet it's locked," he said.

"Bet it's not," she shot back. "And if I'm right you have to take five useless things out of your pack and carry all the extra food we get from here."

"Who decides what's useless?" Adam demanded.

Red thought for a second. "I pick three things and you pick two. Fair?"

"Fine," he said. "And if I'm right then you have to carry all the extra food."

"There's nothing useless in my pack to get rid of," Red said. "Where would I put it?"

"That's your problem," Adam said. "Deal or no deal?"

Red felt a little pang when Adam said that. It was something Dad always said, a phrase from a TV game show that he liked to watch, and for a moment she heard him saying it and could see the twinkle in his eye and she wondered how long it would take for a person's heart to finish breaking.

"Deal," she said.

Adam grabbed the knob. It turned easily and the door swung open.

Red laughed at the expression on his face. "You made the deal. Now you're stuck with it."

"Yeah, yeah," he grumbled. "You pick three things and I pick two."

The back door opened into a small storeroom. To the left there were industrial cleaning supplies and rolls of extra toilet paper stacked on metal shelving next to a miniature desk. Red peered at the contents, always curious about other people's lives. The desk was scrupulously tidy, all the unpaid invoices in a tray marked "unpaid." Red assumed all the paid invoices were in the file drawer. She opened the drawer and saw a line of file folders with months and years marked on the tabs in a neat hand.

A calculator sat next to the tray and a cup with several black Bic Cristal pens—the owner clearly preferred only one type of pen and Red knew the brand because it was the one she liked best, too.

It was an odd thought to make her melancholy, but it did. They had shared something—a small something, to be sure, but it was still a shared trait. They liked the same pen, and now Red would never know what else she and this person might have in common.

The virus hadn't just stopped existing relationships in their tracks. It had taken away the promise of the future, of all the connections that might be made. All those possibilities had been clipped neatly away, loose strings falling to earth.

There were other metal shelves to the right of the door, and these were filled with the store's backstock. Several brands of cigarettes were stacked there, along with boxes of candy bars and beef jerky and potato chips and all the other random snack foods one could find at a mini-mart.

Adam grabbed a bag of nacho cheese chips, opened it, and started cramming them in his mouth like he'd never eaten before.

"At least chew with your mouth closed," Red said.

Adam responded to this by noisily crunching several more chips. Red rolled her eyes and started scanning the shelves for anything with nutritional density.

Beef jerky wasn't bad. The protein at least filled up your

stomach. Nuts were good, too. She rolled down the stock with her eyes from top to bottom.

And when she got to the bottom, she stopped. And sucked in a hard breath.

"What?" Adam asked, chip crumbs falling over his chin.

"Blood," Red said, and pointed.

There was a line of streaky, faded red that went from the door into the shop to the back door they'd just entered. It was rusty and erratic, but it was definitely blood. Red was sure of it.

"It's not blood," Adam said, because he had to argue with her. "It's probably spilled root beer or something. Why do you always have to think of the most dramatic possibility?"

"It's blood," she said, and reached for the door that led into the shop.

"Wait," Adam said, grabbing her hand. "If it is blood, and I'm not saying it is, do you really want to go in there? Somebody probably died of the virus in there, and coughed all over the floor like that lady we saw at the pharmacy."

"If it's blood then someone might be in there who needs our help," Red said.

"Nobody needs our help," Adam said. "That's old blood, if it's blood at all. And you know damn well that nobody with the virus can be helped."

"It might not be the virus," Red said. "But we'll wear the masks and gloves, just in case."

Adam threw up his hands.

She didn't know why she wanted to go into the shop so badly. It went against her risk-averse nature, the intense caution that dictated almost everything she'd done since the virus had first been discovered.

Maybe it was the sensible Ford parked outside and the tidy desk with its pen cup filled with the same pens she liked best. Maybe it was just that she needed to know for sure that she couldn't help, that she couldn't do anything for whoever had made that trail of blood from the back door to the shop door.

Even with their masks on they could smell the rotting flesh as soon as they pulled the door open. Adam halted in the doorway.

"No need for further investigation," he said, his voice muffled under the mask. "That's the smell of dead things."

Red ignored him, kept following the long streaky path of blood. There was something strange about the blood trail, something she couldn't quite put her finger on. It didn't have the splattery look of someone coughing hard, like Probably Kathy Nolan. Anyway, the blood would more likely be on the walls or shelves in that case—not the floor. And the streaks didn't really look like they were made by footprints, or even someone crawling along the floor on their hands or elbows.

It's not a lot of blood, either, Red thought. *It doesn't look like a fresh wound that's bleeding. More like someone got blood on them and was trying to wipe it off.*

Red shook her head. That didn't make any sense at all.

She followed the trail around the counter, and when she saw the body everything made even less sense than before.

The man was lying on the floor behind the counter, which was why they hadn't seen him when they peered in the front door. He was on his back, his brown eyes wide and rigid and terrified.

In the center of his chest there was a giant hole. *Or rather,* Red thought, *there is a hole where his chest ought to be.*

The ribs peeled from the center of the sternum outward, like his lungs had exploded. Whatever organs still remained inside him were a mangled mess. It was almost as if someone had rooted around inside him with the edge of a knife. Red could see the jagged pink edges of organs pushed against other jagged edges.

Even a shotgun blast couldn't do that, if he was shot from behind. At least, Red didn't think so. She was no expert on the outcomes of shotgun blasts.

She considered this very calmly, even though she knew that a normal person would be screaming or running or at least breathing hard. It was as if part of her had unhooked from her body and was floating above her head, looking down on her own wild curly hair and red hood and frozen face staring down at the rigid form of a man who'd had his insides pushed outside his body.

"What the *fuck*?" Adam said.

She hadn't heard him move from the door to her side, and

she didn't jump but her heart took a huge leap forward, skipping over four or five beats.

"I mean, *what the fuck* is that?" Adam repeated.

"I don't know," Red said.

That was probably a first in the history of the world. Red couldn't recall the last time she said she didn't know something. She knew what it looked like, but she wasn't going to say it out loud. It was completely frigging ridiculous and Adam would laugh his head off.

"That's some *Alien* shit," Adam said, pointing at the open chest. "Right? It's that movie you like where the little monster comes out of the guy's chest and there's blood everywhere."

Adam had said it, which meant she didn't have to say it.

"But it's not a monster. It's a virus. Viruses don't do that," Red said, unable to look away from the body even though the sight made her a little sick. Everything inside the man was just a butcher's floor of ground-up meat.

"Something came out of that dude's chest," Adam said. "If it wasn't a monster and it wasn't a virus, what was it?"

"You saw Kathy Nolan coughing on the window of the pharmacy. All that blood. Maybe the intensity of the coughing . . ." Red began, then trailed off. That was almost more absurd than the idea of something

(not a monster, monsters were not real and this she would not tolerate or acknowledge no matter how many horror movies she'd seen, it was not a monster)

erupting out of the man's chest. No virus, no cough, had the power to make someone's chest explode.

Adam was giving her his "I-don't-think-so" look. "Come on, Red. You're the one who watches all those damned movies."

"You seem to know an awful lot about them for someone who doesn't think much of my taste in film," Red snapped. "Look, there's nothing we can do for him."

(what happened to him it had to be the virus but if it was the virus what did it mean was it mutating had this happened to other people what did it mean what happened what happened the virus has mutated it's turned into something else)

"So we should just do what we came here to do—get some food, unload some garbage from your pack, and move on to the campsite," Red said.

She was proud of how even her voice was, how she gave no indication that her mind was galloping in a hundred different directions, imagining possibilities that should not exist.

The virus has mutated. Mutated into what?

Adam looked from the body to her face, then swallowed hard. His eyes seemed a little too wide, but he shrugged. Typical Adam, pretending not to be bothered.

Just like you're doing right now. Maybe if you both pretend hard enough it will be true.

He went back around to the customer side of the counter, away from the body, and grabbed food from the shelves. Red noticed him picking all his favorite snacks—nothing but garbage that wouldn't fill his stomach—but she didn't say a word about it. Instead, she calmly reached past the man on the floor and pulled off several plastic carryout bags.

She handed four of them to Adam. "Put anything lightweight in these, and then double-bag them so we can tie them to the outside of your pack."

He gave her a thumbs-up. "Good thinking."

"Don't think this means you won't have to stick to the deal," Red warned. "You still need to shed some weight from that pack. And replace it with food that has something resembling actual nutrients. But not from here. We'll wait until we can find a grocery store or something."

"You don't think all the grocery stores will be trashed?" Adam asked.

Red gestured out at the empty village beyond the window glass. "It looks like most people either died quietly in their homes or they followed the instructions to go to a quarantine camp. I think we'll find a grocery store somewhere along the way that's not completely decimated."

"All the stores in the cities probably are, though," Adam said. "I bet there are bodies everywhere and everything not nailed down was looted."

"Then we're lucky that we don't have to go near any cities," Red said.

It was a marvel, really, the way they were both talking like everything was completely normal.

They quietly collected their supplies into the plastic bags, both of them pretending that there wasn't a guy with his insides on the outside just a few feet away.

You kind of get used to the smell, Red thought. She supposed it was like someone who worked as a coroner, or in a funeral home. After a while the bouquet of rotting flesh faded into the background.

She wondered how many of the closed doors of this little village hid sights like the one they'd found, people frozen in their last agonies, their faces seized in a final portrait of terror and pain.

They were just tying the plastic bags to their backpacks when they heard the sound of an engine approaching. Red slung her pack over her shoulder and cautiously peered out the window behind the counter. A large black pickup was approaching, the back of the truck overloaded with men holding rifles.

She didn't know if it was the same men who'd come to their house or another group of yahoos or even a government-sanctioned patrol, but she did know that no matter who it was she didn't want them seeing her or Adam.

"Out!" Red said. "Now! Go!"

Adam didn't have to be told twice. He scooped up his pack, the plastic bags full of snacks banging noisily against the outside, and sprinted through the back room. He didn't wait for direction from his sister but ran into the thin weeds behind the gas station.

Red hurried behind as fast as she could. In theory, the fact of her prosthetic leg didn't bother her but in practice it was not the greatest thing for trying to escape quickly.

She heard the truck engine turn off and men's voices shouting and she did not want to get caught, she didn't want to be seen, and half of her brain was worried about what was happening behind her and the other half wondered just what the hell had happened to Adam *(again, it was just like the house all over again, when would he learn to wait for her she couldn't go that fast for chrissakes)* because it was like he'd just disappeared into a puff of smoke and the weeds really weren't thick enough to hide in.

"Here!"

She felt something tug at her right pant leg and saw Adam lying belly-down in a little culvert maybe eight or ten feet from the edge of the parking lot. Red dropped to one knee and then shimmied down beside him, hoping like hell that no one discovered them there because the chance of her getting up quickly and running from this position was exactly zero.

Adam might get away, though.

Adam probably would leave me here. He's already done it twice.

A second after Red managed to get into the channel (and about a millisecond after she realized there was a thin stream of water running through it that soaked the front of her

ese were not Official Representatives of the U.S.
ent. They were individuals who'd collected together
led to act like they had authority. That scared Red
n any patrol of soldiers looking to take them to a
is group would not be answerable to anyone.

hing Red had learned from years of reading and
tching was that people were far scarier than any
zombie or alien or face-eating monster.

was one scene in *28 Days Later* when Jim and
l Hannah met up with Christopher Eccleston's
f-the-army group and the three survivors thought
in a place where they would be safe and then
said, "I promised them women," meaning he
he men under his command.

ver Red watched that movie her whole body came
ng because she knew what that meant, everyone
that meant for Selena and Hannah and their
the calm collected way he said it was far more
than the infected were in that film. Red thought
better to be bitten by a fast-moving zombie.

n who were moving in and out of the station now,
ut in their TV-copying formations with their
hunting gear (because that was what it probably
y overpriced shirts and pants that they bought
bela's or Bean's or Outdoor World so they could
ithout being spotted). They believed they had

clothes) three men came around the corner of the gas station.
They were talking loudly, carrying guns, and wearing
camouflage clothing and military-style boots.

Red couldn't gather too many details from her position on
the ground, but she did note that one of the three men was
black so that meant this wasn't the same group that attacked
their house. *One small favor*, she thought. At least they
probably wouldn't shoot Red and Adam on sight. Probably.

Despite their combat-ready clothing, however, she didn't
think this was a government patrol. Something about the
men didn't seem right, didn't seem like they were military.
They weren't . . . Red couldn't quite put her finger on it, but
they didn't seem cohesive. They didn't appear to be one
body moving in separate limbs, which was the way she
thought of army platoons and whatnot. Not that she had so
much experience of army platoons beyond what she saw in
the movies.

Red had left the back door of the station open—she felt
bad about this but she'd been in a rush and she was a little
surprised that it hadn't automatically swung shut behind her.

Once the three men realized there was an open door their
attitude changed completely.

They went silent, communicating with each other through
a series of hand gestures that were too fast to follow. They
carefully clicked the safeties off their weapons (Red assumed
this was what they were doing, anyway, because right after

that they all put their fingers on the trigger—the one part of a gun Red could correctly identify) and then quickly assembled into a formation with two in front and the third with his back to them and his weapon up. All of a sudden the men had the look of people who would ask questions when it was too late to get answers.

Despite this they still didn't seem like they were Army or National Guard or anything like that—more like men who'd seen that particular formation on TV and were copying it.

Good thing they didn't see us, Red thought. They would definitely have shot Red and Adam just for being there.

The two men in front—Red thought of them as Number One and Number Two—had a quick signed conversation before entering the open door. Then one went high, one went low—again, just like in a cop show.

The third man—Number Three—stood outside with his back to the wall just next to the open door, moving his gun back and forth across the horizon like he was scanning everything in front of him. Red ducked her head a little lower and hoped that her curls blended in with the dirt and the weeds and everything else. Beside her Adam lay perfectly still, like he was afraid to breathe.

Number Two came out again and reported to Number Three in a low voice. Red couldn't hear what he said but she had a pretty good idea that they'd discovered the man with the gutted torso inside the shop. Number Three lowered his

weapon and ran around the fro
shouting something to the other
heard it clearly. She thought it
that didn't really make any sens

Number Three returned w
whom had the same anonymou
first three. Number Three poin
the door. Red didn't know wha
was pavement, after all, and
prints. Had Red and Adam l
inside the store?

No, she would never be s
hurry. Adam might be carele
her heart seemed to beat a litt
men turned to scan the field
barely hidden.

Red could see now that
uniform—rather, it looked
clothing that looked close e
so that they would present

None of them had n
indicate—well, she didn'
indicate because Red knev
as she did guns, but she
usually patches showing
unit, or some other kind

So t
Governr
and deci
more th
camp. T
One
movie w
disease o
There
Selena a
remnant-
they wer
Eccleston
promised
When
over freezi
knew wha
future, an
frightenin
it would b
These
running ab
camouflage
was, probal
online at C
shoot deer

power because they had guns and the imprimatur of authority.

Red bet that most people who bumped into them gave them what they wanted. She also bet that there were more groups like them around, because this was America and the two things Americans liked to stockpile in case of emergency were canned foods and guns.

All the men had entered the building while Red spaced out thinking about movies and other things that she shouldn't be thinking about when they might have to run for their lives. She really did not want it to come to that because running in a prosthetic not specifically made for that purpose would equal Red getting caught by whoever was chasing her. She just couldn't move fast enough.

"Should we try to get away now while they're inside?" Adam said. He whispered it, barely moving his mouth at all, but it sounded incredibly loud in the deep silence all around them and it made Red wince.

She scooted closer so she could talk directly into his ear. "There are probably still men in the front. And the ones inside could appear at any moment. We'd better wait."

Adam's mouth twisted. "The front of my shirt is all wet."

"Better water than blood," Red said darkly.

That shut him up.

A minute later one of the men came out again. It appeared that he was in charge of this crew because he shouted for the rest to come around. Boots pounded on the pavement as six more men joined him in the back.

"Remove anything from the store that's edible or useful," the man said.

"Damn," Adam said, a little louder than he ought to have, but it was easily covered by the sound of all the fake soldiers shouting "Yes, sir!"

Red knew that Adam was thinking they could have gone back into the shop after the group left and perhaps collected more food. That was all over now.

As they watched the men carrying boxes and bags out of the store, Red was forcibly reminded of the Grinch taking the last can of Who Hash. They weren't leaving a single item behind for anyone else to find. Apparently it was now the Apocalypse and screw anybody who couldn't keep up.

Finders keepers and all of that, but Red thought it was a pretty shitty way to be. If they were scouring every store in the area like locusts, then Red and Adam would have to get ahead of them somehow. That wouldn't be easy, since Red wanted to avoid roads and they were walking and these jerks had a giant truck to roam around in.

It seemed like they were in that culvert forever waiting for the men to finish emptying the store. The sun was much higher in the sky and Red felt it beating down on the back of her neck. Her mouth was parched but she was afraid that the slightest movement would draw the attention of the Locust Militia.

Yes, a militia, that's exactly what they are, she thought. *And how many more of them are there? Is this group part of a larger group? And just when the hell are they going to leave?*

Red had hoped to cover the seven miles to that campground during the day, and their long delay here meant that wasn't going to happen. She was sturdy and she had trained up but she could only walk so fast, no matter how much she might want to go faster.

The last thing the men carried out of the shop was the body, wrapped in plastic sheeting. She hadn't noticed them carrying the sheeting inside, so they must have found it somewhere in the store supplies.

For a second Red thought that they were going to dispose of the body in the field, maybe burn it there, and she had a full-fledged panic attack at the prospect of trying to outrun a burning field, possibly while being shot at by pretend soldiers.

But two of the soldiers (she couldn't help but think of them that way even though she knew they weren't real soldiers, and that was the dangerous thing, the way a costume change and certain accessories presented a particular idea to those who looked on) carried the body around the front of the gas station.

One last man came out of the door, then ducked back in—perhaps to do one last check, though for what exactly Red couldn't imagine. It didn't seem that they'd left behind a single crumb. Then he returned to the truck and a moment later Red heard the engine start up.

Neither she nor Adam moved until the sound of the truck had receded into the distance. When she did try to stand up Red found that every muscle was stiff and sore, and she realized she'd been holding her body in a state of clenched tension.

She also realized that the water they'd been lying in did not smell so great now that it had soaked into her shirt. She was still wearing the mask and gloves that they'd put on when they entered the shop, and the combination of the culvert water and her own sour breath made her momentarily nauseated. Red took off the mask and inhaled the smell of dirt, grass, and the lingering scent of gasoline and exhaust.

"Those weren't real soldiers," Adam said.

Red was surprised that Adam had been observant enough to notice that, but she didn't say so. The presence of immediate danger seemed to have thawed the ice between them, at least for the moment. Red also didn't mention that she'd been right to be cautious, that if they had been walking along the road when that truck came along Lord knows what would have happened to them. She didn't say it but she did feel a little smug because it wasn't just Crazy Red being paranoid. Her worry had been completely justified.

"They definitely were not soldiers," Red said. "More like some kind of homegrown militia."

"Well, that was inevitable," Adam said. "Probably collected all of those supplies for their camp full of crazies. They've probably got five wives each and intend to have a full standoff with any real government patrol that comes to take them to quarantine."

"Adam, that is downright fanciful," Red said.

"Sounds like something you'd come up with, doesn't it?"

Red hit him hard in the upper arm and he said, "Ow!" but grinned at her.

"It does sound like something I'd say," she admitted.

"But why did they take the body?" Adam said.

Red's mouth twisted. "I don't know. Maybe for quarantine?"

"None of them were wearing masks," Adam pointed out.

"You're right," Red said. "I can't believe I didn't notice that. I was so focused on their soldier trappings."

Adam gave her a quizzical look.

"You know, their fakey uniforms, the boots, the guns."

"The fact that they drove up in a Ford F-150 should have told you straight off that they weren't real soldiers," Adam said. "I wonder how they fit all the stuff from the store and all those guys in the flatbed."

Red shrugged. "I don't know anything about cars. They all look the same to me."

"Even you should be able to tell that wasn't a government vehicle. The plates were wrong, for one thing," Adam said.

Red inwardly marveled at the details that Adam thought important enough to note. It never would have occurred to her to look at the license plates.

"Wait, how could you even see the plates?" Red asked, thinking about the few seconds he'd had to observe them. "From that distance?"

"You don't need to see every detail," Adam said. "The plate is different from every state plate—usually it's plain white with just the plate number and it will say 'U.S. Government' above the number. I could see even from a quick look that the truck had our state plate on it."

"Huh," Red said. "Well, points to you but we still don't know why they took the body with them."

"Maybe they're performing bizarre experiments on it. You know, *bringing zombies to life*!" He said this last bit in his movie-trailer voice.

"Even I don't believe in zombies," Red said. "At least, not human ones. There are those weird mushrooms that take over insects, though. Not mushrooms, fungi. I saw a documentary once—"

Adam held up his hands. "I don't want to know about any real-life zombie shit. I do not. Because I am already going to have nightmares about that guy's ripped-open chest and the thing that crawled out of it."

"Nothing crawled out of it," Red said. "I told you, this is a virus. Viruses don't crawl out of people's bodies. They stay inside and multiply."

"So the virus made his lungs spontaneously explode?" Adam said. "Seems more likely that there would be a creepy little animal inside waiting to burst out."

Red didn't want to argue about it, and part of the reason she didn't want to argue about it was that she wanted to think all of the possibilities through, one by one.

That might mean acknowledging something you don't want to believe, Red. Acknowledging that a tiny virus has mutated into something that could do that. It was funny how her inner voice so often sounded like Mama, and how she would argue right back at it like Mama was standing there in front of her with her debate face on.

I'll acknowledge it when I'm damn good and ready.

And right now she was not damned good and ready. She never would have said "damn" in front of Mama, though. Mama hadn't cared much for language like that.

CHAPTER 9

The Dearest Thing

AFTER

The snow that woke Red in the early hours of the morning wasn't anything that would have worried her Back in the Old Days. The Old Days, of course, weren't that old, but a few flurries that didn't stick to the ground wouldn't have been anything to fuss about when she had a roof and a furnace and lots of thick blankets as proof against the weather.

Now the few fat flakes were worrisome portents of things to come. They meant that she wasn't walking fast enough, wasn't making good enough time, that her path to Grandma's house might be stopped in its tracks by a snowstorm that she would have to ride out in a backpacker's tent.

It wasn't yet dawn but she bundled up her hammock and sleeping bag and ate a protein bar.

Oh, for a pancake, a Danish, a pile of bacon next to eggs

just out of the pan. Anything except protein bars and granola
bars and energy bars.

Red never wanted to eat anything bar-shaped again for
the rest of her life. Even a candy bar seemed repulsive.

She took out her flashlight and carefully picked her way
back to the trail. That is, she took out her flashlight after a
good five-minute argument with herself over whether it was
safe to use it, as the beam might act as a beacon for anyone
in the vicinity.

Finally Red decided that if there was anyone about they
would also have to use some kind of light and therefore she
would see their light and be able to turn hers off to hide and at
that moment the woods were about as dark as they could be.

She needed to stop getting stuck in circles like that, she
thought, needed to stop second-guessing and third-guessing
for danger. Yes, it was potentially dangerous out in the
woods. But it was less dangerous than being in a city or other
area where there were lots of people and she needed to
remember that.

Once she reached the trail again she consulted her
compass and started off in the correct direction. The sun
came out, but it only gave off a weak cold light. Red found it
hard not to take the sun's lack of warmth personally. The
least the damned sun could do was actually shine and warm
things up so it wouldn't snow on her.

The day passed as so many of them had, with Red

trudging along in the silent wood. Many of the birds were gone now, flown to warmer climes for the winter. A few crows persisted, calling to their fellows perched on nearby trees. Crows always sounded angry to Red, like they woke up every morning with their throats stuffed with bile, but it was just the way they called. They might be singing love poetry to one another, for all Red knew. She didn't really know about birds.

The steady pace with nothing much to look at but trees, trees, bushes, more trees lulled her into something like sleepwalking—just putting one foot in front of the other, thinking about nothing in particular.

Then there was movement in front of her—something bigger than a squirrel, but not big enough to perceive as a threat (Red assumed at this point that basically every adult human was a threat).

Red blinked. Once, twice, and fought the urge to rub her eyes and blink again. Because she thought she just saw—was actually fairly certain she *did* just see—two little kids with dirt-streaked faces and leaves artistically arranged in their hair dart away from the path and into the brush.

She doubted her eyes only because they were so quiet. Red had never known an American kid who was capable of moving like that. They always barreled, leapt, sprinted, falling over and shouting and laughing and crying but generally doing everything as noisily as possible. But not these two.

They'd slipped across the path and into the undergrowth with only the faintest crackle of dead leaves underfoot, hardly more noise than the average chipmunk would make.

The brush they'd disappeared into was thick all along the edge of the path Red walked on, a tangle of low evergreens growing in every direction. She'd never seen so many little evergreen bushes in the woods—usually they were ruthlessly manicured and set to border annual beds on someone's front lawn. These were about three quarters of Red's height (admittedly, not a very high height) and perfect for hiding. Especially if you were a couple of kids on your own in the woods.

Red slowed her pace, because the kids had been a little ways off when they disappeared and she wasn't completely sure where they'd entered the brush. She didn't want to count on hearing them—they seemed like they'd gotten in the habit of being still and quiet (a good habit when soldiers might be about, or just adults that might want to hurt you)—so she peered into the dirt for evidence of little foot marks along the right side of the path.

Red almost missed them *(no, a tracker you certainly are not)* but just as she was about to pass by she noticed the smooth dragging marks made by knees in the dirt, and just the faintest impression of handprints in front of them.

Maybe the kids were not quite as little as they'd initially appeared. They'd been crawling on hands and knees, although their movement had been so quick she'd first taken them for preschoolers.

She carefully put her right knee on the ground and then leaned on her left foot, in a sort of football-huddle-crouch. It was difficult to squat all the way down because of the way the prosthetic attached to her knee, but she was able to get low enough to see that there was a well-worn trench just under the bottom of the bush.

Red considered flattening herself to her stomach to look underneath, but then realized that was a recipe for getting stepped on if the kids decided to burst out of their hiding place. Instead she carefully parted the branches, hoping not to startle them.

"Whoa," she said.

Behind the shell of the branches there was a huge open gap inside, almost like a natural tent or shelter. The kids were huddled up at the far end of the gap, about five feet away from her. There was a pile of filthy blankets coiled like a nest near their knees, and a small backpack that looked like a repurposed school bag. The pack was open and Red could see a few granola bars piled on top of some dirty clothes.

It was hard to gauge their age, especially with their dirty faces and no idea of their standing-up size, but they looked like they were maybe between eight and eleven. She didn't want to make any assumptions about their gender, either, since they both had that shaggy-haired-haven't-seen-a-barber-since-the-world-ended style.

The two of them had their arms wrapped around each other, and Red noticed those arms were very thin. They weren't wearing jackets or hats, only thin T-shirts, and they must have been cold even with the blankets. She wondered how long they'd been out here, and what they'd been eating besides granola bars, if anything.

"I won't hurt you," Red said, and then winced. What a stupid frigging thing to say. It was the first thing the bad guys always said in the movies when they were *about* to hurt you.

The mystery kids seemed to think so too, for they inched farther away from her.

"Sorry, that was dumb. Let's try again. My name is Red. Fancy meeting you out here in the middle of nowhere," she said, and smiled, and hoped they thought her lame joke was funny and nonthreatening.

"Your name's Red?" one of them asked, ignoring the lame joke altogether. "How can your name be Red? Nobody is named after a color."

The other one shushed him/her.

"Don't talk to her," the second one whispered, trying not to move his/her mouth too much.

"Well, my name's not *really* Red," she said. "That's the name that I go by. My real name is too awful to contemplate."

"Contemplate?" asked the kid who'd spoken first. That one seemed chatty.

"Shush," the second one said, again attempting to pitch his/her voice low enough so Red wouldn't hear. Unfortunately, it was so quiet out in the middle of nowhere that any sound, however tiny, seemed like the clash of cymbals. "Don't you remember that we agreed not to talk to strangers?"

"Contemplate means to think about something, or to look at it," Red said, pretending she hadn't heard that last bit.

"It's a word that means two things? I know about those words. I learned some of them in Language Arts at school."

"Riley!" the second child said, clearly fed up with the other child's persistent chatter.

Well, that didn't help narrow down whether it was a boy or a girl. Riley was one of those names that could go either way.

"Riley is a cool name," Red said. "A lot cooler than mine."

Riley had unclenched from the tight embrace of the other child and inched toward the opening where Red's face peered into their shelter. This kid clearly had the friendly gene. Red bet the other kid had to stop Riley from telling their life story to any stranger they encountered. The second child hung back, gazing suspiciously at Red.

"What *is* your real name?" Riley asked.

"It's . . . Cordelia," Red said, with a dramatic pause between the two words.

Riley laughed, a high joyous sound that seemed like it didn't belong in that terrible world. It cut through the oppressive air of the forest and hung there like a magic spell.

"That's not so bad. We have a great-aunt Hilda, and I think Hilda is much worse than Cordelia. Cordelia is kind of pretty."

"Mama certainly thought so, although she usually just called me Delia. She was a Shakespeare professor and she named me after a character in one of his plays."

"Our mama worked at the Walmart," Riley said. "But then she got killed by a man who was mad that there was no more medicine in the store."

This was stated with a bald matter-of-factness, as if the child were a news anchor reading off the day's tragedies at six p.m.

"I'm sorry to hear that. What about your dad?" Red asked.

"Riley!" the other child said, but the admonition didn't stop Riley from continuing. Red bet if she stayed still long enough Riley would tell her all about his/her favorite movie, pet, the last time he/she had pizza . . . the kid just had that kind of vibe.

"He got the Cough and then he died. At first I thought it was better that Daddy wasn't killed like Mama, because that was terrible, thinking Mama would come home and then she didn't because some crazy person shot her over something that wasn't even her fault," Riley said. "But then Daddy got the Cough and there was so much blood. We couldn't even go near him because there was so much blood, and that made me sad because I wanted to at least kiss him good-bye but we couldn't go near him, we might have got the infection. Where's your mama and daddy?"

"My mama got the Cough, too," Red said.

She hesitated, wondering if she should tell them the rest of the truth. Her mama had gotten the Cough, it was true, and it probably would have killed her if that pack of jackals hadn't come along. It might be enough just to tell them that.

Then she realized that protecting little kids from the truth was a relic from an old world, and that these kids had surely seen just how bad people could be since the Crisis started. Their mother was killed for no damn reason whatsoever. They knew the world wasn't a shiny cotton-candy fair ride. There was no reason to lie.

"My mama got the Cough," Red said again. "And probably my dad would have gotten it too, and they both would have died from it. But before that happened some men came along to our house and attacked them."

She felt something clogging her throat as she said this, unable to speak of it with the same detachment that Riley had. It didn't really matter how much time passed, because the deep and profound unfairness of it all surged back on her every time.

Mama would have gotten sick and died anyway but at least that was a normal, natural thing in a world infected with a deadly virus. It was not normal or natural for people to come to your house wanting to kill you for stupid reasons.

Riley scooted a little closer, close enough that Red could have reached through the gap in the brush and touched that solemn little face.

"And they were killed?" Riley said, with the same respectful hush that you might use in church.

"Yes," Red said, because that was all that she could manage.

She'd thought she had processed it, dealt with it, put it all behind her. She'd thought she wouldn't drag all that hurt with her like a suitcase with a broken wheel. But she was still dragging it behind her, even if she couldn't see the tracks. "Me and my brother got away."

"Where's your brother?" Riley asked. "How come you're all alone?"

"My brother is gone now," Red said.

Riley nodded, seeking no further explanation. It was a world of terrors, after all. "Did your mama get the Cough that makes you explode?"

"Explode?" Red said. If she'd had antennae they would have stood up. As it was she thought some of her curls tried pushing out from under her woolly hat.

"Some of the people with the Cough, you know, they explode. Like their chests bust open," Riley said. "Not all of them."

"Riley, shut *up*," the other child said.

"I haven't seen anyone with the Cough do that," Red said cautiously. "What is it like?"

"Well, after the person coughs a lot of blood—I mean a *lot*, like a milk gallon of blood, maybe even more than that," Riley said, waving his/her hands around to demonstrate the pool of blood, "then they split open right here."

Riley gestured down the center of his/her ribs.

"And then everything kind of peels in a really gross way. I never saw anybody's ribs before except in a skeleton in the Pirates of the Caribbean ride and that doesn't count because it was fake."

("That's some Alien shit," Adam said, pointing at the open chest. "Right? It's that movie you like where the little monster comes out of the guy's chest and there's blood everywhere."

"But it's not a monster," Red said, unable to look away even though the sight made her a little sick. Everything inside the person was mangled, no discernible organs, just a butcher's floor of ground-up meat. "It's a virus. Viruses don't do that.")

There had been those funny markings on the floor near the body, the ones that Red thought at first were something slithering away, and then she'd checked her too-active imagination and decided it was just the man's clawing fingers because Red wasn't any kind of crime scene investigator and what did she know about interpreting blood on the floor and it was absurd to think something had come out of the man's insides.

"What happens after that?" Red asked.

"We didn't stay anymore after that," Riley said, glancing back at the other child. "It didn't seem like a good idea to watch. We might have gotten sick, too."

"I have to agree," Red said, but only part of her brain was

there, listening to the conversation. She was thinking of Probably Kathy Nolan.

(You saw someone coughing up blood like that, coughing up a milk gallon of blood, coughing all over the window of Swann's Pharmacy like she was about to burst open)

"Daddy didn't have that kind in him but one of our neighbors, Mrs. Mikita, she had it. We went over there after Daddy died because she said she would take care of us but then she started coughing and we knew we'd have to go soon anyway but we wanted to stay in a house for a little while longer because we weren't sure what to do if we went outside, all our relatives live far away."

Riley trailed off, eyes staring into the distance at some memory Red didn't share.

"But Mrs. Mikita, she coughed like that? And you saw her chest break open?" Red prompted.

"Yes," Riley said. "We had to leave the house then. We just ran out as fast as we could because the way she was coughing it almost seemed like she was going to cough blood right into our mouths. And I didn't want my chest to do that. We didn't even have our jackets or food or anything really."

Red thought there was probably a lot more to the story than this, but Riley no longer seemed inclined to talk about it.

"You guys must have come a long way to get here," Red said. The nearest town was at that dangerous crossing she'd been dreading, and that would be a good walk to kids of this size.

"I dunno how far it was but it seems like we've been walking *forever*," Riley said, and said they came from a town about twenty-five miles or so away, by Red's calculation.

"Stop *telling* her all this stuff!" the other child said. "It's not any of her business."

"You're right," Red said, quietly impressed that a couple of kids could get so far with basically no resources. "It's not my business. But since I'm alone and you're alone maybe we could walk together for a while, what do you say?"

Red would never have said this if they were adults. She knew that. Because she couldn't trust other adults not to harm her. But it was a long lonely walk that she was on, especially without Adam

(don't think about Adam)

and even if she wasn't lonely there was no way she could leave these two children in the middle of the woods. They would starve to death, or someone with ill intent would find them.

"How do we know you're not working with the soldiers?"

"Soldiers?" Red asked. She wasn't sure if they were talking about the homegrown kind or the real military.

"Those soldiers that go around collecting people in trucks?" the second child said, his/her voice doing that uptalk thing at the end like it was half a statement and half a question. "They have dogs."

The child's fearful tone told Red that these two had been

chased by those dogs. It was miraculous that they'd managed to get away—get away from the infection, get away from the soldiers, get away from the dogs. Red wanted to hear that story, wanted to know exactly how they got to where they were—two little kids miles from anywhere.

Why hadn't she and Adam seen more bodies like the one in the gas station? Of course, they hadn't seen that *many* dead bodies to begin with. They'd seen the ones stacked up in their own town and burned in the center square. For the most part the places they'd passed through had been swept clean of people, living or dead, as if a fairy had come through with her wand and magicked them all away.

Or maybe some guys in a truck picked them up and took them away for some nefarious purpose of their own.

The kids stared at her expectantly, and she realized she'd never responded to the second child.

"I'm not working with the soldiers," Red said, coming back from the place where she'd gotten lost in her own brain. "I'm just trying to get to my grandma's house."

"Is your grandma nice?" Riley asked, and Red couldn't miss the wistfulness behind the question.

"She's the best grandma in the world," Red said. "She always has our favorite kind of drink in the refrigerator when we come to visit, and she puts cedar blocks in all of her dresser drawers so that your clothes smell like the forest. And she makes pizza dough from scratch and cooks the pizza in a brick oven outside and it tastes better than any pizzeria could ever make. But all grandkids think their grandma is the best, right?"

"Our grandma was the best," Riley said. "She made one million kinds of cookies at Christmastime—chocolate chip and oatmeal raisin and sugar cookies shaped like Santa and snickerdoodles and . . ."

"Ri-*ley*," the second child said, obviously weary at this point.

Red didn't see any point in chiding Riley, but the second kid seemed to feel it was important to try.

"Do you . . . ?" Riley trailed off, looking uncertainly at the second child, as if expecting him/her to object. "Do you have any food?"

"I do," Red said. "And I'll share it with you, if you'll come out of there and walk with me a bit."

"No," the second child said, and snatched at Riley's wrist, trying to pull the other one back.

"Get off, Sam," Riley said.

Sam. Another maybe-a-boy-maybe-a-girl name. So, maybe two sisters, maybe two brothers, maybe one of each. Red didn't care so much which except that she wanted to stop thinking of each kid as him/her.

"We're not going with you," Sam said, nice and loud so Red couldn't make a mistake.

Red recognized the technique—it was used in a lot of self-defense classes. Sam was "using her voice" (or maybe his voice) to protect herself and her sibling—speaking up, not letting anyone run over her. It was a good thing to teach kids, and Red was glad Sam felt confident enough to do it. But it meant that she had some more work to do before the two of them would agree to come out from under that shrubbery.

What Red wanted was to find a place to camp for the night and build a fire, and she needed a decent clearing for that. This place was far too flammable, what with all the low brush, and there was no place to pitch her tent except right on the path. She didn't cherish the idea of another exposed night in her hammock.

And there was not a chance in hell that she was going to leave these two hungry kids out here in the middle of nowhere. They might die of starvation (although they did seem fairly enterprising; they might figure something out even if it involved eating pine needles) or get picked up by a patrol or . . .

Or worse. A lot worse. Red had no trouble at all thinking about what the worst might be, with gangs of men roving about and no law to stop them. There are things far more terrible than dying.

The kids were probably safe enough in the woods, but they'd have to venture into populated areas to find food, and that was where the horror would be. Those men, like the men who'd killed Dad and Mama, weren't the types to go tramping through the woods in hopes of slim pickings. They would stick to towns and cities, scooping up survivors. So as

long as Red (and Sam and Riley) kept far away from houses
and shops they would be okay.

But how long could they stay away from houses and shops?
How long could they live on increasingly stale granola bars?

"Listen," Red said, because she sensed that trying to ease
into Sam's trust would be too time-consuming. She might be
there all day trying to wheedle the kids into coming with her.
Better to be straight up about it. "I've got lots of food in my bag,
and a tent, too. And I know how to build a fire. I'm not going
to hurt you, and if you come with me I'll share my tent and my
food and my fire and then maybe you can walk along with me
awhile, because I'm alone and I don't want to be alone anymore."

Red kept her eyes on Sam as she spoke, because Sam was
the one she would have to convince. Riley looked ready to jump
out of the shrubbery the second Red mentioned the food.

"How do we know you're *really* alone?" Sam asked, eyes
narrowed.

"What do you mean?" Riley asked. "There she is, all by
herself. Obviously she's alone."

"No 'obviously' about it," Sam said. "She could have
followed us and left behind her buddies and when we go to a
place to pitch the tent those buddies will jump out and . . .
hurt us."

The last bit was said in a very small voice, a tiny voice that
knew something of how kids might be hurt by adults trying
to trick them.

"I don't want to hurt you, and I don't have any buddies. Truth. I do have a whole box of spaghetti and jarred tomato sauce," Red said. "And I can't eat them all myself."

"*Spaghetti,*" Riley said, and there was so much longing in that word—a longing not just for food but for shelter, a table, a family, warmth. "Do you have meatballs, too? Because spaghetti and meatballs are the best."

"No way, lasagna is the best," Red said.

Riley stuck out his tongue. "Mama always put beef in the lasagna and also melty cheese. I don't like melty cheese."

"The beef is the same as the meatballs, only not rolled up," Red said. "And how can you not like melty cheese? Melty cheese is like the only reason for living. Don't you like grilled cheese sandwiches?"

"No way! Gross!" Riley said.

Red gave Sam an incredulous look. "Who doesn't like grilled cheese?"

"He doesn't," Sam said, though she still hadn't lost her suspicious glare. "He never liked anything with cheese on it."

He. Okay. Riley was a boy. One down.

"Do you like grilled cheese?" Red asked Sam.

"She *loooooves* grilled cheese," Riley said. "She loves it so much she wants to marry it."

"Shut *up,* Riley," Sam said. "Who wants to marry a grilled cheese?"

She. Sam was a girl. A brother and sister. Just like Red and Adam. Except that they were together, and Red and Adam were not.

Don't think about Adam.

"How can you eat pizza if you don't like melty cheese?" Red asked Riley.

"He eats pizza *without cheese*," Sam said, whispering the last two words as if they were a bit of scandalous gossip.

"*No,*" Red said, giving Riley a horrified look. "Just bread and sauce?"

"Bread and sauce and pepperoni and olives," Riley said, and Red and Sam both said "ewwwww" together and they all started giggling.

"So will you come with me?" Red asked. "I know it's what all the adults say, but I really am not going to hurt you."

"Come on, Sam," Riley said in a wheedling tone. "Spaghetti! Don't you want spaghetti?"

Sam looked from Riley to Red, then waved her hand at Red. "Go away for a minute so we can talk in private."

Red hesitated, because she didn't want Sam to grab Riley and dart into the woods when her back was turned. But if she didn't show that she trusted them, then the kids might never trust *her*. If she seemed too eager to keep an eye on them, then Sam might think she was a kidnapper or something.

So she nodded and stood up and tried not to fall over as she did, because her thighs had stiffened while she was semicrouched on the ground and it was never easy to get up and down to begin with.

"Go down the path a little!" Sam said. "I don't want you to listen."

Red clomped off noisily so that Sam and Riley could have their conference. She didn't need to eavesdrop to know what it was about—whether she was trustworthy, and if the promise of a spaghetti dinner was worth risking their freedom. She'd have had the same conversation with Adam if the two of them had been alone in the woods at that age. Hell, she'd had multiple conversations with *herself* along the same lines in the last few weeks.

It was always the same debate—absolute safety or some degree of comfort. How long could a person go without eating warm food or having shelter over their head? How long before they decided to risk going into an empty house, a depopulated town, a looted store, an abandoned car? How long before they couldn't bear to be alone anymore and thought it might be safer to join a group of friendly strangers?

And what if that house wasn't empty, or that town was the base for some militia? What if that group of friendly strangers only showed their teeth because they were sharks?

Yes, Red could understand Sam's caution. Red wished she could show the younger girl some proof that she was as safe as she claimed to be.

If they came along with her, that would be a start. That

would at least be enough to show Sam and Riley that she didn't mean them any harm. And eventually she could convince them to continue on to Grandma's house with her. Maybe showing up with these two would help Grandma forget that Red didn't have Mama or Dad or Adam with her.

Or maybe it wouldn't, because you couldn't just replace a person you loved with someone new.

Maybe Sam and Riley could help Red in that department, too. Because the longer she walked on her own in the forest, the more she felt set adrift from the real world, the human world. Without people to help her remember, it would be easy to stop being civilized altogether.

She was already in the habit of viewing every person she met as a potential enemy, and even though it had probably saved her several times over, it was hard not to feel a little ashamed of that. People were supposed to give a shit about each other, especially in times of need.

Trouble was, most people were all too willing to bulldoze anyone who got in their way when they wanted something. *Just look at that story Riley told about their mom*, Red thought. She worked at the Walmart and she got killed because the store ran out of something through no fault of her own. That was the kind of world they lived in now. There would be no heartwarming stories of communities coming together to assist the elderly or take care of orphans or anything like that. Everyone was out for their own damn self, and Red, too. She didn't want to die, so she was willing to do what she had to do to make sure that didn't happen.

But she didn't want these kids to die either, if she could help it. Though taking them on, even temporarily, presented its own set of difficulties. Starting with the fact that she had a one-person backpacking tent and one sleeping bag and as far as she could tell Sam and Riley only had a bundle of smelly blankets.

Well, she would deal with that when it came time to deal with it. She wasn't that tall and the kids were skinny, so maybe they could all squeeze in to the tent and Red could use a space blanket while the kids got in the sleeping bag. It would at least be warm with three bodies inside the tent, even if two of those bodies were small.

Red was so lost in the potential logistics that she didn't even hear the two of them come up behind her. She didn't jump when Sam spoke, but it was a near thing and she had to school her face before she turned around.

"All right, we'll go with you," Sam announced. She carried the backpack of granola bars and had put on a gray sweatshirt with a Gap logo across the front that was much too large for her. Red bet she'd scavenged the sweatshirt somewhere along their walk.

Riley also had a sweatshirt that was too big for his thin frame, although it at least looked like a kids' size. Sam's was something that had once belonged to an adult.

Jackets, Red thought. They needed jackets and sleeping bags and she would have to try to find a larger tent. And of course they would have to find more food and the kids would have to carry some of it.

Yes, there would be problems, but Red liked solving problems. Besides, she'd spent so much time fine-tuning her own pack that she knew exactly what Sam and Riley would need.

But they would have to go into a town, or a house. And that would mean danger.

You know what Dad would say about crossing bridges before you get to them, Red.

So she nodded at Sam and Riley and said, "I'm glad you're coming with me."

"It doesn't mean we're staying with you forever," Sam said, her mouth set in a way that Mama would call "mulish" and Red recognized it because her own mouth made that shape on a regular basis.

"I understand," Red said, and she did. Sam was reserving their right to take off in the middle of the night, or not continue north when Red wanted to continue north. She wanted to know that Red would respect their wishes and not order them around or try to force them to do anything they didn't want to do.

"Okay," Sam said.

They fell in beside her, Riley next to Red and Sam on the outside.

"I can't wait to have spaghetti!" Riley said. "And that means we can have a fire, too, doesn't it?"

"Dang skippy," Red said. "Can't boil the water without a fire."

"And then we'll be warm *and* we'll have spaghetti. Do you know that our dad used to like to eat the dried spaghetti?" Riley said, his nose scrunched up.

"I don't want to say your dad was weird," Red said. "But that's kind of weird."

"I know," Riley said. "It's totally weird. My mom used to yell at him because he would come in the kitchen when she was cooking and pick at the dried spaghetti before she could put it all in the pot and every time she would say, 'If you want to eat dried spaghetti then I won't even bother cooking,' and he would say, 'But you don't want your kids to starve, do you?' and then she would smile and tell him to get out of the kitchen and he would steal some more dried spaghetti on the way."

"She doesn't want to know our whole life story, Riley," Sam said. "You don't have to tell her every single thing that comes into your head."

Riley ignored this, as Riley seemed to do whenever Sam told him not to speak.

"How come you walk funny?" Riley asked. "Is your leg hurt?"

Red didn't think her limp was that noticeable, but maybe it was if you were down close to her leg like Riley was. Or maybe she was just used to it after so many years and it was obvious to people who'd just met her.

"Ri-*ley*!" Sam said, and she sounded really annoyed this time. "That is just rude."

Red waved her hand to show that it was all right. "It's okay. I have a little bit of a limp because I have a prosthetic leg."

"Prosthetic?" Riley asked.

Red stopped and pulled up her pant leg so Riley and Sam could see the metal tube at her ankle. Riley's eyes lit up so bright that Red thought she saw stars in them.

"You're a *cyborg*?" he asked.

Red laughed. "Nothing that cool, sorry. It just means that I have a fake leg to help me walk."

"Oh," Riley said, his face falling. "What happened to your real leg?"

"Some jerk hit me with a car and part of my leg got stuck under the tire," Red said.

"For real?" Sam asked.

"Yes, for real," Red said. "When I was eight years old."

"Hey, I'm eight years old!" Riley said, then added, "I bet it hurt."

"It hurt later," Red said. "When the car actually hit me I got knocked out so I didn't feel too much of anything."

"Once I fell off the high monkey bars on the playground and my ankle got twisted up under me and it really hurt," Riley said. "Like really bad. I bet it was worse than that."

Red didn't really remember the pain in her leg, because when she woke up her lower leg was gone. But she didn't tell Riley that, who seemed eager to find a connection between them.

"It was worse than that," Red said.

"Was it like, super gory? Like the skin and muscle and everything came off your leg and that's why they had to give you a fake one?" Riley asked.

"Come on, Riley, that's gross," Sam said. "And she doesn't want to talk about that."

"I just wanted to know," Riley said.

"You don't need to know every single thing," Sam said. "And you don't need to *tell* every single thing either."

"How far away is your grandma's house?" Riley asked.

"Still a pretty long way," Red said.

She definitely did not want to tell them numbers and miles because they might decide then and there to leave her. The thought of a hundred-plus-mile trek had been intimidating to the adults in Red's family. It would sound like the other side of the universe to these kids, probably.

They walked on for a couple more hours, Riley chattering continuously about whatever came into his head and Sam occasionally interjecting to tell him to stop giving away so much information.

There was no particular point to this constant admonishment that Red could see, but Sam seemed to think it important to try. Red wondered if Riley's friendliness had gotten them into trouble before. Then she decided that if it had, the trouble wouldn't have been too serious, else not even the promise of spaghetti could have convinced Sam to leave their makeshift kingdom under the shrubbery and join Red.

They found a good place to pitch the tent, a nice cozy clearing with trees all around. Red worried, as she always did, about the possibility of the smoke from their fire being spotted from the road. They were getting closer and closer to the town. Still, the town was necessary now. The kids would need a lot of supplies that they didn't have.

This, Red thought, was what life was now. It wasn't an exciting adventure, or even full of the banality of a daily routine. It was about logistics—finding food, carrying food, adequate shelter, stressing about the weather, fretting about people she might encounter. She'd never worried so much before, and she knew very well that the addition of Sam and Riley to her party (such as it was) would just make her worry more. But there wasn't a chance she was going to leave them in the woods with nothing but some granola bars and a pile of dirty blankets.

She built a fire, and made the spaghetti with tomato sauce, and then realized she only had one fork and one plate and one spoon.

So that's more things we need, Red thought, and decided to write down a list after supper so she wouldn't forget anything.

Both kids were looking at the pot with the kind of longing that they might have given to a toy store or a Dairy Queen, back when the world was sane. But now they just wanted something that was hot and would make their stomachs full and it made her so sad to see that, because kids *should* be able to save that look for something stupid like an ice cream cone or a new video game.

She pulled out the fork and the spoon and the plate, then decided the plate was extraneous and put it aside. She held up the fork and the spoon in her fist and said, "Who wants what?"

Sam was quicker off the mark and grabbed the fork, leaving Riley with the spoon.

"No fingers," Red said. "I have to eat out of that pot when you're done."

They reached toward the pot at the same time, scooping up as much pasta as they could get and shoving it into their mouths.

"Don't choke," Red said, alarmed at the quantity of spaghetti stuffed into Riley's cheeks. "Chew your food."

She didn't think they even heard her. They were in a kind of sharklike feeding frenzy; their only awareness was that there was food in front of them and they needed to eat it. Red thought sadly of the food she'd left behind in that cabin. At the time she thought it would be too much extra weight, and that she could get two or three dinners out of one package of spaghetti. The way that Riley and Sam were gulping down her prized discovery meant she probably wasn't going to get a single bite.

She shrugged to herself, because she had eaten well (all things considered) for most of the trip and it wouldn't hurt her to have a can of soup again. Red pulled out her notebook and pen and started composing a list of things she needed to find for Riley and Sam when they got to the next town.

After a surprisingly short amount of time both children seemed to reach their stopping point. In unison they dropped their utensils into the pot and leaned back, holding their bellies.

"I'm so fuuuulllll," Riley said, pointing to his stomach. "Look at how fat I am."

"You're not fat," Red said, peering into the pot. There was enough left for her, maybe a tennis-ball-sized portion. "But you will probably have the mother of all poops in a little while."

Riley giggled at that and Sam did a kind of half-smile, half-frown. "Mama said we're not supposed to talk about bathroom things at the table."

"My mama said the same thing," Red said. "But do you see a table?"

"That's right, there's no table," Riley said. "So we can say 'poop' and 'pee' and even burp if we want to."

Red held up her hand. "No burping. Burping is gross."

"Especially your burps," Sam said, shoving Riley's shoulder. "They're like the grossest things you've ever heard."

And so naturally Riley felt compelled to share his super

gross burp, which was long and loud and wet and made Sam and Red shudder and shout at him to quit it.

Later they all squished into the tent, Sam and Riley in the sleeping bag and Red wrapped in two of the space blankets that she'd packed *just in case* and she was feeling pretty smug about it just at that moment.

Riley watched with interest as Red rolled up her pant leg and unclicked her prosthetic and removed the socket and liner. There wasn't a lot of light in the tent, just a small flashlight's worth while everyone got settled down, and he squinted at her stump in the gloom.

"It looks kind of like Frankenstein," Riley said.

"I guess it kind of is like that," Red said. "They had to cut off the bottom part of my leg and then seal it up."

"So the rest of your leg wouldn't squish out," Riley said.

"Why are you *so disgusting*, Riley?" Sam said. "And anyway, Frankenstein is the name of the doctor, not the monster."

She seemed to be deliberately keeping her head turned away from Red's leg, so as not to seem rude by staring. *Or maybe she's afraid to see it*, Red thought.

"'Frankenstein's the doctor, not the monster,'" Riley said in a high-pitched, mimicky voice that was sure to spark a sibling argument. "Why do you always have to be such a know-it-all, Sam?"

"All right, that's enough," Red said, smooth and even but

with just enough firmness behind it to indicate that enforcement would follow if obedience didn't.

Just like Dad used to do, Red thought, and the two settled down.

Now that they were all in the tent Red was uncomfortably aware of everyone's scent, and that scent was pretty damned ripe. It would be hard to give them a proper bath, but she had baby wipes in her bag and she was going to make sure they used them. And maybe she could heat some water to wash their hair, too.

Red turned off the flashlight and rolled onto her side, the blankets wrapped tight around her to keep warmth in. The ground underneath her was rocky and cold, and she wouldn't have noticed it as much with the padding of her sleeping bag. She shifted a little, listening to Sam and Riley rustling inside the bag, and soon they were both asleep.

Red heard their quiet breaths, long and deep and even, and something else, too—an echo, a memory of a voice that wasn't even there.

Why do you always have to be such a know-it-all, Red?

CHAPTER 10

Sound and Fury

BEFORE

"Why do you always have to be such a know-it-all, Red? Why do we always have to do things *only* your way?" Adam complained.

They were on their stomachs, peering down from the top of a hill to a town below in a little valley. They'd been there for a half hour or so, by Red's reckoning, but she wasn't going to expose herself on the side of the hill until she was sure there was no one lurking down there with a high-powered rifle.

Though how she would be aware of such a thing if the person was indoors she didn't know. She hoped her spider-sense would tingle or some such thing, that her innate sensitivity to danger would warn her before they got their heads blown off.

Innate sensitivity to danger, my ass, Red thought, and for once the voice in her head didn't sound like Mama but a more incredulous version of herself. *You're no X-Man, or Sarah Connor, or any other damned superhero from a movie. You're just a girl who's scared to death and thinks she's smart.*

There had been no movement below, just like every other residence or village they'd come upon thus far, but she wasn't taking any chances. The memory of that homegrown militia methodically clearing the gas station mart had stuck with her, and she felt strongly that if those men had come upon her and Adam then, the fake soldiers would have boxed them up and put them in the back of the truck along with the potato chips and beef jerky. If they didn't kill them first. Red always considered the possibility that for people like that homicide was a viable option.

"There's nobody down there, Red," Adam said. "If this was their base we would know. There would be activity, vehicles parked in obvious places. It's just another abandoned town and this sun is hot and I have had enough. I'm getting skin cancer on the back of my neck."

Adam stood and arched his back, then stared at his pack without picking it up.

"What?" Red said, coming slowly to her feet.

All her muscles felt frozen in place. She'd been holding tension in her body while they watched the town and she needed to stop that, because the walk was hard enough without adding more stress.

She needed to practice some deep-breathing exercises or

something, because if she clenched up like this every time they came to a town, the exhaustion would crack her sooner rather than later. Red rubbed her molars with her tongue. Her tooth enamel wouldn't make it, either, if she didn't stop grinding her jaw.

"I don't want to put my pack on again," Adam said. "I just don't."

Red, who'd never taken hers off, shrugged. "Sorry, little baby. You have to."

"I'm tired of carrying my damned house on my back like a turtle," Adam said. "It's stupid that we're walking. Like really stupid. Every time we cross a road it's clear. There are no abandoned cars and no army blockades like you predicted so there is no reason we should be walking. We could be in a car and be there in a few hours."

"With what gasoline?" Red asked. "How are we supposed to get gas when every pump we've passed has been turned off because there's no electricity?"

"There's got to be a way to get it out," Adam said. "How are those militia guys driving around if they don't have gas?"

"They probably have a stockpile of it somewhere," Red said.

She didn't add that all of her arguments were still valid for the same reasons she'd made them in the first place, or that just because they hadn't seen a blockade didn't mean they didn't exist. They hadn't encountered one because Red and Adam had been keeping to the woods.

Adam made some barely distinct grumbling noises that definitely included the words "fuck this," but he put on his pack.

The hill was very steep, and Red found she didn't have time to fret over what might happen when they reached the bottom of it. Hills were the bane of her existence—they forcibly reminded her that her balance was not the same as everyone else's. Steep hills required a lot of concentration and careful stepping, because one root, hole, or rock could equal a Jack-and-Jill-type disaster.

"Why *haven't* we seen any cars, though?" Adam said.

"We have," Red said.

Adam waved his hand. "I'm not talking about those military guys. I'm talking about regular people, people like us."

Red puffed out a breath. It was hard to think about what Adam was saying and focus on not falling flat on her face at the same time.

"Well, we've seen a few other people," Red said, thinking of the one awkward evening spent at a campground about a week before.

There had been another party there, an older couple with a very small boy, and the woman (the grandmother, Red assumed) had given them such a suspicious glare that Red and Adam hadn't even tried to do more than say hello. Red didn't know if that suspicion was because they were black (possible) or just because the old woman was cautious (likely). Red and Adam had chosen a site that was as far from the other group as possible, and in the morning they were gone.

"We've seen other people on foot, like us. But I can't believe your average American would choose to walk rather than get in a car. Our whole lives are organized around our cars," Adam said. "Drive-ins, drive-throughs, parking lots, highways, freeways, pay at the pump—everything is designed to get us in our car and keep us there."

Whenever he said stuff like that, Red felt she didn't give Adam enough credit for being perceptive. Mostly she felt his intelligence was unequal to her own because he was lazy, not stupid, but occasionally he came out with a gem like this one.

"And most people don't like to walk, or exercise. So when the shit rolled down the hill they would have put all their stuff in their car and driven away," Adam said.

"Yeah, but to where? To a camp? To their country estate? I mean, where do you think people out here would go?" Red said, gesturing toward the little village nestled in the valley below. It was a postcard waiting to happen, all snug and slightly antique and surrounded by green hills and sunshine. "People in a city fleeing—that would make sense. They might think that getting away from a large population would help keep them from getting sick. And then you'd see all those car pileups and people just abandoning their vehicles and deciding to walk because of the gridlock. But out here there is no gridlock, so if folks decided to drive away they probably didn't have any trouble doing so."

"So tell me again why we didn't?" Adam asked.

"Because at some point we would have come to a bigger town, or city, and then we would have encountered that gridlock," Red said. "Or those blockades. It's safer this way."

"It's slow as hell, is what it is," Adam said. "And I'm tired of lugging this shit around and eating nothing but canned soup and peanut butter sandwiches."

Red felt the retort on her tongue and swallowed it. Adam was in a combative mood and she didn't need to roll in the weeds with him just because he felt like arguing.

When they reached the village, Red saw that a close-up view made it a lot less picturesque. Every building had peeling paint or stood at the slightly crooked angle that indicated subsidence or had shingles falling from the roof. The houses were clustered tight together, like cattle fearful of wolves.

The main street had the required secondhand store, bursting at the seams with spindle-leg chairs and creepy porcelain dolls. Red had never been much of a doll girl. She didn't see the appeal of a plastic figure with strange-smelling hair and dead eyes, and even as a child her interest in clothes (and therefore doll dress-up) was nil.

There was a cobbler next to the secondhand store. Red peered with interest into the windows of the cobbler's shop.

"Do people really go to cobblers anymore?" she asked. "I

mean, most shoes don't even have the kind of soles that can be replaced."

"We're looking for food, Cordelia," Adam said. "The cobbler shop isn't going to help us."

Out of curiosity Red tried the door. It was locked up tight. Both the cobbler shop and the secondhand store were completely untouched, windows intact.

"Like the owners closed one day and just never came back the next day," Red murmured. She suspected at least some of the owners were rotting inside the houses. Not everyone would have survived long enough to leave.

Adam had gone on ahead, because his stomach was always his priority. He was about four storefronts ahead of her when she saw him stop suddenly.

"Damn!"

"What?" she asked, hurrying along a bit to catch up with him.

In response he pointed at the storefront before him. There was a green awning with white script on it that read *Albertson's Grocery*. But the double doors to the shop were broken open, and even from the sidewalk Red could see that the store had been scavenged already.

"Damn," Red repeated, then automatically checked around to see if there was a person in the immediate vicinity who had done the scavenging.

"There's no one here," Adam said, rolling his eyes. "This

looks like the work of those militia guys. Which means there won't be so much as a crumb left inside."

"But we should check anyway," Red said. "There might be something."

The smell hit them a few feet inside. Adam gagged and Red immediately dug for the masks that she kept in a handy pocket. "The mask isn't going to cover the smell," Adam said, but he took it anyway.

"Hang on, I have an idea," Red said, dropping her pack on the ground. She dug through until she dredged up the jar of Vicks VapoRub that she'd taken from Swann's Pharmacy—so long ago, psychologically speaking, that it seemed like a scene from another life.

She rubbed some of it under her nose and reapplied the mask, then handed it to Adam. He looked at the jar doubtfully.

"Go on, give it a try," she said.

He copied her and gave an impressed nod as he handed the jar back.

"What made you think of that?" he asked, then added, "Some movie, I bet."

"*The Silence of the Lambs*," Red admitted. "There's a scene where everyone's come to look at a body and they put stuff under their nose so it doesn't smell so bad."

"I never thought I'd be grateful for your horror movie habit," Adam said.

"You watched it," Red said.

"Yeah, but I only remember the part where Hannibal Lecter put the guy's skin on his face," Adam said. "Because that was just *wrong*."

"Like the killer making a skin suit out of women isn't wrong?"

Red noticed that both of them were using voices a half-pitch above their regular ones, what she thought of as cocktail-party voices. And she also noticed that neither of them had come out and said, *The smell means there's at least one body in here*, even though they were dancing around it by talking about a serial killer movie.

"Let's start on the left and work our way to the right," Red said, pointing at the aisles. "All the packaged food is always in the middle of the store, so if there's anything left it will be there."

"It would go faster if we worked separately from each side," Adam said, but there wasn't a lot of conviction in his tone. Red knew he didn't want to be alone when he found the body.

It's just foolishness, because a dead person can't touch you or hurt you, Red thought. But foolishness didn't matter when the dead had been the boogeymen of humanity since the dawn of time. People feared the dead because they feared becoming one of them, but Red thought that there were worse things than death. Death meant you didn't have to worry about staying alive anymore and that seemed like a comfort, especially now when staying alive was the primary concern of every moment.

"I don't think we should separate," Red said. She held fast to this rule, because separating was always wrong in an apocalypse situation—even if it was only one of them on the right side of the grocery store and the other one on the left. Something Would Happen, and then they would no longer be Red and Adam, and a solo traveler would be left behind. Red didn't want to be left alone, even if she and Adam didn't always get along.

"We'll be in the same building," Adam said, but his protest felt half-hearted, and they moved together to the left side of the store.

The cash registers were on that side, so they quickly checked the impulse-buy shelves, even though Red knew if there was anything it would be of the sugar-salt-fat variety, nothing properly filling. But Adam was a damned bottomless pit at home when he wasn't walking several miles a day, and now he was hungry pretty much every fifteen minutes so even a random, nearly expired Snickers bar would be something.

There was nothing there, though, not even a pack of gum. That didn't bode well for the rest of the store, but Red felt that they should check. Adam took the higher shelves. Red was five foot one and he was a full foot taller, which meant she would have needed a rolling ladder to see the rear of the top shelves.

She used to have to stand on the bottom shelf to reach items on the top shelf, back when she used to do normal things like go to fully stocked grocery stores and buy food with money that was more than just worthless bits of green paper.

And Adam used to make fun of her if he saw her taking clothes out of the washing machine, because she'd have to reach so far inside that it seemed like she might just fall headfirst into the basket and he would have to pull her out by her flailing legs.

They were halfway down aisle six (cereal, granola bars, tea and coffee, according to the sign) when Red and Adam saw them. There were two corpses this time, not just one. The stench was so pervasive (despite the Vicks under their noses) that they hardly noticed an increase in the smell until they were practically upon the bodies.

"Why are they stuffed onto the shelves?" Adam said.

It was an odd detail to latch onto, but then Red figured Adam's brain needed to grab something or else he might start screaming his head off. She knew that she was in that condition herself.

"They" were a man and a woman, anonymously middle-aged, white, and naked. In this condition it was easier to see the caverns where their chests used to be—the broken ribs (jagged at the edges), the ripped muscle, and the spray of dried blood that had decorated their remaining skin like a modern art painting. The man's lips were pulled back from his teeth, frozen there in a permanent grimace.

Someone—or a few someones—had pushed the bodies

onto the second shelf from the bottom, one on each side of the aisle so that they faced each other. Red was at a loss to explain why anyone would do this.

"And they're just like that other guy," Adam said. "The one in the gas station. Which means it wasn't some fluke thing and there really is a parasite bursting out of people's lungs. Look, there's the slither marks on the floor, too."

Adam pointed to the end of the aisle in front of them. There were bloody trails there, leading away from where they stood and toward the back of the store.

Red took a deep breath. She wasn't ready to believe in chest-bursting monsters even if *Alien* was one of her favorite movies. "It doesn't make sense. How can the parasite get inside their lungs in the first place?"

"They inhaled it," Adam said. "It's the virus. They inhale it and it makes people cough because it's growing inside their lungs and then when it's too big it busts out."

"Adam," Red said patiently. "I told you before, viruses don't grow that way. They're like a trillionth of an inch long to start and they don't get larger. They're not tapeworms that get bigger and bigger inside you."

"Why not?" Adam asked. "You're looking at the evidence."

"I'm not looking at anything," Red pointed out. "I see two bodies with open chest wounds and some marks on the floor. Until I actually see an alien life form crawling on the ground I'm not buying it."

"Then let's follow the tracks," Adam said.

"Oh, let's not," Red said.

"Afraid you'll be proven wrong?"

"No, just afraid that we'll waste our time with this when we should be looking for food. I think we might have to break into one of the houses nearby and see if they have anything stored. There's nothing left here."

Red hated breaking into houses, because it felt like such a terrible violation. Of course it was necessary. They needed to eat and it was likely that the owners were dead or rounded up into quarantine camps. But it never stopped feeling wrong.

"I want to see where the tracks go," Adam insisted.

Red sighed. She recognized his "digging-in-my-heels" voice and decided it was better to play along for a few minutes and get it over with so that they could move on to more important things. Like finding food, which seemed to occupy a huge portion of their lives now.

She was getting that itchy feeling again, the one that made the back of her neck prickle. There hadn't been anything *obviously* wrong with this little run-down village, but that didn't mean wrong things weren't hiding in the seams.

"Fine," Red said, then grabbed his shoulder before he could stride forward. "Hold on, idiot. If you really think there's a monster lurking in the shadows, you don't go charging forward without something to defend yourself."

"Right," Adam said. "Like what?"

It was *so hard* not to roll her eyes right out of her head sometimes. Someone ought to give her an award for dealing with Adam.

"Don't you have a hunting knife?" Red asked. She'd seen him using it not too long ago.

He dropped his eyes and shuffled his feet and he looked just like one of her babysitting charges caught eating extra dessert.

"I, uh, lost it," Adam said.

Red narrowed her eyes. "How did you—wait, never mind. I don't want to know. It'll just make me want to beat you and we don't have time for that."

"I think I left it at one of our campsites," he said. "By accident."

"I just told you not to tell me," Red said, unhooking her hand axe from her belt. "Get behind me, dummy."

"Hey," Adam said. "I'm not a dummy."

"What do you call a person who leaves an essential piece of equipment on the ground?" Red said.

Adam ignored this. "I should be in front."

"Why?" Red said.

"Because I'm . . ." he began, then trailed off when he saw her expression.

"A *boy*? More able-bodied?" Red offered, but her tone was silky and dangerous. "You don't have a weapon, and I'm not giving you mine. So get behind me."

She moved along carefully, not because she was worried

about something hearing them (they'd already made plenty of noise arguing) or a monster popping out in her face but because she didn't want to miss the tracks. The lines on the floor were clearly demarcated close to the bodies, but they faded out pretty quickly once Red and Adam rounded the corner of the aisle.

She stopped, bent over, peered closer. "I don't know. It looks like the tracks are disappearing. If they are tracks in the first place—the kind of tracks you mean. They could just be marks from where someone dragged those bodies on the ground."

Red was trying not to think about the bodies. This wasn't because they were horrifying but because she wanted time and quiet so she could contemplate what she'd seen. She wished to take out her mental picture of the Other Guy (as she now mentally tagged the man at the gas station) and compare it side by side with the couple on the shelves.

Maybe they had it all wrong. Maybe it wasn't an alien or a lung parasite or some other completely unbelievable thing but instead was some serial killer who opened people up and pulled their organs out. Adam would scoff at this because he seemed (surprisingly) invested in the idea of an out-of-this-world monster, but the idea of a human one was a lot more plausible to Red.

A human who can peel back bone and bend it like metal? Are we talking supervillain now, Red?

No, she definitely did not need another potential option to contemplate. There were drawbacks to watching too many genre movies.

She was about to propose that instead of following streaks of blood on the floor, they go back and examine the wounds more closely when Adam shouldered her aside.

"Let me see," Adam said, crouching down with his nose nearly touching the floor. "Yeah, they're fading. But it looks like the tracks went toward that back room."

He indicated a door with no handle a few feet away from them. The door was the type that you could push in either direction—handy if you were carrying a box of produce or a cart full of goods to restock the shelves.

Also useful if you were a handless lung parasite and you needed to hide away in a dark space.

She shook her head. *Don't get caught up in his fantasy, Red. The thing that killed most people is a regular old virus, the kind that you can't see without a slide and a microscope. This thing that's tearing open chests is something else, and it's not supernatural.*

While she was woolgathering Adam popped back up and made for the door with no regard for his own safety.

"Hey!" she said.

He turned around, his hand on the door ready to push it open.

She held up the hand axe. "What are you going to do if

something freaky jumps out and tries to eat your face?"

"Scream like crazy and run," Adam said. "Which is what you're always saying people should do in those movies you watch. I'm no kung fu master. I'm not going to try to stay and fight it."

He pushed open the door and went into the back room, leaving Red muttering to herself.

"Sure, and what's going to happen to your one-legged sister while you're running away? That's probably part of your plan, to leave me here to get eaten and then you can hitch a ride on someone's truck and you won't have to walk anymore."

She pushed on the door, hesitated (because she was born with an overabundance of caution even if Adam wasn't), realized that if there was anything or anyone inside that Adam would be yelling his fool head off already, and followed him.

The room was much bigger than she expected, a little warehouse attached to the back of the store. It was lined with aisles of metal storage shelves attached to the concrete floor. There was a strong scent of off-produce—the wet rot reek of greens, the halfway-to-cider fermentation of apples, bananas well past their banana-bread usefulness. Red could see flies buzzing around several of the boxes in the aisles directly before her.

Red couldn't see Adam anywhere, which was no surprise. It would never occur to him to wait for her.

"Adam!" she called.

"Yeah?"

"Where the hell did you go?"

"Aren't you following the tracks?"

"I'm not a damned bloodhound, Adam."

She heard movement on her right side, and Adam stuck his head out of one of the aisles several rows away. "Here."

Red moved in that direction, peeking at the floor as she did so. She couldn't see any marks that indicated they were heading in the correct direction. What she did see were boxes of dried goods on the shelves. Not a lot, but there were several unopened cases of soups and other things that could be useful.

"Hey!" Red called. "Did you see all this food?"

"Yeah, the soldier-boys must not have had enough room in their trucks for everything," Adam said. "Come look at this."

Not enough room in their trucks, Red thought, and that made something go *twang* deep inside her brain. Before she could latch onto that alarm and explore it further she was next to Adam.

He pointed to a hole underneath one of the storage shelves. It looked like something had chewed through the concrete.

"There," Adam said triumphantly.

"What about it?" Red said.

"The trail leads here and there's a hole, so whatever came out of those people went in here."

"It looks like a rat hole. And Norway rats can chew through concrete," Red said. "In fact, those streaky marks on the floor probably *are* from rat tails. I don't know why I didn't think of it before."

She shuddered a little, because she really hated rats. She didn't like mice, either, to be honest. As a child she'd turned away from books with rodents as the main character (and there were a surprising number of these, as if children's authors thought every kid was in love with small furry animals even if they were disease-carrying monsters) because just the thought of their slithery little tails made her sick.

"Rats didn't bust out of those corpses," Adam said.

"I don't think anything *did* bust out of those corpses," Red said. "I think maybe a person did it."

"That doesn't even make sense," Adam said. "The chests look like they exploded from the inside, not like they were cut from the outside."

"Do you have a medical degree? How do you know?" Red asked. "It makes a lot more sense that rats came and nibbled on the corpses and left those tracks. And that would also account for the mangled insides."

"Then where are the rat paw prints in the blood?" Adam asked. He gestured toward the hole in the ground. "I say some freaky alien thing grew inside their lungs and then broke out and ran away in here."

"And I say you have no proof," Red said. "But if something like that did happen, you probably don't want to put your face so close to the hole."

Adam stood up so quickly that his pack banged into the shelving behind him and knocked over a bunch of paper towel rolls.

"Look, whether it's rats or aliens there's no creatures now," Red said, glad for the mask that covered her mouth so he didn't see her grinning at him. "So let's collect the food we need and get out of here."

Adam shot one last suspicious glance at the rat hole (Red was going to think of it as a rat hole and nothing else, because the other option was absurd and that was that) and then followed her.

They spent some time figuring out how many cans of soup they could each realistically carry. Red wished for the meal pouches she'd started off with but splitting them with Adam had made them disappear fast, and this was not the kind of grocery store to carry those types of goods.

They collected some more granola and cereal bars and packaged nuts, then hoisted their packs back on. Adam moaned immediately.

"Oh my Christ, it's so much heavier," Adam said. "What the hell? Do we really need to carry all this?"

"I just don't know how many times I have to ask you if you want to eat on a regular basis," Red said.

"I am never going camping ever again," Adam said. "Once we get to Grandma's house I'm never leaving."

Red didn't say that when they got to Grandma's house

there would probably be just as many, if not more, tasks to stay alive. Adam was not ready to hear that. But they wouldn't have to carry their packs every day, and Red could admit (quietly, to herself) that this *would* be a relief.

She covered her ears and said, "You whine more than a four-year-old without a nap."

Adam said something that was indistinct because her fingers were pressing into her ears.

"La, la, la, I can't hear you," Red said.

He grabbed at her, trying to take her hands away from her ears, and she darted away through the door into the main part of the store, laughing.

She always remembered that afterward, that she and Adam were laughing when she walked out and there was a man holding a rifle pointed at her face.

CHAPTER 11

The Hurlyburly

BEFORE

Trapped, Red thought. After all her plans and all her schemes and all her caution they were caught anyway, pinned like butterflies on a board.

The man was shouting, telling them to get down on their knees and put their hands on the back of their head and Red followed his instructions but everything inside her had gone numb.

Still, some remnant of hope and caution made her tug her shirt hem over the axe hanging off her belt so they couldn't see it. She didn't see how she'd possibly be able to overwhelm a man with a rifle with that little blade but if she kept it hidden then maybe, *maybe*, it would come in useful later.

What do you think you're going to do, Red—leap up and battle this guy to the ground like you're a movie superheroine with martial arts skills? More likely he would just break your wrist and take the axe away.

Still, no point in advertising its presence. And having the option to defend herself made her feel better.

He called to someone else—Red wasn't really paying attention to what he was saying and anyhow the blood was filling her ears now and how could she have been *so* stupid as to not set one of them out to watch while the other went into the back room?

Because then you would have been separated, and Not Separating is the golden rule.

Why had she indulged Adam's stupid idea about chest-exploding monsters? Why were they playing around when they came through that door instead of being careful?

She was *always* careful. She was *always* cautious. If they had been listening they would have heard the rumble of truck engines outside. It was pretty clear now from the amount of activity that she could see through the window that there was a long line of them, and that they were filled with soldiers—real soldiers this time, with proper uniforms and patches and name tags and all the accompanying gear (which included more guns than she ever wanted to see in her life).

Soon there were three more soldiers around them, each man holding his weapon trained on Red and Adam like they were the most dangerous criminals in America. Nobody spoke after the first guy (and they were all guys, Red noted, not a woman among them and that wasn't a good sign) called his buddies over.

Red didn't say anything because she was not volunteering any information to anybody no matter what the circumstances and she was pretty sure Adam wasn't speaking because he didn't want to get shot if he startled one of them.

Red and Adam remained in position with their hands on the backs of their heads. Part of her wondered how she was going to get back up again because kneeling like this on a hard floor was really not good for her left knee and she was worried that if she struggled or stumbled when rising that these men would interpret it as aggression and shoot her out of hand. It would be such a stupid waste to get shot for a dumb reason and then Adam would be all alone, too, and Lord knew Adam needed someone to look after him even if he was older than her.

Her brain ran around in circles like this, her inner monologue on babbling mode because there was nothing else for it to do.

The soldiers appeared to be waiting for someone. They didn't speak to Red or Adam or to each other, just kept their weapons trained on their prisoners.

Prisoners, Red thought bitterly. If they were just going to get caught they probably should have driven as far as they could. Maybe their parents would still be alive and they could all be prisoners together.

No, Red, don't you think like that. Don't try to double back and say if only we'd done this or that. *Choices were made and right or wrong they can't be unmade.*

Red could see the broken double doors of the store from her position on the floor. Two men entered. They both wore camouflage uniforms with caps instead of helmets and carried sidearms but no rifles.

Each man appeared to be over six feet tall, but one was several inches taller than the other. He was easily the biggest person Red had ever seen who wasn't on a professional basketball team. His height was so distracting that she almost missed the little leather bag he carried in his right hand.

Oh no, she thought. There was nothing in that bag that she wanted. She knew with a blinding certainty that he would open that bag and out would come a needle or a bottle, a little something to make her sleep or make her pliant.

And after that she and Adam would be loaded onto a truck just like a box of soup and taken to some quarantine place teeming with miserable people, people screaming to be let out or just wandering in a resigned zombie shuffle, people wondering why nobody was helping them and why they were being treated like criminals when all they'd done was follow instructions and gone to where the government told them to and now they were trapped and there were high fences and guards on catwalks and it was all supposed to be for their protection but it didn't feel like it, it felt like maybe it was so the soldiers could be protected from them.

Red hadn't followed the rules, hadn't done what she was told, but she was still going to be stuffed into a bag and taken to that place anyway. Adam didn't care, probably, because Adam had wanted to go there in the first place and she'd bet that he'd be thrilled to pieces not to have to walk anymore.

If it comes down to it and I try to run, I bet he'll stay behind.

Her heart hurt at the thought of this, because she'd tried so hard to keep them together. Maybe it was selfish, and she was sure Mama would yell at her for even thinking this, but she felt she'd rather leave Adam behind than let the soldiers keep her.

And he would probably be happier that way, really. He'd never seen the wisdom of her plan.

The two tall men approached—Red tagged them Tall and Taller—and the soldiers surrounding Red and Adam moved apart deferentially to make room for the newcomers in the little circle.

"What have we got here, Corporal?" Tall asked.

"Caught them coming out of the back room." This was the first man, the one who'd stopped Red and Adam laughing.

Red didn't like the way he said it, said "caught" like they'd been found covered in blood with a massacre at their feet. But she bit her tongue because she wasn't going to give them so much as a sigh.

"Where are you from?" Tall barked.

Adam looked at Red, and Red looked at Adam, and by

silent consent they decided Red would do the talking.

"Why do you want to know?" Red said.

She could sense Adam's silent groan, could practically feel the words emanating from his brain to hers.

Why can't you just answer the man's question, Red? Why do you always have to be smart?

And of course her response to that would be, *You had to know I would be like this.*

Tall frowned at her. "What's your name, young lady?"

"And I say again, why do you want to know?"

"I don't think much of your manners," Tall said.

"And I don't think very much of yours," Red said. "You're holding guns on us when we've done nothing wrong. You're demanding information without giving any. If you want to have a polite conversation you need to rethink your methods."

"Red," Adam said, but very low, almost just a breath.

She didn't know why she felt bolder now than she had a moment before, but it was probably because she felt the soldiers with rifles wouldn't fire in the presence of their superior officer without an order.

And because Tall was trying to find out who they were and where they came from, it was unlikely that he would have them shot for no particular reason. So she'd relaxed a little—not her guard, but her terror of dying in a hail of bullets. And once she relaxed, her natural inclination to push back against authority came to the fore.

Tall looked at her for what felt like a million years but was really only a few seconds. She stared right back and let him see that she wasn't playing around.

Now, in a movie the next thing to happen would be shouts and threats and then one of these big old soldiers would shoulder his rifle and drag me off in one direction and Adam in the other and we would be tossed in dirty cells with no water until we talked.

But it wasn't a movie, and Tall was a human being even if he did look like a walking stereotype with his grizzled hair and severe expression. And that was why Red was surprised when he ordered all of the men away except Taller. The corporal who'd initially found them gave Red and Adam a doubtful look, but his CO shook his head and told him to go so he went, too.

Red didn't know what was going on outside but there was a lot of activity. She heard vehicles driving up and down the street and lots of shouting.

"Stand up, young lady," Tall said, and gestured to Adam. "And you, too. What are you, brother and sister?"

"Yeah," Adam said.

Red twisted her mouth, because she didn't see any reason for Tall to know that. But it had probably been an automatic response from Adam. She pulled her right foot forward so she could brace on it and then put both hands on her knee and pushed off until she got her prosthetic foot safely underneath her.

Tall caught the flash of metal at her ankle and said, "What happened? Accident?"

"Clearly," Red said.

Tall gave a short laugh. "Suspicious little thing, aren't you?"

"Yes, she is," Adam said.

Red gave her brother a sidelong look that was meant to convey *Shut the hell up*, but he didn't get the message.

"Well, you are," Adam said. "Suspicious of everyone and everything."

"I can't say I blame you. It's safer to be suspicious of everyone, especially now," Tall said, and for a moment he seemed less Intimidating Military Guy and more Tired of Everything Guy.

That little flash of vulnerability made Red feel sorry for him, just for a half a second, because probably he was getting told to do XYZ by someone who ranked higher than him and that person was getting told by someone who ranked higher than *him* and so on and so on.

Although Red didn't know who might be handing down orders from On High anymore. Was the president even still alive? Or the vice president?

"Who's in charge if the vice president is dead?"

She didn't realize she'd said it out loud until Taller responded.

"The Speaker of the House," he said. His voice matched his body, a deep low rumble that rose up out of his chest. It seemed like it had a long way to go to reach his mouth.

He was quite a bit younger than Tall. They both had an assortment of stripes and patches and ribbons, although none of those things made any sense to Red so she had no idea of their actual rank.

"Is the president still alive?" she asked.

Tall's face reverted back to his military mask. "No."

"How about the vice president?"

"I answered one of yours, you answer one of mine. What's your name?" he asked.

"Seriously? We were just talking about *The Silence of the Lambs* like an hour ago," Red said.

She could feel Adam rolling his eyes. She didn't even need to see him. Tall gave her a blank look, but Taller snorted.

"Quid pro quo," Taller said. "It's a thing the FBI agent and the serial killer do in the movie."

"I don't watch movies, but I did study Latin in military school," Tall said. "Fine. *Quid pro quo.*"

"My name's Red and his name is Adam," she said. No need for last names. And since he wanted to play along she'd give him some information. There was a lot that she wanted to know.

"Red?" he said. "That's your name?"

"I said so, didn't I?"

Tall looked at Adam, but Red snapped her fingers under his nose.

"Don't you look at him for different information," she said.

"It's me and you here. My name's Red and his name is Adam."

The left corner of his mouth turned up, just a little. "All right, Red. It's you and me, then."

"Who's in charge now if the president is dead?"

"The secretary of state," Tall said.

"That means a lot of people must have died, right?" Red said, trying to remember the order of succession. She'd seen it once in high school social studies class, but social studies was never her best subject. "Because he's pretty far down the list, I think. That's not a real question—just a rhetorical one, so don't answer it."

He seemed amused by her attitude. She knew it was because he didn't see her as a threat, and he was likely humoring her because she was a very small woman with an oversized personality. Normally she'd be pissed because she couldn't stand men who acted that way, but she wasn't above using it to her advantage. Like now.

"What are your names and ranks?" Red asked.

"I'm Lieutenant Regan and this is Sergeant Sirois. What are you and your brother doing in this sector?"

"Looking for food," Red said. "And we didn't know it was a special area."

"This whole sector has been evacuated and closed off to the public," Regan said.

"She got you, Lieutenant," Sirois murmured. "That wasn't a question."

"Tricky, aren't you?" Regan said, and she heard a little touch of admiration in his voice.

Red shrugged. "If you say so."

"All the roads leading into this area are clearly marked," Regan said.

Red just gave him a bland look. She wasn't going to tell him where they came from or how they got there. Surely he could see their backpacks and do the math, and she wasn't a dummy to be tricked by a statement. Anyway, it was her turn to ask a question.

"Why is this sector closed off?" Red asked. "And what's a sector anyway?"

"Two questions," Sirois said.

"Who made you the referee?" Red asked, giving him a filthy look. "Fine, just answer the first one."

"I'm afraid that information is—" Regan said.

"Don't say 'classified,'" Red said, cutting him off. "Let's not turn this into any more of an apocalypse movie cliché than it already is."

"Unfortunately, that *is* the word that we use," Regan said. "It's not information that I can share. And because you're not supposed to be here and said information is need-to-know, our little game is up. If you don't want to tell me why you're here or where you came from that's fine, Red, but I have to remove you from this zone."

"Remove us to where?" Red asked, though she already

knew. She just wanted him to say it out loud so she wouldn't hear the cage door slamming.

"To a quarantine camp, of course," Regan said. "Which is where you're supposed to be in any case. All noninfected citizens are required to relocate to the nearest quarantine camp."

"Why?" Red said. "We're not infected. So why send us into a prison?"

"It's not a prison," Regan said.

"If you're not free to leave, then it's a prison," Red said.

"It's for your own safety—" Regan said.

"That's a load of bullshit. It's to make things easier for you, or for whoever is in charge of you," Red said, her voice rising. "It's a hell of a lot easier to control the population if said population is neatly portioned into the geographical location of your choosing."

She felt her face warming, her heart pounding faster. She didn't want to go to any camp. The thought of the net closing around them sent her blood into jittery Panic Mode.

"That's enough, Red," Adam said, holding his arm in front of her. "Sorry, Lieutenant."

Red hadn't realized she'd been getting closer to the lieutenant's face as she shouted. He hadn't moved a centimeter, which meant he wasn't concerned in the least about her as a physical threat.

That made her unaccountably angry on top of everything else, because he thought she was just an amusing little bug.

When he was done toying with her then he would put her back in the bug box where she belonged.

She thought about grabbing her axe off her belt and waving it in his face, just to prove a point, but she wasn't that dumb. He had a gun and she was sure he was trained to use it.

Even if he didn't kill her (and dying was not on her agenda for the day) the last thing she needed was an injury—especially if they were going to get away from the convoy or whatever it was called. And she *was* going to get away. No man was going to put her in a camp.

"Now, Red and Adam, Sergeant Sirois is going to do a quick blood test to see if you are, in fact, uninfected as you claim," Regan said.

"You'd know if we were infected," Red said. "We'd be coughing."

"Some people don't show symptoms right away," Sirois said. He pulled something that was shaped roughly like a staple gun out of the little bag he carried.

Red took three steps back. Adam looked from Sirois to Red.

"What's in that thing?" he asked.

"Probably a tracker," Red said. "So they can find us if we get away."

"You really don't trust anyone, do you?" Regan asked.

"Tell me again why I should trust a guy who's telling me he's going to put me in a truck and take me someplace I don't want to go."

"Enough, Red," Adam said. "The game is over. Stop trying to pretend that it isn't."

He pushed off his pack and rolled up the sleeve of his shirt.

"Do your thing, Sergeant," Adam said.

Red narrowed her eyes at him. Of course Adam was giving in. Adam had been waiting for an opportunity to give in this whole time. He'd never wanted to walk or get to Grandma's or do anything that might be construed as vaguely nonconformist.

And it wasn't a surprise, either, because Adam had always been a conformer. He liked the music on the radio and the top twenty Nielsen-rated TV shows and shopping at the same places all the white kids liked to shop. He went to a party college where he could major in business—just like everyone else who wasn't really sure what to do with their life. He got average grades and drove an average car.

When did I start drowning in bile? Red thought, shocked by the stream of thought that had burst inside her. She never realized how much contempt for him she'd been holding inside, and it made her feel sick and ashamed.

He was her brother, after all. If his choices were boring then they were his choices and he was the one who had to live with them, not her.

But I can still be angry that he's happy we got caught, Red thought. *Because that's not just about Adam. It's about me, too.*

She thought about the trenches she'd dug, the barbed

wire she'd put up around her heart when Adam blamed her for their parents' deaths. And she fortified her defenses because she was certain she was going to need them.

Sirois put the little staple gun machine up against Adam's arm and pulled the trigger. A second later he pulled it away and checked the LCD readout screen on the side.

"What does it do?" Red asked, her tone loaded with suspicion.

"It takes a small blood sample and determines if you are infected," Sirois said.

"I didn't know we had technology like that," Red said. She was still pretty sure that the gun was actually implanting something inside them

(like a tracker)

and not doing something as benign as taking a blood sample.

And anyway, if they're so worried about us being infected . . .

"How come you aren't wearing masks?" Red asked, finishing her thought out loud.

She backed up a little more as she said this, because Sirois was approaching her with the tracker/staple/blood sample gun and she was not going to submit without a fight. In fact, there would be no submission at all. If he wanted to shoot her with that thing, then he was going to have to hold her down.

Sirois stopped, and Regan gave her a sharp look.

"What do you mean?"

"If you're so concerned about infection, then why aren't you wearing masks?" Red asked, gesturing to her own mask. She'd almost forgotten it was on her face, and she yanked it down to her neck.

"We've been immunized," Regan said.

His tone was bland and his face was blank but Red knew he was lying. Even if no other muscle on his face gave him away, his eyes said that he was lying.

And if he would lie about that he'd lie about anything.

"There's no vaccine," Red said. "Before the lights and the Internet and everything else got turned off there was no vaccine, and I know for damned sure that nobody has found one in the last few weeks."

"How would you know that?" Regan asked. He sounded genuinely curious about her answer.

Red held up a finger. "First, tons of people have died, and that means lots of smarty scientist types also died. So you've got brain drain right there. Fewer people to try to find a cure or a vaccine decreases the odds."

"Go on," Regan said.

He seemed, at that moment, like a professor encouraging a bright student in class. It was like there was no urgency, no shouting men outside, no Sirois standing there with his magic gun poised.

"Second, it's a lot harder to find a vaccine quickly without technology. And technology is also in short supply these days."

"Edward Jenner found a vaccine for smallpox by observing milkmaids in the eighteenth century," Regan said.

"Yeah, and the vaccine that he created had nothing like the efficacy of current vaccines," Red said. "Most vaccines were discovered and/or perfected after 1950 using modern methods and technology, and those methods have only become more refined in the last sixty or so years. Man, don't use an outlier as your example. That kind of shit pisses me off."

The corners of Regan's mouth twitched. Sirois gave her a curious look.

"Are you a med student?" he asked.

"No, I just like science," Red said.

"She's a *liberal arts* major," Adam said. "No special concentration."

"I haven't decided yet," Red said. "And I probably would have been better off taking a survival class or something at this rate."

"You seem very well informed," Regan said. "For a liberal arts major."

"I told you, I like science. And I've been accused of a lot of things—"

"Paranoia, stubbornness, a general unwillingness to entertain the opinions of others . . ." Adam said.

"—but none of those things are stupid," Red said with a glare. "I know that no vaccine was developed for this disease, so don't lie to me and tell me that you're immune. And you're not wearing masks, so that toy over there is not taking blood because you're worried that we're infected. You're worried about something else."

Regan and Sirois exchanged glances. Regan seemed to be weighing what to say next.

"The infection is manifesting differently in this sector than it is everywhere else," Regan said. "Because of that we do the blood test. We perform it on ourselves as well. I promise you that it really is a blood test and not a secret government tracker."

"What's it testing for?" Red asked.

"The presence of certain agents in the blood," Sirois said.

"I told you, I like science, so if you explained to me what you were looking for I would probably understand," Red said slowly. She was thinking it through now. "Whatever it is you're looking for isn't contracted like this cough that's killing everyone, is it? That's why you're not bothering with masks. It's not airborne."

Regan slowly shook his head side to side.

Red looked at Adam, and then back at Regan and Sirois. Sirois still had the blood-testing gun up in what Red thought of as a drawn position, like he could lunge at her any moment and stick it into her exposed arm.

"Is it . . . ?" She stopped, took a breath, because the whole thing was crazy, even crazier than some blood-spattering cough that killed everyone and also because once she said it out loud she knew Adam was going to whoop because it was his theory and he was right. "Is it some kind of parasite? Is it nesting inside people?"

"That's right!" Adam said. "I told you that was some *Alien* shit coming out of people."

"What have you seen?" Regan said, and took a step forward, looming over both of them. "Tell me now."

The change in him was instant and astonishing. Gone was the professor pose, the kindly soldier. He wasn't even the barking stereotype he'd pretended to be when he first walked into the barren grocery store. This was a hunter, a killer, a man accustomed to getting his way and doing whatever it took to get it.

"People with their chests busted open," Adam said in a hurry, like he was trying to get the words out before Red told him not to say anything (which she certainly would have done because she still didn't see the value in sharing information with people who wanted to lock them up).

"And tracks on the floor," he continued, despite her side-eye glare. "There's two of the bodies in this store, if you hadn't noticed the smell."

"We find this smell everywhere," Sirois said. "Because of the victims of the Cough that have been left behind."

"Two bodies with open chests?" Regan asked, and when Adam nodded he said, "Show me."

Some kind of parasite, Red thought as they all trooped

obediently in the direction of the bodies. *Not an airborne disease like the Cough. But where did it come from? And how did people get infected?*

At least the bodies have distracted Regan for now. Maybe I can get away without being implanted by the tracker gun.

For she still believed that it was implanting something rather than testing—the idea of an instant blood test result within that little machine seemed more like science fiction than reality.

You don't think planting trackers is just as sci-fi? Red, when are you going to stop thinking that stuff you read is real? This was Mama's voice, of course—the voice that told her to stop letting her brain run away hand in hand with her overactive imagination.

Stop worrying about the gun and start worrying about how you're going to get away, Red thought.

They arrived in the aisle with the bodies. As soon as he saw them Regan told Sirois to call somebody on the radio and collect the corpses.

"Those other guys were collecting them, too," Adam said.

For chrissakes, is Adam going to tell them every freaking thing?

"What other guys?" Regan asked. "Where did you see them?"

And so of course Adam named the town and the date that he and Red saw those other men and how they seemed like a militia but not real military.

"They aren't," Regan said. His lips pressed tightly together. "What else did they do? Did you talk to them?"

"They can't have, Lieutenant, otherwise they wouldn't be here," Sirois said.

"Are they kidnapping people?" Red asked, looking from one man to the other. "Why would they be doing that?"

Sirois seemed to realize he'd said too much, and neither of them answered her.

"Why would they take that guy's body?" Red asked. "Are they doing some kind of tests?"

Sirois shook his head at her. "Sorry, that's not something we can tell you."

He did seem genuinely sorry, which made her more angry. How could their stupid orders be more important than people's lives? Why was everyone so flipping secretive?

Uh, pot, meet kettle. You're not exactly forthcoming yourself.

But it was different when Red didn't tell them something. They were just being nosy, trying to herd her into a box. When she held back information she was just keeping herself and her *(stupid)* brother safe.

Of course, said stupid brother seemed willing to tell their life story to these guys.

"How are we supposed to protect ourselves from these people if you don't give us any information?"

"You won't have to worry about protecting yourself anymore," Regan said. "We'll be protecting you."

"Like hell," Red said. "I don't trust me with anybody but me."

"Show me the tracks," Regan said to Adam.

And with that, Red was Dismissed. Their little game was over and Regan had determined that Adam would be cooperative, so she was out. Fine. She had more important things to think about. She was getting the hell away from them and all she needed was the right time to do it.

Adam went to one knee to show Regan the slithery tracks in the blood trail.

"Did you follow them?" Regan asked.

"Yes, into the back room," Adam said. "And I found a hole in the concrete back there. Red said it was just a rat hole but I don't think so."

"Can you show me?" Regan asked. "Sirois, stay here with the girl."

Now she was just The Girl, an annoying appendage without a name. Red tried to burn a hole in the back of Regan's neck with her eyes. She caught Sirois giving her a sympathetic look.

Well, she didn't want anyone's damned sympathy. And she certainly didn't want Sirois to remember that he had the magic staple gun in his hand and that Adam had submitted to his ministrations but she had not.

"So it's something like a tapeworm," Red said, as if the intervening conversation had never happened. "A parasite.

But tapeworms don't get inside people's lungs. The digestive system and the respiratory system aren't even connected in a way that would allow a tapeworm to get from your intestines to your lungs."

Sirois gave her an admiring look. "You really do know a lot."

"That's grade school biology." Red sniffed. "Don't try to pretend you're impressed. And anyway, I noticed you didn't actually answer my question."

"You didn't actually ask a question," he said.

Red drew her dignity around her and gave him her best glare. "I would think that the question was implied, but fine—if you want to be like that. If this . . . if whatever you're talking about is like a tapeworm, then it wouldn't be in the lungs, because biology doesn't work that way. So how did it get there?"

"Who said it did?" Sirois said.

"My dumb brother," Red said. "And you still didn't answer the question."

"Why does your brother think the . . . why does he think it's in the lungs?" Sirois asked.

I noticed that, Red thought. *I noticed that you have a name for this thing and you were going to name it until you realized what you were doing.*

"He told you why," Red said. "Because one time he was in the room when I was watching *Alien* and apparently it scarred his brain."

"Well," Sirois said.

He looked like he was contemplating Serious Thoughts. Red assumed he was trying to determine how to tell her things without actually telling her things. That let her unbend a little, because if he wanted to share some kind of information despite his "orders" then he probably wasn't that bad. Probably.

But that didn't mean she was going to trust him. Especially since he would shoot her arm with that tracker gun in a second if Regan said so.

"So, if you know about the digestive system and the respiratory system, then you know that the actual stomach organ is placed higher up in the body than most people think it is."

Red nodded. "Right. When people say 'stomach' they think of their belly button, but that's more where the intestines are located."

"The stomach and liver are actually nestled pretty close to the lungs," Sirois said.

"Okay," Red said.

"And if something large, say, burst out of someone's stomach with enough force, then it would probably throw the rib cage open as well."

"And it would make a mess of the lungs on the way out," Red said. "But that's assuming that such a creature does exist. And I'm not going to lie—it sounds ridiculous. Parasites don't behave that way. Sure, things like tapeworms can get pretty big inside a human, but they normally like to stay there. Why would you leave if you had a good thing going? Your person is going to keep providing free energy while you just camp out inside their body and eat it all up."

"Guinea worms leave the body," Sirois said. "So it's not unheard of for human parasites to leave their hosts."

Red held her hand up, because she wanted to get her ideas in order.

"All right. A parasite that grows larger inside the human stomach," she said. She put one finger down as she ticked off each thought.

"And at some point it . . . becomes too large for the organ it's in?"

Sirois nodded.

"So it bursts the bag it's in, just like a baby emerging from the placenta."

"You're doing very well," Sirois said.

"Don't patronize me," Red said. "And when it breaks out of the stomach it emerges with enough force to push the ribs out and scramble up whatever else is in its way."

"Is it acceptable for me to nod?" Sirois said, with a half-smile.

"Yes, if I'm on the right track," Red said. "But here's the thing—what does it have to do with the Cough?"

Sirois shrugged. "Who says that it does?"

"So it's not related to the Cough, which is still a dangerous pandemic that has killed thousands of people," Red said.

Sirois nodded again. Red gave him an expectant look.

"What?" he asked.

"What is it and where does it come from and why does it behave unlike other parasites? Again, the questions are clearly implied."

"Well, I thought our pleasant conversation would come to an end soon, and now it has," Sirois said.

"Are you trying to say that information is classified without saying it's classified?"

"I know how much you dislike the term," Sirois said.

"You do understand that the key information here is the information you're suppressing?"

"Where do you get your gall from?" Sirois asked. He didn't sound offended—just curious. "Most people would be cowering before the authority of the military in this situation."

"Cowering isn't my thing. I rarely submit to anyone's authority," Red said. "And you can't discover anything if you don't ask."

"Fair," Sirois said.

"But it really sounds absurd. I hope you realize that," Red said. "I mean, the stomach isn't really a hospitable place for a parasite. Stomach acid exists for a reason—to break things down. That's why most digestive system parasites hurry on to the intestines. And nematodes and cestodes don't have the kind of musculature you'd need to push bones out with that much force."

"You really do like science," Sirois said. "I don't think I've ever heard anyone say 'nematode' in casual conversation."

"I remember things that I read," Red said. "So?"

"So what?"

"So do you want to tell me just what these creatures are really, and why the government is so determined to find them that it's sending the military out to sweep the back end of nowhere?"

"I'd like to tell you, but . . ."

"It's classified," they both said together. Sirois laughed, but Red scowled at him.

Then he sighed, and waved the gun in his hand. "And I know you've been hoping that I'll forget about this, but I still have to test you."

"How do you know I've been hoping you'll forget?" Red said. She would do anything to stall the inevitable.

"You have one of the most expressive faces I've ever seen," Sirois said. "Never play poker, because you tell like anything."

"I see," Red said.

She didn't scowl, even though she wanted to. It annoyed her that whatever she felt was so obvious on her face, because she'd always thought of herself as one of those cool, stony-faced characters that gave nothing away.

"I'm sorry, Red," he said, and reached for her arm.

She tried to dance backward, but evading a determined

someone's grip is not the easiest damned thing when one of your legs doesn't dance too easily.

He grabbed hold of her wrist. "I don't want to hurt you. But I will if you don't stop moving."

"I'm sure you're violating a whole lot of my civil rights," Red said.

"Civil rights went out with the electricity," Sirois said. "You're just lucky you met up with us and not someone else's command. Regan is more human than most of them."

Red tried to turn her arm, to twist away, but there was no give in his grasp and anyway if she did get out of it she would likely just fall down. She could feel how off-balance she was, thanks to both her leg and the heavy pack and the awkward way she was standing. The only thing keeping her upright was Sirois's hold.

I can't even escape from one soldier who doesn't mean me any harm, Red thought, infuriated with her own helplessness. *How the hell am I going to get away if I meet someone who does want to hurt me?*

She'd taken a self-defense class that had been offered on campus, but for some reason she couldn't remember a single thing she'd learned at the moment. Her brain and her gaze had narrowed to just one thing—the gun in Sirois's hand.

No no no don't let him do it I don't want whatever he's got in there it's not fair I tried so hard I thought I was so smart I was going to be the one that got away I did everything right from the start so how did this go wrong how how how no no no

And then something happened that she should have expected (as she thought later) because in every Apocalypse Comes story it always does.

The world exploded.

CHAPTER 12

A Walking Shadow

AFTER

Red and Riley and Sam hid behind an abandoned truck at the edge of the town. They were in a field of vehicles, most of them rusted and lacking wheels. These were Seriously Abandoned, not the recent refuse of people fleeing the Cough or the government or the militias or whatever. Red knew about as much about cars as she did about guns—that is to say, not very much—but she knew enough to tell that most of these cars were thirty years old or more. She wondered if this was once a used-car lot that had been sacrificed to nature.

Red had convinced the two children that they needed better gear if they wanted to continue on, with or without her. Sam had seen the wisdom of this (Red suspected that she, too, was worried about the coming winter and had no wish to subsist on increasingly stale granola bars), but Riley had glanced fearfully from one to the other.

"What if someone tries to get us?" he asked.

"I know. There are a lot of monsters out there, and all of them look like humans," Red said. She could lie, or dismiss his fears, but that wouldn't be fair. "But don't worry, I'll be there to protect you."

Human monsters were everywhere, roaming free without the leash of civilization to hold them. And those human monsters were the reason Red and Sam and Riley were huddled up next to a rusty old door instead of entering the town.

There were three of them, all men. They seemed youngish—younger than middle age, but older than teenagers. This she could tell by the way they walked, with that loose-limbed swagger that so many young men had.

She wasn't worried about the swagger. She was worried because all three carried rifles.

Why does everyone have a fucking gun? she thought. Red didn't want to take Riley and Sam anywhere near those young men. She was confident that she could protect herself, but she didn't want to endanger the kids, especially since she didn't know how they might respond in a high-stress situation. It was best not to risk it, even if Sam and Riley seemed more together than most kids.

There wasn't a main street or a town proper like so many of the other places Red had passed through already. Rather, there were several houses clustered together (but not too close together, because this was America and a large yard was a God-given right) on the state road.

There was a chain convenience store/gas station about half a mile from where Red and the children stood. No sign of a convenient sporting goods supply or anything like that. Red imagined that there was a mall within a fifteen-to-twenty-minute drive where most of the residents did their shopping. That meant they'd have to find what they needed in these houses, because Red wasn't going to wander across the countryside with two kids in tow in hopes of discovering a Walmart.

The three youngish men had small backpacks, not huge carry-everything packs like Red's. Red and Sam and Riley had just reached the Field of Abandoned Metal when they saw the three men come out of one of the houses a short distance away. Red had pushed the kids behind the biggest vehicle she could find, although the men didn't seem to be concerned at all about anyone sneaking up on them. Maybe that was the kind of stupid confidence you got when you carried a gun.

What if I had a gun and ill intent and shot you three dummies while you strode in and out of houses like you own the world?

And while I'm on the subject, she thought, *why have I seen so few women?*

There were three possibilities—first, more women had been infected by the Cough and died and thus there were fewer female survivors.

Second, more women had done the sensible thing and gone to the quarantine camps as they were told to do by the numerous announcements before the television broadcast went off the air forever.

If they had children they probably had sprinted there— Red was sure that any mother with young children would do her best to make sure her kids didn't get sick. Keeping your child away from infected people was a good way to do that, and most people didn't view quarantine camps as free-floating prisons the way Red did.

Third, any remaining women out there had been spirited away to become handmaidens for the militia weirdos.

Red didn't like any of the possibilities but was somehow sure that the last possibility was more of a sickening probability.

All the more reason to keep myself and these kids away from any human contact, she thought.

The men had checked in a few houses, but in a lazy, undisciplined sort of way. Red wasn't sure if they were looking for food or other supplies or if they were looking for survivors or what. They had the vague look of a group out on patrol, but a very unserious patrol. This was not a well-ordered militia like the men Red and Adam had seen at the gas station.

She hoped very much that they had not already stripped all the houses bare of useful things. Food was the biggest priority, of course. It did seem that they left several of the houses untouched, so maybe Red would be able to find what they needed.

Or maybe they didn't bother going into all the houses because they'd already been scoured clean by the Locust Militia.

Red shook her head. She didn't need to get off onto one of her worrying-about-all-the-permutations rants inside her head, because she needed to be present for Sam and Riley and because stressing about every possible negative outcome would paralyze her into doing nothing at all. So she decided she wouldn't worry unless she had to, and the only thing she was worried about were those three slow-moving guys.

"Oh my Christ, when will they fucking leave already?" Red said under her breath.

Apparently she hadn't said it low enough under her breath, because Sam gave her a shocked look and Riley clapped his hands over his mouth to hide his giggle.

"You said a bad word," Sam said. Her scandalized expression was something akin to a Victorian spinster spotting a bare ankle on an unmarried maiden.

"You've never heard that word before?" Red said, disconcerted. She thought all kids knew every dirty word in existence. There were a few young children in her own hometown who knew words that she'd never heard of before.

"I've heard it. I just know you're not supposed to say it," Sam said. "There is an impressionable child here."

She jerked a thumb at Riley, who stopped giggling.

"Hey, I'm not impressionable," Riley said. "I'm only two years younger than you. And Red can say whatever she wants, because she's a grown-up. Daddy always said that."

"And Mama always told him to watch his language in front of us," Sam said loftily.

"My mama used to tell all of us—me and my brother and my dad—to watch our language," Red said. "It didn't take, though."

"What does that mean?" Riley asked.

"It means nobody listened to her mama," Sam said.

"Anyway," Red said, because she really didn't want to get into a protracted conversation about cursing with an unusually prim ten-year-old. "Once these slowpokes get out of town we can start checking the closest houses, okay?"

"It's getting late, though," Sam said, squinting up at the sun. "We thought we'd be able to check the houses and then get back into the woods to set up camp, remember? I don't know if we'll be able to do that. Maybe we should go back and try again tomorrow."

Red could see the wisdom of this plan. She really could. The trouble was that she didn't want to go backward at all—only forward. The long walk was hard enough without going in circles.

The woods that they wanted to be in were about three miles or so beyond the point where they currently stood. They had left the trail early in the morning before sunrise and picked their way carefully along the road, ducking into the shallow culverts if they heard anything suspicious.

"Suspicious" had turned out to be several white-tailed deer who'd given them bland stares as they passed by, and a very fat raccoon carrying a large dead frog in its mouth. Sam had made a puking noise at this.

"Honestly, the frog is probably better for him than people's garbage," Red had said.

Sam shook her head. "Frogs are gross, and eating them is even grosser."

"What, you don't like Kermit?" Red asked.

"The raccoon is eating Kermit?" Riley said, and his eyes welled up.

Oops, Red thought. *Not the right audience for that kind of joke.*

The crossing from the forest to the town had been Red's biggest concern, because they were completely exposed to any passing vehicle. Having made it to the town unscathed she really hadn't expected to find anyone in it. Practically every town she and Adam had been in had been completely free of people—because it had been scoured either by Regan's men or by the Locust Militia.

Maybe we're out of Regan's sector now.

Red wished she'd taken the time to find out just how big the sector was, because that would be useful information to have right now. It would help her avoid Regan's group, at least. Too bad there hadn't been a handy map hanging around for her to steal before she escaped.

Well, the circumstances were fairly urgent. There wasn't time for data collection.

"Red?"

Sam was looking at her expectantly, and Red realized she'd gone off on a tangent in her brain *(again)* and never acknowledged what the girl had said.

"I think," Red said slowly, thinking it through as she spoke. It would be okay. It would probably be safe. "I think that we might try sleeping in one of the houses. Just for tonight."

Riley's eyes lit up. "We could sleep in a real bed. With warm blankets."

It made Red's heart break just a little to hear him say that, to hear him speak so hopefully about a bed and warm blankets—basic things a kid should not have to worry about.

"What if there are dead bodies in the houses?" Sam asked, her voice just above a whisper.

"I'm not going to sleep in a house with a dead body, don't worry," Red said. "There might be some that have bodies in them, though. We can't expect that everyone will have left the area before they got sick. But I bet that at least a few of them will be empty. Everyone was told to go to a quarantine camp, and most people are the law-abiding types and complied."

"Why didn't you?" Riley asked.

"I'm a rebel," Red said, and Riley laughed, but Sam

looked at her in a funny way, like she knew Red's answer was no answer at all.

There was a little dip in the road about a mile away, and Red watched the three silhouettes of the men disappear and then reappear on the rise. She couldn't hear their voices anymore, despite the silence that hung all around, and that meant they were far enough away for safety.

She couldn't worry that they might be back later, or that they were only a patrol that was part of a large group. Or rather, she *could* worry about such things but knew that worrying wouldn't stop anything that was going to happen. Several weeks on the road had convinced Red that Fate had her own plans and didn't consult humans before she laid them.

"All right, let's start checking houses," Red said.

First they looked for houses that already had open doors or windows, for Red thought it better to enter houses that already looked derelict rather than signal to anyone who might be checking that someone had done some fresh breaking and entering.

After trying a few of these Red quickly realized the flaw in that plan. If someone had gone to the trouble of opening the house, then they'd also gone to the trouble of taking all the food they could carry. There wasn't anything edible left in those first few residences—not even a stray Cheerio for a colony of ants to carry away.

There were some useful things to be found here and there, however.

In one home there was a pink bedroom with a dresser stuffed with underwear and shirts and jeans and leggings just Sam's size. Sam was inclined to wrinkle her nose at these—"They're all covered in hearts and glitter"—but Red convinced her that personal taste in fashion was less important than having clean clothes that fit.

In another house Red found a stash of camping equipment in the attached garage, and was able to cull out another backpacker's tent for the kids and a good-sized pack for Sam to carry. They ditched the school backpack—there was nothing in it but the granola bars and a dirty blanket. There was also a two-person kayak in the garage, which Riley desperately wanted to take with them.

"There are no rivers nearby," Red said, nonplussed by his sudden desire to paddle.

"But we might find some," Riley said. "Look, it has wheels. We could pull it until we find a river to put it into."

"Who's going to pull it?" Red asked.

Riley gazed at her hopefully.

"Forget it, kid," Red said, ruffling his hair. "Most days I can hardly pull myself along."

The fourth house they entered stank of decomposing things, and they backed out of it without ever going past the foyer.

Finally Red decided that breaking a window was going to be necessary. She chose a low white bungalow-type house, only one story. It had black shutters on the front windows and the shutters were pulled closed. There was a short driveway but no garage and no car. Red assumed the owners had fled long before.

"Why that one?" Sam asked. "It looks poor compared to all the other houses."

She gestured at all of the two-stories with their wooden decks and aboveground pools and play sets in the yards.

Red nodded. "Right, and because it looks poor no one has gone near it. People just assume there's nothing inside."

"Our great-aunt Livia has a house like this," Riley offered. "But all she has inside is crocheted stuff and like, one million cats."

"She has three cats," Sam said. "That's not even close to a million. Everything is covered in crochet, though. That's pretty much all she does—watch TV and crochet."

"And she only watches boring TV," Riley said, rolling his eyes. "Like the most boring TV ever—people baking cakes or making pasta or whatever or shows where a bunch of people sit around a table and *talk*."

"It would be so much better if there were explosions and stuff on every TV show," Red said.

"Yeah!" Riley said. "I like shows with superheroes and villains, but I hate it when the heroes are always like, kissing girls or thinking about kissing girls or moping around because they can't kiss the girl they want to kiss. That's lame."

"It's not lame," Sam said. "Lots of people like to kiss each other. It's normal."

"I don't want to kiss anybody," Riley said, sticking out his tongue in disgust. "It just looks messy."

Red thought this was pretty rich from a kid who didn't seem to care at all about his personal hygiene.

"People like it, and someday you might, too. Red, do you have a boyfriend?" Sam asked. She looked like she was hoping Red would back her up and say kissing was not lame.

"No," Red said. "I used to have a girlfriend, though."

"Oh," Sam said. Red could see her reshuffling her worldview. "That's cool, though."

"Thanks," Red said.

"But you liked to kiss your girlfriend, right?" Sam asked.

"Sure," Red said. "When people are in love they like to kiss each other."

Riley made gagging noises. "*Love*, gross."

They could have gone on arguing, Red supposed, except that Sam finally seemed to recognize that Riley was too young for this conversation and rolled her eyes.

The truth was that Red was attracted to men and women but hadn't dated much. Most people were frankly not interesting enough for her to bother with, and it was hard to find people in her little town—or even from the college—

who liked the things that she liked. She'd often thought she might care more about dating if she lived in a city and her pool of potential mates was larger.

Besides, it was hard for her to lower her guard around other people enough to form any kind of real intimacy. She was always on the lookout for someone who might see her as a prize or use her as a fetish because of her prosthetic leg.

They circled around the back of the bungalow. There was a large window covered with a white sheet just above a dryer exhaust.

A good place to break into, Red thought. A little glass wouldn't hurt the laundry room. She always tried to be polite when entering other people's houses—there was a possibility that they might come back to them one day, after all—and she disliked the idea of accidentally breaking some precious heirloom as she stepped through the window frame.

"Should I find a rock?" Riley asked.

"To break the window? No, I'm going to use this," Red said, and took her axe off her belt.

She turned the blunt side toward the window and then waved at the kids, who stood at her hip, watching.

"Get away," she said. "You don't want to get cut by broken glass if it flies in every direction."

"I'd rather you didn't do that. Apart from the risk to your kids it's very hard to get a good glazier to come and fix windows these days."

The voice was strong and firm but a little scratchy, like a well-played record, and it made Red jump and nearly lop her own ear off with the blade of the axe, which was facing her. Sam and Riley clutched at the hem of her coat.

Red lowered the axe slowly, spinning the blade face out so she could use it if she had to. She turned to face the voice, which was not easy to do with two small people clinging to her.

Don't let anything happen to Riley or Sam. Please, whatever happens, let them get away.

She expected to see one of the men they'd spotted earlier, and that there would be a rifle pointed at her head. But instead there was an almost comically benign-looking gray-haired man not much taller than Red peering at them out of dark inquisitive eyes.

He was wearing a neatly pressed blue button-down shirt under a gray cardigan with soft-looking khaki pants and worn navy blue Converse sneakers. His hair was cut short on the sides, longer on the top, and combed back from his forehead. He looked like he was getting ready to walk to the grocery store, or do some light gardening.

How did he get his shirt pressed without electricity? Red thought, then said, "Who are you?"

The corners of his eyes crinkled a little bit. "Don't you think I should be the one asking that question? You're about to break into my house, after all."

"Oh," Red said. "Um."

It wasn't often that she was at a loss for words. *A first in the annals of history*, Adam would have said.

Now is really *not the time to think about Adam.*

"I'm sorry," Red said. "We thought nobody was here."

The man nodded. "A reasonable assumption, given the circumstances."

He looked at her expectantly. The silence stretched out between them. Red wasn't really sure what to do. Should she just take the kids and go? Would he try to stop her?

Riley and Sam were both trembling, their faces hidden in her coat. She was able to pat Riley's head with her free left hand but could only give Sam an awkward bump of her elbow since Red still had the axe in her hand and she wasn't ready to put it down yet. The man seemed friendly but that didn't mean anything.

"I see that the lack of civilization has made you forget the rules of civility. Very well. I shall go first. My name is Park Dae-Jung, though most people call me D.J."

He gave them a little bow, hands at his sides.

"Uh," Red said. It was really quite extraordinary, the way she could run her mouth in the face of an army but when confronted with a harmless-looking old man she could only manage single syllables.

She cleared her throat. "Um. I'm Red. This is Riley and this is Sam. It's nice to meet you, Mr. Park."

That last bit sort of trickled out so that by the time she

said "Park" it was almost swallowed up. This, somehow, was more surreal than anything that had happened to her since the Crisis began.

"And all of you have just one name, like Prince or Madonna. You may call me D.J., not Mr. Park. I see now that you are far too young to be the mother of those children. A sister, perhaps?" He went on without waiting for an answer. "You probably have several questions, and I'm assuming you were attempting to break my window because you were hungry."

"Er. Yes," Red said.

"Well, I have plenty of food inside and you are welcome to join me for lunch."

Mr. Park—*no, D.J.,* Red thought—looked at them expectantly.

"I'm assuming you don't want to get caught when those young men return on the second circuit of their patrol," D.J. said. He glanced at his watch. The brown leather band was cracked with age. It looked like the old-fashioned kind you had to wind every day. "You do have some time. They usually don't circle back for a couple of hours."

"The same men?" Red asked. "Why would they do that?"

"Oh, it's not always the same men," D.J. said. "But there are always three of them, and they come through here every couple of hours or so. None of them are especially attentive about checking the houses, but if you're out in the open even they will notice you."

Red felt Sam shift and the little girl's gaze lock onto her face. If what D.J. said was true, then that meant the area wasn't safe for them. Three men came through the town every couple of hours on a kind of patrol. That meant that they were affiliated with some group that had established this as part of their "territory." Red wondered where their home base was.

"Their territory can't be very big if the patrols are returning here every couple of hours," Red murmured.

She'd said it more to herself, just thinking out loud, but D.J. answered her.

"I agree," he said. "But the fact remains that they do return. And I should warn you that they are more diligent about examining the open houses at night. It seems they think that travelers might be squatting in them."

"What do they do if they catch someone in one of the houses?" Red asked. She had a good idea of the answer, but it was best to know for certain.

D.J. looked from Sam and Riley back up to Red's face and quirked an eyebrow, like he was asking if she really wanted him to say it in front of the children.

"Go ahead," Red said. "It doesn't help them to hide terrible things. They've already seen plenty."

"They kill any men they find and take the women and children," D.J. said.

Red felt Sam and Riley press harder into her sides.

"Red, let's go inside, okay?" Riley said. His voice was muffled because most of his face was still hidden in her coat.

She hesitated, because it wasn't in her nature to trust anyone and because for all she knew this man might be the leader of the patrolling gang.

"I have nothing to do with that group," D.J. said, correctly interpreting her expression.

Damn, I thought my poker face was getting better.

"I assure you that I am just what I seem—an old man, living alone. I promise that if you come inside my home you will come to no harm from me."

He seemed sincere. He *sounded* sincere. Still, she looked down at Sam and tapped the girl's head with her elbow.

"What do you think?"

Sam thought about it for a moment. Even though Red and Sam had only known one another for a couple of days Red already could tell that Sam was like her—the type who considered every possible move before moving her chess piece. Sam was weighing the risks and rewards, just as Red did.

"I think we should go inside," Sam said. "I don't want to get caught by a patrol."

D.J. smiled and held out a hand to indicate they should enter.

"After you," he said.

Even though everyone was on board with the decision, it took a minute to get them shuffling in the right direction.

Neither child would release their hold on Red's coat, and she was still holding the axe in her hand.

"Sam, let go of me for a second, all right?" Red asked. "I want to put the axe away."

Sam stepped back but she watched Red's fingers sliding it into the loop at her waist. As soon as the axe was secure Sam grabbed Red's hand. Red got her feet moving in the right direction and the kids came along, moving like a many-footed sea creature that drifts along the ocean floor.

D.J. seemed unconcerned by this, patiently waiting until they reached the door.

"You've got to let go of me or we'll never get through," Red said, but gently. Sam's hand was damp inside her own.

Sam nodded and released her, but Riley shook his head.

"You have to let go or we've got to turn sideways and crab-walk in," Red said.

"Crab-walk," Riley said.

She thought it a little strange that Riley was acting so shy when he'd been more than willing to reveal his life story five minutes after he met Red—and he was the one who'd first agreed to go into the house. Maybe he was different around men.

Or maybe D.J. Park isn't as trustworthy as he seems, Red thought.

Paranoid, a voice in her head whispered, and it sounded a lot like Adam's voice.

Red and Riley scooted inside, and D.J. followed, closing the door behind him. He took his shoes off immediately and slid his feet into house slippers.

The door was a modern, well-insulated type and fitted securely in the jamb without making a sound.

That explains how he got outside without us hearing him.

They stood in a neat little kitchen tiled in varying shades of cheerful yellow. The cabinets and appliances were all white and gleamed as though they'd just been cleaned that morning. The floor was hardwood, and though it was well-kept Red could see the marks that came from feet walking in the same patterns over the years.

She also noticed something else—the faint but distinct hum of electricity.

"You have a generator?" Red asked.

D.J. smiled. It was a ready smile, Red noticed, natural and given at the slightest provocation.

"You're wondering why there isn't more noise?" he asked.

Red nodded. Sam had come close to her again once Red and Riley had made their way through the door, but she hadn't grabbed Red's hand or coat again. It was almost as if she were trying to prove to herself that she didn't have to.

"I have a natural-gas-powered standby generator," D.J. said. "It's designed to run quietly and come on automatically when the grid goes down."

"Yeah, but it's been weeks," Red said. "Where are you getting the gas from?"

"I had a stockpile," D.J. said.

Red waited for more information, but none was forthcoming.

"I also have water that draws off a well," D.J. said. "And that means there can be tea with lunch. Or perhaps hot cocoa?"

He looked at Riley when he said this. Riley unclenched a little.

"With marshmallows?" he asked eagerly.

"Yes," D.J. said. "My grandchildren also love marshmallows."

There were acres of sadness in those five words and that, more than anything else, convinced Red to trust him. So she slung her pack off her back and dropped it at her feet. Riley took that as the signal that they were staying.

"You can put your things in the laundry room," D.J. said, indicating a doorway next to the refrigerator. "There are hooks for your coats and a bench where you can remove your shoes."

"Oh," Red said, then made a shooing motion at Riley and Sam. "Go ahead, put your stuff in there."

D.J. gave her a mildly inquiring look as the kids went into the other room.

"I have a prosthetic leg," Red said. "I know my shoes are muddy and it's rude for me to have them on, but it's difficult for me to walk around without my shoes because the foot was made for the angle of a shoe."

CHRISTINA HENRY

"What did you do when you were at home?" D.J. asked. It wasn't accusatory, just curious.

"Well," Red said, tugging at her ear. "I would just take my leg off. I had crutches to help me get around in the house."

"And you don't have them with you," D.J. said. "That is a problem. I don't have any crutches."

Red didn't want to take her leg off, not really. She could technically walk with the prosthetic and a bare foot but it was slippery and really difficult to keep her balance.

At home she liked to take the prosthetic off because it meant she could relax—not unlike the way most women felt about taking their bra off at the end of the day. But she didn't want to relax that much here—what if they had to leave quickly? What if those men found them here and they got taken away and her leg was left behind? She'd really be screwed then. It wasn't like she could grab any old prosthetic to replace it, assuming she could find such a thing in the first place.

"I do have a cane," D.J. said. "Would that help you?"

Red realized she'd need to unbend a little. She'd accepted this man's hospitality and as such she also had to accept his house rules.

She decided to keep her leg on once she removed her shoes. D.J. disappeared into another room and returned with an ordinary wooden cane with a curved top and a rubber bottom. Red stood carefully, putting more weight on the cane than on her left leg. Riley and Sam and D.J. all watched her while she did this.

"I should have sold tickets," Red said, unable to keep from sounding cross. She hated it when she was treated like a sideshow.

"Apologies," D.J. said. "I just wanted to ensure that the cane was a good solution for you. I will prepare lunch now."

His response made Red feel churlish. Riley and Sam followed D.J., but not before Sam gave Red a look that told her she should apologize too.

"What should I apologize for?" Red muttered to herself. "I'm the one who was being stared at."

She left her backpack in the laundry room with her shoes. It was the first time in months that it had been out of arm's reach, and she felt the loss of this more than her missing limb. The pack had become a very heavy security blanket.

D.J. took a package of ground beef out of the refrigerator. The normalcy of this action struck Red hard enough that she felt her eyes well up.

That's stupid, she thought. *Why is a package of beef making you cry?*

She knew why. It was because it was a Thing People Used to Do, buy groceries and store them in the refrigerator and cook them, and seeing it made things feel ordinary again when they were not. Just seeing a working refrigerator was enough to make Red feel sentimental, especially when all of the food she'd eaten for weeks had come out of boxes and cans and wrappers. Sometimes she felt she'd kill for the taste of fresh lettuce, and she'd never been the biggest fan of salads before the Crisis.

D.J. glanced from the package of beef to the kids and up at Red. "I was going to make bibimbap, but perhaps hamburger would be better? I have some rolls in the freezer and the rice can stay in the cooker for a while."

"No way, I love bibimbap," Riley said excitedly. It was the first time he'd seemed like himself since D.J. had caught them trying to break into his house. "Mrs. Mikita used to make it for us all the time when Mom and Dad both had to work the late shift."

"Mikita?" D.J. said. "That doesn't sound like a Korean name."

"She was Korean but her husband wasn't," Sam explained. "She also made a lot of pierogies."

"That's an interesting combination," D.J. said, his eyes crinkling as he smiled. "Well, I'm afraid I don't have any fresh vegetables for the bibimbap, only pickled and frozen ones."

"The important question is . . ." Riley said, his voice comically dramatic, ". . . is do you have kimchi?"

"Of course I do. Although I can't say that's a question most American kids would ask," D.J. said.

"I'm a weirdo," Riley said cheerfully.

"You sure are," Sam said.

"The only weirdo here is the person who wants to marry a grilled cheese," Red said.

Sam stuck her tongue out at Red, who responded in kind.

"And what about you?" D.J. said to Sam. "Do you also like kimchi?"

"It's okay." Sam shrugged. "It's not my favorite thing but I'll eat a little."

D.J. looked at Red, who said, "I'll eat anything. Especially after weeks of canned soup and granola bars."

"Will you all wash your hands, then? The washroom is through there."

The three of them trooped to the bathroom. Sam and Riley took their turns and then ran back to the kitchen to watch D.J. cook. Red really did cry when she got her chance to use the toilet. She never realized how much she appreciated running water and indoor plumbing.

She took a little extra time washing up, because now that she was indoors and out of the open air she could smell her own body odor and it was not pleasant. She hated to impose more on D.J.'s hospitality but she wondered if he would let her wash her hair and give Sam and Riley baths.

By the time Red was back in the kitchen the process was well under way. Riley shadowed D.J. as he prepared all the elements of the mixed-rice dish. Sam sat at the table with her chin resting on her hands. There was an expression on her face that Red couldn't quite interpret. She slid into the chair next to Sam's.

"Everything all right?" Red asked, but quietly so the other two wouldn't hear.

"He used to do this to Mom," Sam said. "He'd follow her around the kitchen and ask a million questions and help as much as he could. Mom used to say he was going to be a chef someday."

Red didn't say anything, because she knew that Sam wasn't just mourning for their lost mother but for their lost life, for a life that would never exist in the same form again. Even if someone found a cure for the Cough and the electricity came back on and some form of order was restored, things still wouldn't be the same as they were before.

Soon they were all sitting around the table digging into bowls of rice and meat and vegetables. Red wasn't sure she actually tasted any of it, because as soon as the first bite hit her tongue she realized just how hungry she was. It was the same for Riley and Sam, who shoveled food into their mouths like they'd never seen food before.

Luckily, D.J. didn't seem to notice their appalling manners. He just kept refilling their bowls until they all sat back with their hands over their stomachs, groaning.

"That was sooooo good," Riley said.

"The best meal I've ever had," Red agreed.

D.J. looked pleased, and waved away their offers to help clean up.

"Perhaps you'd like to use the bathtub while you're here?"

D.J. said. It had the air of a delicate suggestion, and Red thought he would probably open the kitchen window as soon as they left the room.

"Good idea," Red agreed.

"You can wash your clothes as well," D.J. said, glancing at his watch. "Although it might be best to wait until the next patrol has passed through. The washing machine is a little noisy, and I'd rather not attract their attention."

Red still had a lot of questions about these patrols, and how D.J. had managed to evade their notice. But the offer of a bath was too good to pass up.

Red knew from her babysitting experience that eight-year-old boys didn't do the best job in the world washing themselves even when they didn't have weeks of grime caked onto their skin. Despite Riley's loud protests of "Privacy! Privacy!" she went into the bathroom with him once the tub was full.

"For crying out loud, Riley, I don't care about your private parts," Red said. "I care that your hair has bugs in it."

"Really?" Riley asked. He didn't look disgusted, only curious. "Bugs?"

"Who can tell under all this dirt?" Red said, pouring a very generous amount of shampoo into her hand. "You could have potato plants growing in there for all we know."

It took three good washes for Red to get Riley's hair in roughly acceptable condition. At least he didn't smell like a dog that had rolled in a garbage heap anymore.

Sam was less particular about Red's presence and seemed to welcome the offer of assistance with her hair.

"I want it to stop itching," she confessed as Red scrubbed her scalp. "I think it's just dirt but I keep thinking it's lice."

"It's probably not lice," Red said. "If it is, the easiest thing to do is cut your hair. We don't have any treatments handy."

"Maybe you could cut my hair even if there isn't lice. I used to have short hair anyway," Sam said. "It's a lot easier because I'm a swimmer and it just goes right under my swim cap without fuss."

Her voice faded out at the end, like she was realizing that she'd probably never swim laps in a pool again.

When it was Red's turn she scrubbed herself all over four times and then wrapped up in one of D.J.'s towels. She was reluctant to put her filthy clothes back on her clean body.

Sam had some clean things because of the pink bedroom find and it turned out that one of D.J.'s grandkids was a boy who'd left behind Pokémon pajamas just a smidge too big for Riley.

D.J. knocked at the bathroom door just as Red finished toweling off her hair.

"I have a sweat suit that will fit you," he called through the door. "I'll hang it on the knob."

Red unwrapped the towel and as she put on the sweat suit she noticed just how much weight she'd lost in these weeks. Her ribs were visible just under the skin, and her thighs looked like long ropy bands of muscle with no fat to pad them. She turned around and checked her butt in the mirror. Even that appeared pretty sad—*there's hardly any butt left*, she thought.

There were marks on her shoulders like calluses from carrying her pack every day, and despite wearing lightweight pants meant for hiking there were red-purple stripes at her waist where the waistband chafed. They weren't fresh, like blisters—rather, they had the look of skin that had been repeatedly damaged in the same way.

The sweat suit was baggy on her but it was soft and clean, and Red just stood there for a minute marveling at how good it felt to be completely washed all over. Early on, when it was warmer, she'd taken a couple of dunks in streams and rivers. Lately she'd just been freshening up with baby wipes when she got up in the morning, and after a while it really didn't matter how many wipes you used if your clothes hadn't been cleaned in weeks.

She went looking for Sam and Riley and D.J., and found the latter sitting in the kitchen drinking a cup of tea.

"Where are the kids?" she asked.

"I have a spare room for when my grandchildren visit," D.J. said. "It's down the hall and to the left, two doors past the washroom."

Both children were sleeping. The room had a queen-sized bed with a plaid comforter and cozy-looking flannel sheets. It was surrounded by bins of Legos and a large bookshelf packed with books for kids of various ages. Some of the Legos were on the floor, which meant that at least one of them had played some (probably Riley) before climbing onto the bed.

Sam was snoring lightly, propped up a little on the pillow with a book splayed open on her chest. Riley was stomach down with arms wide, taking up as much space as his little body would allow.

Red returned to the kitchen and accepted D.J.'s offer of tea. She felt surprisingly relaxed. Her brain wasn't circling every terrible future possibility, wasn't screaming that all of this was a trap, wasn't contemplating what would happen tomorrow or the next day or the next day. Maybe she was too tired and too full to do any of that, and her old paranoid self would return as soon as they left this house and the lean times returned.

They sat in companionable silence for a while. D.J. didn't seem to expect anything from her, not even conversation.

When her tea was almost finished Red said, "Tell me how you've managed to avoid these patrols."

D.J. shifted a little in his chair and gave her a half-smile. "What you really wish to know is why I'm here and how long I've been here and what I know about the patrolling group so that you can avoid them. You want my whole story."

"Well, yes," Red admitted.

"And will you tell me your whole story in return?" D.J.

asked. "It's been some time since I had someone to share stories with."

Red heard the many days of loneliness in his voice and knew how that felt, knew how the hours had loomed long and empty once Adam was gone. Even if he didn't speak Adam had at least *been* there. And then he wasn't, and she was just a girl in a red hood alone in the woods.

"I suppose my story is not unlike many since this strange event began," D.J. said, and sighed. "I have two children, a son and a daughter. They each live on a different coast, in large cities far away from me. Of course I understand that they must go where the work is but it's hard to have them so far away, especially since my wife passed on last year.

"My grandchildren, my son's children, they come to stay with me every summer for four weeks and it is the highlight of my year, as you can imagine. I didn't know that this summer would be the last time I saw them."

He fell silent then, and Red waited. It wasn't her place to say meaningless things in the face of his grief. She knew how much she hated sympathy of any kind, how stupid awkward words given only out of obligation made her feel worse.

"If I could have seen into the future I would have kept them here," D.J. said. "Of course I would have, because it was safer here—fewer infected people to start with, and no riots and no traffic jams full of people trying desperately to leave their city. That was the last time I spoke to my son, you know. He and his wife and the children had packed what they could in their car and were sitting in traffic trying to get out. His cell phone battery was dying and he told me that they were coming here, that he hoped they would be here within a week. Naturally they never arrived, and now they never will."

"Don't say that," Red said, and surprised both of them with the fierceness in her voice. "Don't decide that they haven't made it, that they'll never get to you. I'm going to my own grandmother's house. It's taken me seven weeks to get this far, and I've probably got at least another twenty or thirty days to go, but unless someone stops me I'm going to make it there. So don't give up on them yet. They might be out there, somewhere, moving very slowly but knowing that you're waiting for them."

D.J. blinked, and Red saw that his eyes were full and wet and she looked at the cabinets instead of his face because they didn't really know one another well enough to share tears.

"You're right, of course," D.J. said, and then repeated it. "They might still be on their way. They could arrive any day. Though now with the patrols I worry that they would walk into a fate worse than the Cough."

Like Mama and Dad, Red thought. If they had to die at all she would have much preferred them to get sick, even though the Cough itself was beyond terrible. But she didn't say that, because it wasn't time for her story yet.

"I never heard from my daughter at all. I can only assume that she became ill early on. They said, on the news, that people who became sick were largely incapacitated within twenty-four hours. And she lived alone . . ."

She lived alone so she probably died alone, Red thought. It was very likely D.J. was thinking the same thing, but she wouldn't make him say it.

"At any rate, when everyone was told to head to the nearest quarantine camp I decided not to go. There was still a chance that my son and his family could arrive here and I wanted to be here if they did. And besides—I'm not the sort to be happy behind barbed wire, even if it is there to protect me."

"Me neither," Red said.

"I had the generator, and my water is drawn off a well instead of a municipal water system, so I thought I could stay here for quite some time, especially if I laid in supplies. And I did, very early on. I have always been cautious. Long before people started to panic I was stockpiling fuel and food.

"But I knew that remaining undetected was even more important than supplies. First, I closed and locked all the shutters in the front and then boarded all but one of the front windows. I wanted to make it difficult for anyone to try to break in, but wanted a way to see into the street if I needed it.

"Then on a day when I noticed several of my neighbors loading their cars to leave I packed a small bag with food and water, got into my car, waved to my neighbors and told them

I was heading to the nearest camp. I drove about fifteen miles away and left the car in a fairly isolated parking lot near the state forest. I then walked back here and returned to my home under the cover of night, relatively certain that anyone I knew would assume I was gone for good.

"For some time—perhaps two weeks or so—I saw nobody at all. As far as I knew everyone in town had either gotten sick or left. I occasionally walked up and down the road looking for signs of other survivors, but saw no one.

"Then one day I heard an engine, followed by voices out in the street—many voices, far too many voices to safely approach. I went to the window and looked out and saw two large pickup trucks filled with young men."

"How many, do you think?" Red asked.

"How many men?" D.J. asked. "Two or three in each cab, and another eight to twelve in the bed of each. Somewhere between twenty and thirty. And they were all armed."

Thirty young men with guns somewhere out ahead of her path. Red did not like that. It would be easier to avoid them if she didn't have Sam and Riley, but she did have Sam and Riley and so she would have to find a way to get around.

But going around means extra miles, extra days.

She would have to find a way, even if it meant extra miles and days. It was either that or leave Grandma alone forever. Red was not going to let her grandmother wait by herself, twitching the window curtain at every sound, hoping against hope that her family was returning to her *(like D.J.)*.

So the boys with the guns would have to be dealt with. And she would deal with them. Somehow.

"These young men dispersed throughout the area. They broke doors and windows in some of the houses, but only if they were easy to get into."

"Did they try this house?" Red asked.

"They tried, but only the front, which was as I'd hoped. I hadn't bothered fortifying the back, assuming that anyone who came around would move on to the next house rather than continue to try here. My house is modest compared to others in the area, and I thought they wouldn't think it worth the effort."

"That was what attracted me," Red said with a little smile. "I figured the larger houses had already been raided."

"Besides," D.J. said, and he smiled a very grim smile. "If they had broken in they would have regretted it. I am not incapable of defending myself."

Red knew what he meant, and she sighed. "Not you too."

"Not me too what?"

"You've got a gun, right? The gun's going to fix all your problems."

"Well, no, but it can fix a certain kind of problem. The kind that comes to my door looking for trouble. You don't have a gun with you?"

"I don't like guns," Red said.

"I don't like them either, but I do acknowledge their occasional necessity," D.J. said. "How are you supposed to protect those children without a gun?"

"You think a gun is going to help me more than my brains?" Red asked.

"No, but—"

"No buts. I don't like guns. The only point and purpose of a gun is to kill, and I am not going to carry something that's only for killing. Let's move on."

He gave her a strange look, like he didn't understand her. That was perfectly fine with Red. Most people didn't understand her and she wasn't looking for their understanding, anyway.

"So the men tried your door, couldn't get in, moved on?" Red prompted.

"Yes," D.J. said. "I admit I was slightly confused by their behavior. Nothing they did seemed systematic. They broke into some houses, took useful supplies from a few of those, and others they just seemed to want to destroy for no particular reason. After an hour or two of this they climbed back in their truck and drove away."

"But it wasn't the last you saw of them," Red said.

"No," D.J. said. "The next day a group of three men came through on what was clearly a patrol. And the patrols continued every day at approximately two-hour intervals."

"They've obviously got some kind of base nearby," Red

said, more to herself than D.J. "You never tried to find out where they were coming from?"

He shook his head, and flushed. "I didn't want to know, if I am honest with myself. I know what they are doing and that they are not good people. If they found me out on the road or near the place where they are encamped, then they would shoot me on sight. I thought it better to stay here, out of their reach."

Where it is safe. He didn't say it out loud, but he didn't need to.

"You can't save everybody," Red said.

"Perhaps I should have tried to save some," D.J. murmured. "People have passed by this house and decided to stay the night in one of the open homes. Those people are always, always caught by this group and their patrols. I could have warned them."

"And if they didn't listen?" Red asked. "What if you warned them and then they told those men that you were here in this house? What would have happened then?"

"Yes, I understand what you are saying," D.J. said. "But somehow I feel I should do—should have done—more. There were children. Sometimes, there were children."

"If you had done more you might not have been here when we needed you," Red said.

"I haven't done anything so extraordinary for you," D.J. said.

"Don't kid yourself," Red said. "A bath feels pretty extraordinary after so many weeks on the road."

D.J. laughed, but it was a sad laugh. Red felt somehow that their presence was making him regret his choices in a way he might not have otherwise.

"We should wash your clothing now," D.J. said. "As I said, the washer is somewhat noisy. The next patrol will come through shortly, and though they largely stay on the road there's no use attracting their attention. And we can't use any of the electricity after dark. The patrols are . . . worse after dark."

They hadn't discussed it at all, but somehow a botched break-in had become a lunch invitation that became a staying-for-the-night invitation. Red wouldn't have tried to move Riley and Sam in any case. She expected that they would sleep through dinner and into tomorrow.

D.J. showed Red how to use the washing machine and then left her to it. As she poured extra laundry detergent into the basket she wondered (in the random way that she sometimes did) what was going to happen to all the laundry detergent with no electric washers. It wouldn't have the same currency as food, even if there were people like D.J. who could function off the grid.

Her own grandmother was one of those people—her cabin in the woods was just as self-sufficient as the house Red stood in. Red worried about her grandmother, even though most days it seemed she didn't have a second to spare a worry for anyone but herself. And her grandmother was far more capable, far more prepared for the current circumstances than ninety-nine percent of the population.

And now I have Sam and Riley, too.

Red hoped they would stay with her. It was nice not to be alone anymore.

About forty minutes later Red was about to transfer the clothes from the washer to the dryer when D.J. stopped her. He'd gone into the front room for a while after their talk. Red hadn't wanted to intrude so she sat on the bench in the laundry room with one of the two books she'd packed. The cover of *The Blue Sword*, which had been loved to death even before this trip, was hanging by a tattered edge.

For a little while she pretended she was at a Laundromat, reading while she waited for her clothes, and that when she was done she could go to a diner and have a greasy burger and more fries than she could eat and a chocolate milkshake.

Then D.J. came in and said, "Would you come up front, please?"

He led her into the front room, which was as neatly polished and organized as the kitchen. Three large bookshelves overflowed with books—some titles had been stacked on the floor in front of the shelves. The floor was hardwood, like the kitchen, and worn to a loving patina. A couch and two chairs were clean but used—no plastic furniture covers here, Red thought. It looked like a room where guests were welcome, where kids had jumped on the cushions, where life had been lived.

The windows were all boarded up except for one, as D.J. had told her. This one had curtains that hid the shutters from the inside. The shutters had narrow slats that made it possible to peek out onto the road below.

"Look," he said.

The sun was going down outside—the days were getting shorter, after all—and the patrol was out again. This time there were six of them instead of three, and they moved with more purpose. Red watched them systematically checking each house, looking for signs of life. One of the men walked up on D.J.'s lawn and flashed a light toward the house.

Red flattened herself against the wall beside the window just in time. She didn't know if her silhouette was visible through the shutters but she wasn't taking any chances. Once the light moved away she went back to her viewpoint.

"Nobody ever goes in that one," one of the other men called from the street. The group was moving down the road, inspecting the other homes.

The first man said, "Really?"

He was tall and very thin (which made Red mentally dub him Toothpick) and his hair was shaggy and he wore a denim jacket with his denim pants and had a bandanna tied around his neck like a robber's kerchief.

He looked, Red thought, like a refugee from *The Outsiders*

THE GIRL IN RED 297

(which was not a film she would normally watch but her eleventh-grade English teacher had done a Book vs. Movie term and that was one of his selections).

His flashlight (which was really bright, bright like a policeman's flashlight) was on the ground now, and he appeared to be peering at something there very intently.

Footprints, Red thought. Even though it hadn't rained, there would still be signs that someone had disturbed the grass—especially if you knew what to look for.

Toothpick bent over and picked something up out of the grass. Red couldn't see what it was—the slats of the shutters blocked her view of his hand. The object was small enough to go into his pocket, whatever it was.

He cast a thoughtful look at D.J.'s house.

"He's going to come up here," Red said under her breath. "He's going to walk right up to the front door and look around and then he's going to find something that will make him want to break the door down."

But instead Toothpick followed his compatriots, though he did look back once at D.J.'s house again.

"So he'll come back another time," Red said.

D.J. stood a few feet away, watching her. "Did you see the larger patrol?"

Red nodded. "It's really not safe to travel at night through here."

She dreaded the thought of this group coming upon

herself and Sam and Riley in the woods, asleep and vulnerable. Before they could go any farther forward, Red would have to find out just where the group was based and the size of their patrol circle. She had to make sure that her path and theirs would never cross.

"It would be easier to reconnoiter if Adam were here," she murmured.

"Adam?" D.J. asked.

Red looked up. Her brain had gone into planning mode, and she'd forgotten that D.J. was there (and listening) for a minute.

"Adam," Red said, and her heart hurt when she said his name. "My brother. Adam."

CHAPTER 13

Brief Candle

BEFORE

The world exploded, or maybe it only felt like the world, but there was certainly an explosion.

Red and Sirois were knocked off their feet by the percussion. The room immediately filled with heavy thick smoke.

Getting knocked over by an explosion was not, Red thought groggily, like the movies. She did not feel at all like leaping to her feet and running toward the danger the way film heroes did, or even away from it like a movie extra. Mostly her ears hurt, and they made her head hurt, and when she thought about standing she felt a little sick. The smoke didn't help, because whenever she tried to get a good gulp of oxygen to clear her brain she instead got a mouthful of black fog to choke on.

She heard lots of shouting, and the sound of rifles firing, and more explosions. Sirois moaned. He was a few feet away from her, struggling to push to his feet. He touched the side of his head and his fingers came away covered in blood.

Red had landed on her right side, and the heavy pack felt like a snail's shell holding her in place. She had to get up. She had to get away from Sirois before he grabbed her again. She had to find Adam. And she had to take advantage of whatever the hell was going on outside so they could escape.

She rolled to her belly, pushed herself up to her knees, and then paused there, because her head swam and the kind-of-vomity feeling was back again. She coughed, felt bile rising, tried breathing through her nose to make it stop and instead just got a deeper inhale of the chemicals in the air, which hurried on the inevitable.

Red turned her head away from Sirois, because for some stupid reason she didn't want him to see her puking. When she was done she drank some water and then remembered that she had her mask around her neck, so she pulled it up and that made things a little better. At least there was some kind of filter between her and the smoke that poured in through the open doorway.

She grabbed one of the metal shelves and used it to hoist herself up. Sirois had collapsed to the floor again and wasn't moving. Red hesitated, then went to check on him.

His head was turned to one side and she saw the flare of his nostrils that indicated breathing. The head wound wasn't bleeding a lot that she could tell, so the blood cells were doing their clotting thing and he would probably live.

There wasn't really anything else she could do for him—she wasn't a medic, and he was far too big for her to drag even if she knew where to take him. It didn't seem like a good idea to throw him out into the street, where apparently a pitched battle was going on. Her priority was Adam, who still hadn't emerged from the back room.

"Sorry, pal," she whispered to Sirois. "Your buddies should come and find you soon."

She stepped over his body, noted the staple gun/tracker gun/whatever-it-was nearby and kicked it away under a shelf.

A little cloud of smoke entered the back room with her when she pushed open the door but it was otherwise clear. Red pulled her mask down again and breathed deeply. Even the rotting fruit fog was better than the metallic tang of that smoke.

"Adam!" she called, walking toward the place where they'd found the hole in the concrete floor. "Adam!"

Why hadn't Adam and Regan come out when they heard the explosion? What was taking them so long?

Maybe whoever threw that bomb came in the back and dragged them away already and you'll never see your brother again.

"Too many movies, Red," she said. It was more likely that Regan and Adam were having such a fascinating conversation that they hadn't noticed everything shaking and burning.

The outside noise was strangely muffled in that room. The

air was still and heavy and lifeless. Even the flies buzzing around the rotting fruit had stopped moving.

Lifeless, Red thought. *Nobody here to answer.*

"Adam!" she called again, and felt the first sparks of panic.

Where had her stupid brother gone? He was stupid, stupid to make her worry like this.

"Adam!" she called, and she knew he wasn't going to answer but she couldn't stop herself because she could only move so fast, her head was spinning around and she never walked that fast even without this dizziness but maybe if she kept calling he would hear her and answer and then she could stop imagining terrible things had happened to her one and only stupid brother.

She reached the aisle that Adam had ferreted out by following streaks of blood on the floor and there was no one there.

There was no fresh blood. No sign of whatever had made the hole. And no sign of Adam or Regan.

All the panic blooming in her chest came to an abrupt and anticlimactic halt, replaced by confusion.

"They didn't come out the door," Red said. "I would have seen them. It wasn't that far from where I was standing with Sirois.

"Adam?" she called again.

Nothing. Only the vague sounds of guns and shouting outside, like an echo of a war movie playing a few rooms away.

There must be another door, she thought. Or a basement,

maybe. Something that had attracted their attention, and they had followed like Alice and her white rabbit.

Red circled around the perimeter of the room, checking each aisle as she went. Nothing, nothing, and then . . .

"Adam!" she cried, and she ran to him.

He was propped on the floor with his back to a closed door. The door looked like one of those large sturdy ones that sealed off a freezer room.

But the freezer can't possibly be on because the electricity is out, Red thought, and she thought this because it was the only thing for her brain to grasp.

If she didn't then she would have to look and to see and there was blood, so much blood, blood everywhere.

"Adam," Red said, and she knelt beside him. His blood soaked through the knees of her pants.

Yet who would have thought the old man to have had so much blood in him?

She'd only ever read Shakespeare for Mama's sake and it was strange, wasn't it, so strange that it came back to her now as her brother lay dying.

His eyes were closed and his hands were at his sides and his legs splayed out in front of him—

—*or rather what's left of his legs,* Red thought, because his right leg had a big chunk taken out of his thigh *(like something bit him, which was absurd, something with sharp teeth that left sharp marks behind)* and his left leg was almost completely denuded between the knee and the foot. All that was left was the bone and some ragged bits of skin hanging on.

Something had eaten his leg. It didn't look like he'd been shot or hit by a grenade or even carved up by a mad somebody's knife. It only looked like one thing. Something had tried to eat him alive.

"Adam," she said, and she shook his shoulder.

His chest rose and fell, but very shallow, very gentle, like he was a machine that had been turned off and the gears were winding down.

"Adam," she said again. "Wake up, stupid."

Wake up. You're my stupid brother and you're not supposed to die. Mama told us to stay together and we've never had a chance to make up not really we never had a chance to say we're sorry to each other about all the things we said and thought after Mama and Daddy died and Adam you have to wake up because you're the only one I have left and don't leave me don't don't don't leave me

"Red," he said, soft like an exhale.

She thought she'd imagined it, and then he said it again. "Red."

His eyes were closed, and the rest of his body was so still, but his lips moved. She had to lean close to hear him because his voice came from a faraway place.

"It's . . . not . . . what . . . we . . . thought. Not . . . what they said. Don't . . ."

He trailed off, and she waited, and wondered if he would finish before his voice left altogether.

"Don't open this door," he said in one long breath.

That was the last one, the last breath, though Red stayed there for she didn't know how long waiting for another one, her eyes fixed on his mouth and clinging to the hope that it would move again, that there would be another word, that they would be able to say a proper good-bye.

She wiped angrily at her wet face but more tears kept appearing, even though she was *not* crying and her chest *wasn't* racked with sobs that made her lungs burn.

"Stupid," she said, and she didn't know if she was saying it to him or herself.

They shouldn't have separated, not even for a few minutes, not even under the threat of the military. Mama told them to stay together and Red had meant to do that. Because Red knew, had always known, that separation meant Something Would Happen. And it had.

Something had happened to Adam, and to Regan, for the other man wasn't to be seen. Red had to assume that Regan, as a trained soldier, would have shot at whatever it was that chewed Adam's legs to pieces.

For all the good it did him, Red thought.

He was probably behind the door that Adam guarded, and given the lack of noise coming from inside there was a pool of blood in the freezer, too.

A pool of blood, and something that Adam wanted to keep from getting out. He'd stayed there to protect her. His last words had been an order to not open the door.

Red didn't much care for orders—direct statements tended to make her want to do the opposite of what she was told—but she wasn't dumb. Her curiosity was not going to make her push her brother's corpse out of the way and find out what put him in that condition.

If it were a horror movie she would have, because in movies people were always doing things that made no sense. But this wasn't a movie. This was her life. Adam had wanted her to live, and Red wanted to live, so she wasn't going to open that door.

That mystery would just have to remain a mystery forever.

And it was important now to get out without being snared in whatever was happening outside. This little burg had basically no tree cover, so she had to get through the town and to the other side without being seen, being caught, or losing her supplies (which were more precious than ever now that Adam wasn't carrying half the gear).

Her practical brain took over, and it was a good thing that it did because it helped her not look at what was left of Adam.

She didn't see his pack anywhere, and hadn't spotted it in any of the aisles as she searched for him. That meant it had been dropped inside the room he was blocking.

Whatever is in there is gone forever, she thought. Not even the promise of what he carried in his pack could have encouraged her to open that door.

Adam had told her not to open the door. And for once, she was not going to argue with her brother.

But she needed to get out. She pictured the town in her mind—the little valley, the state road running through the middle of it, the rise that she must climb to exit on the other side. No trees, really, except a few dotted here and there on the landscape. And once she was out of the town there would be no cover at all until she reached the forest again, and that was a few miles away.

It sounded like there was a war going on outside. Somehow she'd have to cross this war zone by herself and reach the woods. Somehow. First she had to find a rear exit to this building, because the explosion had occurred at the front and she didn't think it was a great idea to go out through all of that black smoke again.

"Wh-what happened here?"

Red turned around, furious and scared, and her hand went to the axe at her belt. Sirois stood there, his face white as chalk, staring at the blood at Red's feet.

He could have snuck up on you and shot you, Red. If you want to remain the last surviving member of your family, then you need to start using your ears as well as your eyes.

She wasn't going to cut herself a break just because she was standing over her brother's corpse, either. Adam was dead, but she was alive and she needed to stay that way or else Grandma would be alone forever.

"One of your 'tapeworms' got my brother, and probably Regan, too," Red said.

She felt her anger building, and wanted to take it out on this man who represented everything she hated—lies, opacity, pointless bureaucracy, men with guns.

Men with guns killed my parents. And a man with a gun couldn't save my brother.

Red gestured at the thing that used to be Adam on the floor.

"Still going to tell me that information is classified?"

"Where's the lieutenant?" Sirois said.

He seemed unsteady on his feet, although Red didn't know if that was because of his head wound or the blood around Adam or the smoke that he'd surely inhaled while staggering after her.

"I have no idea and I really don't care because my brother is dead," Red said. "And he's dead because your lieutenant dragged him back here to look at a hole in the ground, and whatever was in that hole probably killed him."

"I have to find the lieutenant," Sirois said. "I need to find him now. Outside . . ."

"You do what you like," Red said. "I'm leaving."

Sooner or later Sirois was going to look for Regan behind the door that Adam guarded and when he did Red was not going to be present.

"You can't leave," Sirois said.

Red pulled the axe off her belt. She'd never used it on a person, or anything alive. She'd always wondered if she could. She was angry enough to use it now, because the man before her was not going to stop her.

"I *am not* going to your little quarantine camp," Red said, and held the axe up. "I am going to my grandma's house, and if you try to stop me I will slice off whatever I can reach and leave you here to bleed to death."

Sirois shook his head. "No. I believe you. I believe you'll do it, and I'm not trying to stop you so I can take you away. That's not it. You can't get out right now. That militia has got us pinned in here and they're covering the road in both directions."

Red blinked. "The militia? The fakey soldiers that Adam and I saw?"

The Locusts had returned for the rest of the goods in the store. That was the thing that had twanged her antennae earlier—when Adam said they didn't have enough room in their trucks for the food in the back room. Of course, they would return with empty trucks. And when they returned they'd discovered the army, or whatever branch of the military Regan and Sirois were supposed to represent.

"Yes," Sirois said. He ran his hand over his close-cropped hair. The wound on his head had clotted up, just as Red thought it would.

"Why would they do that?" Red asked, narrowing her eyes.

"Because they see us as the enemy," Sirois said. "They've been getting bigger, collecting stragglers to their cause. They think the Cough came out of a government lab, that everything that's happened is part of some massive conspiracy."

"Is it?" Red asked.

"Of course not," Sirois said.

"Just the part about parasites that explode out of humans and then become something that chews off my brother's legs," Red said. "And the part where you're covering it up."

"The point is that the Cough isn't because of anything we did," Sirois said.

"How do you know?"

"What?"

"How do you know?" Red repeated each word slowly, enunciating every consonant. "If the CDC brewed up something in their lab and it accidentally was let loose in the world, do you think they would tell you?"

Sirois frowned, opened his mouth, closed it again.

"Yeah, you're thinking about it now," Red said. "Fine, there's no massive conspiracy but there are a load of conspiracy theorists with weapons trying to eliminate your whole battalion or patrol or whatever you are."

"Platoon," Sirois corrected absently. "And I need to find Regan, because he's the CO and he's needed right now."

"I'm sorry to say that I think he's been eaten up by

whatever is behind this door," Red said. "Adam told me not to open it, so I am not going to do that. If you insist on doing that so you can visually confirm the death of Lieutenant Regan then feel free, but give me a ten-minute head start first because getting eaten alive is not on my agenda for the day."

Sirois's eyes went from Adam to the door and back to Red.

"You're telling me one of those things is behind that door?"

"One, twenty, who knows?" Red said. "All I know is that I was told not to open it and I am going to take my brother's advice on that score."

She was flippant now because it was the only defense she had, for the longer she stayed in that place with Adam's body the more she felt she might just break down or crack up or start screaming to high heaven and never stop. There was no time now for grief, for curling into a little ball and crying all the water from her eyes.

Sirois stood there. Red saw him thinking, saw his eyes flicker as he turned over the possibilities.

"I'm going to take your brother's advice, too," Sirois said. "He seemed sensible, even if you don't all the time."

"You're only saying that because he submitted to your tracker gun without an argument," Red said. "So now what? You're going to run outside to join the fray?"

"Yes," Sirois said. "It's my duty to do what I can, especially since the lieutenant is . . . missing."

"And what is it that you think I should do?" Red asked.

"Stay in here and cower like a good little woman until you suppress the insurgents?"

"I'd like you to use some degree of care and caution, yes," Sirois said. "I feel responsible for you."

"That's a dumb thing to feel," Red said. "It's a free country, or at least it used to be. Go do whatever you think you need to do and don't think about me again."

"But your brother . . ."

"You don't think Adam was the one doing the planning and decision making, do you?" Red laughed. The laugh had a hard, hysterical edge to it and she stopped right away. "I'm more cautious than Adam ever was. I promise you that."

"Even you can't think it's a smart thing to try to escape with everything going on outside," Sirois said.

"Sure it is. I can use the chaos to my advantage and slip away in a cloud of smoke."

"And what will you do if you get caught by them? I don't think they are the type that will be kind to a woman alone."

"Do you think I don't know what kind of men this world has wrought?" Red said. "Every woman knows. And those men existed before everything fell apart."

She turned away from him then, because they were only going in circles and above all things she needed to get away from Adam's corpse before her brain broke into a thousand pieces along with her heart.

"Where are you going?"

"I'm looking for another exit," Red said.

She carefully stepped around Adam, looking without actually *looking*. There was nothing she needed to see again.

Sirois didn't say anything. After a moment he followed her, catching up in a few strides.

Long legs, Red thought. Then she said, without breaking her stride, "What do you want now?"

She had to crane her neck up to see his face. Now that he was beside her the comical difference in their heights was much more apparent. He had a good foot and a half on her, maybe more.

"I'm going to see you safely away," Sirois said grimly. "I feel responsible for you. I know you said it was dumb, and it's pretty clear you've got brains and know-how or else you wouldn't have gotten this far. But you're right. It was our fault—mine and Regan's—that your brother got killed. So I am at least going to help you get out of town."

"You're going to be my deus ex machina?" Red said. "I don't think so. Look at the size of you. You're going to attract attention when I'm trying to be sneaky."

"You don't think a lone girl in a red hood wandering through a battle zone is going to attract attention?"

Red sighed. There really wasn't anything she could do to stop him from following her like an abandoned puppy. She should probably be grateful that he wasn't trying to drag her away to quarantine, but she wasn't. Mostly she just wanted to be left alone so she could think. How could she think with this annoying person looming over her?

She followed the perimeter of the store until she reached the back.

"Ah," Red said. "That's what I was looking for."

There was a large warehouse door, the metal type that pulled down from the ceiling and was large enough to drive a truck through if necessary. Next to it was what Red thought of as a human-sized door. There was a light-up *EXIT* sign above it, though of course the light was out.

Red went to the smaller door, Sirois trailing behind her. She pressed her ear up against the door and listened. There was rifle fire, shouting, the revving of engines—but it all seemed far away. There was a good chance that all the action was centered on the main road.

If that was the case she could slip away while no one was looking. Of course, "slipping away" was a relative term—in order to slip away she would have to climb the hill that surrounded the town and then go west (and out of her way) in order to escape any watching eyes. She hated climbing hills. It was better than going down, but it was always too easy for her to lose her balance. Once she was away from the town and out of the valley she could circle back to the main road that would lead to the woods.

She pulled a map out of her pack to confirm her route.

"What are you doing?" Sirois asked.

Red gave him a dirty look, not dignifying such a stupid question with an answer.

"Okay, that was dumb," he acknowledged. Then he said, "Do you really think the lieutenant is in that room?"

"I do," Red said, folding up the map again. "Are you going to tell me what's in there with him?"

Sirois looked as if his tongue were rolling up behind his lips.

"Fine, keep your classified information in your mouth," Red said. "And don't follow me."

She grabbed the door handle and pushed down, easing the door open a crack so she could peek outside.

All she could see was the back of the building. The chemical smoke smell returned with a vengeance, even though the source was on the main road. She pushed the door open a little farther, so that she could get a better look in both directions.

To the right there was only the back end of the town, and a couple of abandoned cars. To the left—south, the direction she and Adam had come from

(don't think about Adam)

there were two soldiers holding rifles. They were about twenty or thirty feet away from her and peering through a space in between the buildings. Red couldn't tell if they were the fakey soldiers or the real ones, but it really didn't matter since both sides carried guns and could shoot her for no apparent reason if she was seen.

There was nothing for it. She would have to take her

chances. Two soldiers were hanging around now. It was possible there might be twenty or thirty in a minute.

The rifle fire seemed to be tapering off to the occasional fusillade. Red didn't know if that meant things had been fought to a standstill or if somebody had won, and she didn't care, either. Let them shoot each other.

She adjusted the straps on her pack, made sure they were secure, and double-checked her shoelaces. Red was *not* going to fall on her face because of something stupid like an unlaced shoe. She took a deep breath even though it was a cliché, but oxygen was important when you were about to make a mad dash up a hill and possibly be forced to dodge bullets.

And then Sirois grabbed her shoulder and pulled her back inside. The door slammed shut behind her and made a noise that sounded inordinately loud.

"What the fuck?" she shouted, shoving his arm off her. "Just *what the fuck* are you doing, Sirois? I told you to go the hell away. I was about to escape and now you've probably attracted their attention, you goddamned idiot."

"You can't go out there. You're going to get shot," he said. His eyes flicked down to her leg and back up to her face.

"Oh, that's what this is all about," Red said. She could practically feel her blood reaching the boiling point. "This is because you think I'm a Helpless Little Crippled Girl."

"No," Sirois said, but his eyes couldn't stay on hers.

"Yes, it is," she said, and poked him in the chest. "I am

perfectly capable of taking care of myself. I have freed you of obligation. Stop getting in my way. I'm leaving. And if those guys are outside the door I am blaming you, one hundred percent, because the door wouldn't have slammed shut if you hadn't grabbed me."

Red took her axe off her belt again and held it loosely in her right hand. If those soldiers *were* just outside, then they were in for a surprise.

But I'd really rather not use it, she thought. When she thought about Adam

(don't think about Adam)

and all the blood all around him it was hard to imagine using her axe to hack at anyone. But she would. If she had to.

All she wanted was to leave. She didn't have any kind of stake in this argument between the army and the Locust Militia. She glanced behind her, where Sirois stood watching her.

She flicked her hand at him. "Go. Go away. I don't want you."

"I'm going to follow you out and give you cover," he said, his mouth set in a grim line.

"Fine," she said. "Do whatever you want. Just don't get in my way."

"Actually," he said, "it would be better if I went first."

Red huffed out a breath through her nose and looked up at the ceiling.

"Give me strength," she said, and stepped out of the way

with a dramatic flourish. "Here you go."

"On my count," Sirois said, taking out his sidearm.

"Yeah, yeah," Red said.

He burst through the door like a police officer in a crime TV show, sweeping his weapon right to left. It was so perfectly executed that Red wanted to applaud.

She trundled out in his wake. He was large enough that she could literally use him as a body shield without even trying. If she stood behind him she would effectively disappear.

Her axe was still in her hand but it appeared that it wouldn't be necessary. The two men who'd been lurking on the corner were gone.

"Go," he said, and gestured up the slope.

"I'm going," she said.

She'd only taken a few steps when Sirois called her name. "Red."

"Mother of God," she said, rolling her eyes and turning back. "What now?"

"You know how you said the Cough might have been made in a lab?"

"Yeah?"

"Well," he said, and it looked like it was a real struggle for him to say whatever was trying to come out of his mouth. "I don't know about the Cough. But the other thing—the, er, tapeworm—it did come out of a lab."

She raised her eyebrow at him. "And?"

"And that's all I can tell you," Sirois said. "Besides the fact that you want to avoid them."

"I'd already figured that out," Red said. She started climbing again.

Halfway up she peeked back over her shoulder. Sirois had his back to the hill and was checking both ends of the alley that ran behind the buildings. A soldier came around the corner holding a rifle but he must have been the wrong kind of soldier because Sirois shot him.

She could just see over the roofs of the buildings and into the town now. A plume of black smoke rose from the front of the grocery store (*what had they done? Blown up a truck with a grenade launcher?*) and she saw what appeared to be hasty fortifications made of vehicles facing one another on the main road.

She resolutely turned her back, because she didn't want to know. She didn't want to get caught again. She didn't want to get dragged into some meaningless fight between men who wanted to control the way this new world was going to spin.

As she crested the slope she couldn't shake the nagging feeling that she'd forgotten something, something important. Then she remembered that she'd promised Mama she would stay with Adam.

They were supposed to stay together, Red and Adam. Now Adam was gone and it was just Red, Red all alone with a long way to go in a world full of wolves.

CHAPTER 14

Something Wicked

AFTER

"I don't think you should go," Sam said.

Red said, "I know."

She'd thought long and hard on it but there was really no other option. Someone was going to have to find out where those men had their base and the size of their patrol circle. It was beyond foolish to bring the kids, so of course Red would have to go by herself and they would stay with D.J.

At least they'll be safe and warm and fed if something happens to me.

Leaving Sam and Riley behind broke the No Separation rule, which bothered Red because separation within her party had thus far only resulted in loss. And approaching the base camp of a bunch of gun-toting men who kidnapped women and children smacked of stupidity on top of it.

She wasn't anybody's Chosen One. She wasn't here to

Save the World. And while she'd managed to defend herself
from a few lone wolves she didn't have the least idea how to
manage a pack of them, barring the sudden discovery of
superhero skills.

*Well, you're not going to manage them. You're going to find
out where they're located, and where they travel to every day,
and then you're going to mark those places on the map and avoid
them. There's not going to be heroics of any kind.*

"I really don't like this," D.J. said.

"Yes, I know, everybody thinks it's a terrible idea," Red
said. "Including me. But this is what it comes down to—
terrible idea number one, which is to scope out the camp and
figure out how to avoid them, or terrible idea number two,
which is to walk blindly into their net and get scooped up.
I've already been scooped up once and I'm not letting it
happen again."

"What do you mean, scooped up?" D.J. said, a little
indignant. "Do you mean by me?"

"No," Red said. "I got caught by soldiers once."

"You did?" Riley asked. "How did you get away?"

"I walked," she said.

There was no need to explain about Adam, about Regan,
about Sirois, or about the war between the militia and the
military.

"If you can escape from the soldiers I suppose you'll be all
right," Sam said, unable to keep the doubt out of her voice.

She was too smart to buy Red's brief explanation, and Red could tell that she knew there was more to the story.

"There's really no need for any of you to leave at all," D.J. said. "You can stay here with me for as long as you need."

Riley got up from his chair and went to Red's shoulder, tugging on her sleeve. "Yeah, let's stay, Red. It's so much better here than out in the woods. And we can have kimchi and rice every day."

Red's mouth twisted. She'd thought it might come to this. Sam and Riley were under no obligation to stay with her, and it was probably safer for them if they didn't go any farther. Still, there was a little pang in her heart when she considered leaving them behind. It wasn't easy to be on your own all the time, and the two of them had made her feel human again.

"You can stay, if you'd rather," Red said gently. "But I have to keep going. My grandmother is waiting for me, just like D.J. is waiting for his son. I can't let her wait forever."

"Oh, right," Riley said. "Your grandma. I forgot."

They'd only been together for a few days. It wasn't as if they were lifelong friends. It would be better, much better, for Sam and Riley to stay here.

Except for those patrols that came around every day. And that man, the shaggy-haired toothpick who'd picked something up off the lawn.

That something had been nagging at Red ever since she

saw him, nagged at her in the way little worries do and making it impossible for her to completely relax.

One worry at a time, Red.

"Look," Red said. "They can't be that far away, not if they're coming through here on patrol every day. And it's pretty obvious they're mostly sticking to the roads. Since they don't double back, then they're walking in a big circle, or something resembling one."

She pulled out her map. In order to continue more or less in the correct direction of Grandma's house, she and Sam and Riley would have passed through this collection of houses and followed the state road until it connected with more forest farther north.

This was what she'd been doing all along—frog-hopping from wooded area to wooded area, avoiding settlements if possible. Most people likely weren't aware of just how much land was still wild in the United States, even if that land was only pockets between civilization.

"These guys are not going to want to be far from a road," Red said. "They're using it to transport anyone they capture, and any supplies they need. Despite the walking patrols they'd still be pretty dependent on their vehicles."

"So their camp, or base, or whatever you'd like to call it, won't be in the woods," D.J. said, leaning over the map.

"If they walk along the state road here—and we know they do, since they pass us every day—then they can connect

up with Sparrow Hill Road here"—he pointed to the spot—
"and could follow along it for another mile or so before
turning south again."

"And if they follow the southward road here," Red said,
"they'll come back to the state road, because it curves like a
backward J there before straightening back up this way. How
big would you say that loop is?"

"Perhaps six miles, give or take," D.J. said.

"Six miles. That means a walking patrol doing a twenty-
minute mile could follow the whole loop in about two hours.
And you said that's how long the patrols usually take."

"And since it's not the same men every time," D.J. said,
following her train of thought, "then a fresh patrol can go out
quickly when the first group is ready to rest."

"So if you've got it all figured out," Sam said quickly,
"then you don't have to go out to investigate, Red. We can
just avoid those roads."

We. Red ignored the little candle that lit in her heart when
Sam said *we.* Sam, at least, still wanted to travel with Red.

"But we have to be sure," Red said. "What if we're wrong?
What if they are using a larger area and we're only seeing one
circuit of patrols when they're actually sending out more? I
can't take a chance that anything will happen to you."

"But, Red," Sam said, and she looked down at her hands
folded in her lap as she said this. "You . . . you can't get away
from them really fast."

Red sighed. Sam didn't mean to treat her like Poor Slow Crippled Girl. She didn't really understand that Red could do a lot more than most people thought.

"I don't need to get away from them really fast," Red said. "Because I am going to use my eyes and my ears and my brains to avoid them."

Riley tugged her sleeve again, and he leaned into her arm. "But what if they catch you?" he whispered.

Red thought of her axe, and the things she had done with it.

"I'll make them sorry," she said. "They'll regret the day they tried to catch me."

The next day Red was awake long before the sun was up. D.J. packed her a small sling bag with water and some food and a few other essentials, because she would be leaving her heavy pack behind. Her axe, however, went into its accustomed place on her belt.

She needed to move quickly, and while she was certain she couldn't do the circuit in two hours she was fairly confident that she'd return by early evening—if she discovered the base.

"And if you don't find it by midday," D.J. said quietly, for Sam and Riley were still asleep, "you will return to us regardless and search again tomorrow. I don't want you caught out at night. And those children will fret about you until you're back."

Red had told them they could see her off in the morning, but she wasn't about to wake them. She was a little afraid that they might try to follow her, or that they would cry, and she didn't think she could leave if they did.

Besides, the night before Riley had complained of a sore throat and Red didn't want him getting sick because he didn't rest.

(It's not the Cough, though)

(It's definitely not the Cough because their dad had it and they didn't catch it so it's probably just a regular kid thing a regular sort of cold and nothing to be concerned about and D.J. can give him tea with honey and by the time I come back he will be fine just fine because it's not the Cough)

"I really wish you would take my rifle with you," D.J. said.

"Why, so I can shoot off the only real foot I have left?" Red said. "I don't have the first clue what to do with a rifle."

"I can show you—"

"I told you, I don't like guns," Red said. "I've gotten this far without one and I'm not going to start using one now."

D.J.'s lips pressed together, but he didn't say anything else about the gun.

Red's plan was to follow the road from as safe a distance as she could manage. If she didn't find the base between D.J.'s house and the woods, then she would turn onto Sparrow Hill Road.

"Be very careful there," D.J. said. "There isn't much tree

cover, and the houses are spread much farther apart than they are here."

"I'm always careful," Red said. "To a fault."

It was a little past five, according to D.J.'s watch, when Red left the house. The sun wouldn't be up for another couple of hours, and while D.J. didn't like the idea of her possibly running into the more dangerous night patrol, he also saw the value of darkness. It would be easier for her to travel without worrying about being spotted. And she considered that she had the advantage, because she knew about the existence of the patrols in the first place. Most travelers wouldn't.

The night sky was covered in clouds, and the frost that crunched under her boots told her that if she didn't get back on the road to Grandma's house soon then the impending snow would make that decision for her. She pulled her hat down around her ears.

At first she darted from house to house, staying in the back yards and out of reach of any headlights that might appear on the road. After a while she realized that dashing between buildings was stupid. She'd get worn out faster that way, and anyhow it wasn't as if the houses were especially far apart. She'd be able to hear the approach of any engines or the chatter of the foot patrol easily, especially in the intense silence. Her jacket was made from down and nylon and the rasp of the cloth as her arm brushed against her body sounded like a chain saw.

People made so much *noise*, Red thought. She'd never realized it until all the people were gone. Even where she lived, out in the middle of nowhere, there was a kind of constant background rumble of sound—the far-off hum of cars on the road, the low buzz of lightbulbs overhead, the refrigerator whirring, the rhythmic thump of clothes in the dryer, the sound of the television drifting out the window screen, Mama and Dad talking, Adam tapping away on his phone. Red and Adam had gone camping in some fairly isolated places as well, but even there she'd found there was a surprising amount of noise. You'd have to go to the ends of the earth to escape the sounds of planes flying overhead, for example. And there were very few places in America where there were no power lines.

Red surprised herself by reaching the first turning point at Sparrow Hill Road fairly quickly. She'd forgotten what it was like to walk without a heavy pack dragging her down, and the continual fatigue that had dogged her for weeks had been partially remedied by a bath, food, and sleep in a soft bed.

There was a little strip mall a short distance past the turning onto Sparrow Hill. Red thought that would be an ideal place for a home base if you were a militia. There was a Target and a grocery store anchoring a scattering of other small shops.

The Target and the grocery would be beyond useful—dry goods and clothing and all sorts of other things would be readily available. It was the kind of place Red would choose if she wanted to establish a fiefdom in this broken world.

The locals didn't agree with her, though, for she saw no sign that the gang of kidnappers was anywhere nearby. Still, it would be worth it to come back. There was the off-chance that all the food wasn't taken, and at the very least she would be able to find clothes for Riley and Sam in the kids' department at Target.

She wished she had time to go there now, just to take a quick look around, but that was violating one of the many rules of life in the postapocalyptic war zone. Rule number eight, or whatever—Red had lost track although she thought she probably should write them down—Never Deviate from the Plan. If the protagonist decided on a course of action and then was distracted like a magpie from that course, then Something Would Happen.

Something Would Happen, Red decided as she turned onto Sparrow Hill Road, should be its own rule. Of course, it was the consequence for violating so many of the rules, like Never Separate, so maybe it should just be an addendum to every rule.

Sparrow Hill Road had no particular cohort of sparrows that Red could see, although it did have several rolling hills. She didn't care for the hills, although it was much easier to maintain her balance on the downhill without the weight of the pack.

THE GIRL IN RED 331

D.J. had been right—there really wasn't much cover on this road. The residences were far from one another, and there were very few trees. The houses were mostly set far back from the road as well, with long winding driveways. The only place for her to hide—if such a thing became necessary— was in the ditch that ran along the road.

And that, Red realized, was not a practical solution now that the sun was up. The patrols would have returned to walking in groups of three, not six, but she would be easier to find without the cover of darkness. It would not be a good thing for Red to encounter them. She'd been feeling a little too free and easy, letting her mind wander around.

Red saw two houses maybe a half or three quarters of a mile distant—one covered in blue siding and closer to the road, the other made of brick and tucked a little farther back. She decided she would stop in the brick one—break in, if she had to—and use it to spy on the road for a while.

She was getting that itchy feeling on the back of her neck again, and she didn't know if it was because the patrol really was coming up behind her or if she was just being paranoid. Either way it seemed like a good time to find a hidey-hole and stay there until the patrol passed.

By the time she reached the brick house her neck was so itchy it felt like a mass of spiders were nesting on her spine. Something was wrong, really wrong, and she didn't think it was just her worry-brain working overtime.

Something has happened to Sam and Riley, she thought as she broke one of the back windows on the house with her axe. She was hardly aware of what she was doing, because the fear had taken hold now and logic was no longer welcome.

She climbed through the window—it was low, thank goodness, because she couldn't deal with another problem at that moment. The window was over a kitchen sink, which meant that when Red boosted herself through, her hands went into the basin and her chin banged against the faucet.

Her legs were dangling outside and she thought, *It would be just my luck for them to come along and find me like this, with my limbs hanging out the window. All they would have to do is grab me and pull and there wouldn't be a damned thing I could do about it.*

Red managed to turn her torso to the right and kind of flop onto the counter and yank her legs after. Something ripped as she went through and when she sat up on the counter she saw that the left leg of her pants was ripped from shin to foot. It was a good thing she had a fake leg on that side or her skin would have been ripped from shin to foot, too. She hadn't done a great job of clearing all the glass from the bottom of the sill and had paid the price.

Tearing her pant leg was weirdly calming, because it made her settle down and focus on where she was and what she was doing.

"Stop freaking out for no reason, Red," she said to herself.

The kids were fine. They were with D.J. She was the one who was more likely in immediate danger.

She hopped off the kitchen counter and looked around. The air was stale but it didn't have the rotten reek of dead things decomposing. It was likely the owners had just locked up and drove away. The kitchen had yellow wallpaper with little cartoon geese in various poses—wearing a hat and reading a newspaper, or walking to the market with a basket.

Red supposed it was cute, but since in real life geese were jerks she didn't really see the appeal of anthropomorphizing them and putting them all over your wall.

She couldn't resist checking the cabinets and was disappointed to find nothing but a few stray cans of tuna with expired dates on them.

"How long do you have to keep tuna for it to expire?" she said, wrinkling her nose.

The kitchen connected to a dining room complete with a heavy wood dining set. It had probably been repeatedly polished by loving hands but now there were no hands to do it and a thick layer of dust had formed on the tabletop. In the center of the table was a bouquet of fake flowers composed of artificial greens and purples set in a clear blue vase. Red couldn't even tell what flowers they were supposed to be imitating.

The dining room connected to a living room with hideously orange furniture and a carpet that looked like it was composed of lava flow—reds and oranges smashed together. There were lots of bookcases filled with glass and porcelain knickknacks but no books.

What kind of people had no books? Red judged the occupants and found them wanting.

She reckoned she wasted ten or fifteen minutes fooling around with the window and checking the kitchen cabinets. The living room had a large picture window that looked out onto the road. The angle was perfect—she could see quite a distance back the way she'd come, and if she switched corners it was easy to see another half mile or so in the other direction. After that the road rose into another rolling hill and whatever was beyond it was hidden.

The picture window had blinds and a sheer curtain and heavier curtains over those—orange, of course. While Red didn't understand why anybody would want to spend so much time contemplating the stuff that covered the windows, she appreciated that it gave her plenty of camouflage. There was even a handy chair to sit in just at the angle she needed to watch the road.

She thought the walking patrol should come along any minute, unless they'd passed by while she was in the kitchen. That would be unfortunate, because her plan was to let them get about fifteen minutes ahead of her and then continue on.

After that she thought she would find another good place to watch the road and hopefully follow them to their base. Sparrow Hill Road was not a good place for following because of all the exposed land.

She dug in the bag that D.J. had given her and found a small container packed with cold rice and egg, and another container with a peanut butter sandwich.

Red ate the cold rice and egg and watched the road. She wished she had a watch, but before the Crisis she'd only had one of those fancy smartwatches and those were useless bricks without electricity to charge them and cell grids to provide necessary information like time.

But the satellites were still out there, circling around sending back data, right? Red thought. She wondered if there were people who knew more about electronics than she did, out there still sending and receiving information. There were probably radio and Morse code people communicating all over the world.

It was only Red and those like her (which was, to be fair, probably most people) who were helpless without their smartphones and Internet connections. Hell, it was only because of her father's insistence that she learn that Red could read a map. She knew that most adults around her age only knew how to follow Siri's turn-by-turn directions.

She finished the rice and tried not to twitch the curtains. Where were they? D.J. had said the patrol came through every two hours, like clockwork. Red was certain it had been more than two hours since she got on the road, and even accounting for their different starting points she should have seen them by now.

Something Has Happened, she thought, and the back of her neck started itching again.

"But that something doesn't have to mean that D.J. or the kids are in danger," she said. Her voice sounded unnaturally loud in the silent room.

It could mean that Regan's group had met up with the Kidnapping Militia and they were fighting it out, just like in the town where Adam had died. Or it could mean that the other militia, the crazy Locust Militia that took all the available resources, had encountered the Kidnapping Militia and *they* were fighting it out. Or the Kidnapping Militia had decided that it was pointless to stay in the area and had moved on to another one.

There were loads of possibilities. Those possibilities didn't have to include Red's friends in jeopardy.

And you are not a comic-book hero with some kind of special sense for danger. You are just an overly imaginative woman in a potentially life-threatening situation and the tension is getting to you.

"Yes," Red said, agreeing with her internal monologue. "You're just getting yourself Into a State for no damned reason."

She saw movement from the direction she'd come from—a group of figures, made blurry by the distance. The patrol.

"See?" Red told herself. "There they are. Everything's fine. You just didn't calculate the time correctly, or they were delayed by something else."

There was some satisfaction in seeing them, too, because it meant at least some of her assumptions about their patrol loop were correct.

Except that as the group approached she could see that there were four figures instead of three, and one of those figures was very small.

Small and wearing a pink hooded coat that looked a lot like the one Red had found for Sam in the house with the pink bedroom.

She stood up, ignoring the way her heart slammed in her chest and her breath came fast and frantic. Red squinted at the group—like that would make her see more clearly. The little figure had a shaggy brown haircut

(just like Sam)

and bright blue sneakers

(just like Sam)

and the larger figures were laughing and pushing her shoulder so that she stumbled. Every time she stumbled they would laugh harder.

The group got closer and closer, and when they passed the house with the blue siding Red clearly saw their faces and one of them was small and twisted with fear and wet with tears and of course it was Sam's.

Red was seized by a sudden and urgent thought—*I can't let them take her to the camp.*

If they took Sam to their base she would be gone forever, for Red didn't have a band of freedom fighters to liberate a child from imprisonment in a camp full of armed men.

So it was important—no, it was *imperative*—that she get Sam back now. And to get Sam back she would have to kill those three men who were laughing and pushing her and probably thinking terrible thoughts about what they would do with a little girl.

One of those men laughing and pushing Sam was Toothpick—the guy Red had spotted on D.J.'s lawn. Red wondered if he was the reason that Sam was taken. But if that was the case, then where were D.J. and Riley?

(not dead please not dead don't let anything have happened to them)

No. She wasn't going to believe in anything without evidence seen by her own eyes. And it wasn't time for reconstructing possible scenarios. Red had to save Sam.

She would have to surprise them, which meant moving fast, and moving fast just wasn't Red's best thing.

"Don't think about it too much," she said, unhooking the axe from her belt.

Red took off the small bag of supplies that D.J. had given her and also pulled off her noisy coat. After a minute she reluctantly put her red hood on top of the coat. A bright red hood might attract attention if one of them saw a flash in the corner of their eye.

She went to the front door and unlocked it and hoped like hell it wouldn't squeak or squeal when it opened. Red pulled the door just an inch and peered through the crack. The opening faced the direction the group was heading and she waited for them to walk by on the road, hoping that none of them observed the open door as they passed.

The brick house wasn't right on top of the road and of course they were distracted by Sam so chances were good that they wouldn't notice.

But that Toothpick guy, he's pretty observant. He might notice.

They crossed into Red's range of vision a few seconds later. She noticed that the Toothpick wasn't quite as toothpicky when viewed from the side. He had a little round gut that protruded from his bony ribs like he'd swallowed a water balloon.

The other two men looked younger than him—late teens, early twenties was what Red figured. She thought this was kind of young to be a rapey scumbag, but then she supposed it was important to the recruiters to get them while the boys were still impressionable.

Anyway, it was the Toothpick she was worried about. He was a known quantity and he was the closest to Sam. It was possible that he might grab her and try to hold her hostage if Red attacked.

This is stupid, Red thought. The chances of her overwhelming all three of them and getting Sam away safely were absolutely minuscule. But she had to try. The alternative wasn't worth considering.

So she didn't think too hard about what she was doing or how she was doing it. Red just pushed the door open and ran as fast as she could down the front yard as soon as the group had their backs to her.

The yard was a little downhill slope toward the road. She felt like she would lose her balance at any moment, but luck was on her side and she didn't trip.

Sam also chose that moment to let out a particularly loud wail, which meant that the sound of Red approaching on the road behind them was masked.

"Shut up!" Toothpick shouted, cuffing Sam across her right ear.

The other two laughed as Sam cried out. None of them were that tall—not even the Toothpick, whose extreme thinness gave an impression of more height than he actually had. She could reach all of their necks. She was sure of it.

Red swung her axe.

It sank into Toothpick's neck and though Red had never relished the idea of killing anybody it felt deeply satisfying to feel the blade slicing through the taut stretch of his skin and into the place where his blood ran free.

She was angry. That was a surprise. She was really angry,

not just scared for Sam or for herself. She was furious, actually—furious that somebody like this was still alive and walking around when her family was dead.

It was always men like this, men who thought that they could take what they wanted and leave the broken scraps of people behind. Men like the ones who'd driven up to her house with rifles with the intent to kill them all. Toothpick and his pals were just like them, just part of a club where anyone who wasn't in it got used up and run over.

Red wasn't sorry to kill them at all. Not at all.

Toothpick's jugular vein opened and blood was everywhere in a hurry but Red didn't stop to see how much. She just yanked the axe out again and did the same thing to the second guy.

Mama's dead. Dad is dead. Adam was eaten up by a monster and here you are, walking around like you deserve to be alive, and you don't.

She had to work fast, had to keep the element of surprise on her side, because if she didn't then they would shoot her. Shoot her, but maybe not to kill. And then she'd be dragged off to their camp and so would Sam and she didn't want to think about what would happen to them there.

The third guy had half a second to react and started to turn toward her, raising his rifle as he did, but she wasn't having any of that and she embedded the axe in his neck too. The slightly changed angle meant that she got more of his vocal cords and the muscle made the axe blade stick and it took more effort to pull it out but she managed.

There was blood hot in her throat and blood hot on her face and her hands but they were down, they were all down, and all that remained was Sam standing there with her eyes as big as her face.

All three of the men had dropped their rifles as they fell, and Red picked up Toothpick's and threw it into a ditch several feet away. Sam stared at Red as if she were an apparition while Red grabbed the other two rifles and did the same thing.

"Get away!" Red shouted. She wanted Sam out of arm's reach.

Sam ran down the road about ten feet, then turned back.

The third man was down and still. The second man was kind of gurgling but he didn't seem like a threat.

Toothpick, of course, had rolled to his back and was grabbing at the seam that had opened in his neck and trying to talk.

Red slammed the blunt side of her axe into the front of his skull without any hesitation.

And then she did it again and again and again because he was a monster, a wolf in the woods who took little girls away and ate them all up and she did not want him to get back up again.

You're a wolf and I'm a hunter. I'm no Red Riding Hood to be deceived by your mask. I know what you are.

She wanted him down. She wanted him done. She didn't want him to come after them.

"Red," Sam said, and her voice was closer than expected.

Red paused. There was blood and brain all over her axe and on her shirtsleeves and her pant legs. There was probably some on her face, too.

"Red, he's dead now," Sam said.

She looked like she was trying valiantly not to throw up.

Red stared down at the mangled remains of Toothpick's head, and the nice lunch that D.J. had packed for her came right back up again. She turned her head to one side and as she did she heard Sam run a few feet off, copying her.

Red stood up and gestured toward the house.

"My bag and jacket are in there," she said. "There's water."

Sam took her cue and ran off to the house to collect Red's things while Red stared down at her handiwork and tried to think of the best thing to do.

This made five people that she'd killed. Five people since she'd left home with Adam, just trying to get to Grandma's house.

Who's the wolf in the woods now?

It sounded like Mama's voice, and that made her heart hurt because Mama had to know that Red would never have chosen this. She was just trying to keep Sam safe.

Sam came flying back with the water and Red's hooded sweatshirt.

"Thanks," Red said. She didn't feel like herself without her red hood.

Red poured a little of the water into her hand and gestured for Sam to do the same so they could clean their mouths.

When they were finished Sam looked at Red and Red looked at Sam. Red wanted to give her a hug but she didn't want to get their enemies' blood all over the little girl's pink hoodie.

"What happened?" Red asked.

Sam's face crumpled up, and then Red had to hug her because she was sobbing like she would never stop.

"I was s-s-s-so s-st-stupid," Sam said. "I t-t-tried to f-f-follow you."

Red leaned back so she could look into Sam's face. "Why would you do that?"

She didn't add, *That* was *really stupid*, even though she definitely wanted to. Red was proud of her restraint. If it had been Adam she wouldn't have been able to resist.

That's the first time you've been able to think about Adam without feeling angry.

She wanted to take a minute to feel that, to examine that emotion from all sides, but Sam was talking again.

". . . wanted to help you," Sam said, wiping her face. "I was really worried about you being out here by yourself. Which is the dumbest thing ever because you were by yourself for a long time before you found me and Riley."

Red nodded, and Sam continued.

"I was awake when you left. I had it all planned out. I left a note for D.J. and Riley so they wouldn't worry and then I went out the bedroom window about ten minutes after you left. I thought I could catch up with you."

"D.J. is probably out of his mind worrying about you," Red said, imagining how he must have felt when he found that note. She didn't acknowledge her own relief that Riley and D.J. were unharmed. "Although I bet Riley is jealous because he thinks we're having an adventure without him."

"Some adventure," Sam said. "I managed to get myself kidnapped."

"Tell me how you did that," Red said.

"Well, like I said—I thought I could catch up with you," Sam said. "But you were moving a lot more quickly than I thought you would be."

"I'm not carrying my pack," Red said.

"I didn't think about that," Sam said. "Anyway, I was trying to follow you and I thought I was being pretty smart, staying in the shadows and everything."

"You had to be pretty smart to get you and Riley to where I found you," Red said. "Don't sell yourself short."

"Well, the sun came up and I was getting thirsty because I was dumb and snuck out the window instead of planning properly. I know how you are about planning."

Sam had only known Red for a short time but she already knew that Red's defining characteristic was thinking ahead.

"Anyway, I came up to that intersection where there's a Target and a little outdoor mall?"

Red nodded again.

"And I thought I could go into one of the stores and get some water. I was going to go back then, back to D.J.'s house, because I knew it had been too long and I wasn't going to be able to catch up to you. So I looked all around and I didn't see anybody in any direction. I started running toward the Target and then out of nowhere there was a gunshot. I knew it had to be them but I thought maybe I could still get away if I ran fast enough. I thought it would be hard for them to find me inside the store."

"It was a good plan," Red said. "There would have been lots of places for you to hide in the Target."

"It doesn't matter if it was a good plan," Sam said miserably. "Because I tripped on a pothole in the parking lot like a dummy and by then they caught up with me."

"Were they coming from the direction of D.J.'s house?" Red asked.

"I think so," Sam said. "I didn't really look once they started shooting at me."

"Did they ask you any questions?"

"Yeah, a lot of them. Like who was I with and where did I come from and stuff like that. I didn't tell them anything, though, even though they slapped me," Sam said proudly. "That skinny guy punched me in the stomach, too."

"I'm glad I beat his head in," Red said.

"Red," Sam said, and she tugged on Red's shirtsleeve. She seemed younger than ten all of a sudden. "I'm glad that you found me."

"So am I," Red said.

Then there was a strange noise from the direction of the bodies, and Red stood up and pushed Sam behind her.

None of them could still be alive, could they?

She had to make certain. She couldn't let any of them get up again. They might report back to their fellows that there was a woman and a child wandering around in their territory.

"Run toward the house!" Red said.

She was going to ensure that the men were definitely dead and then she was going to drag their bodies into the ditch. Red didn't want Sam watching while she did that.

"They're going to get us again," Sam moaned. "They're going to get up and take us away."

She clutched Red's pant leg with white-knuckled hands.

"No, they aren't," Red said.

She was going to make damned sure of that. She should have beaten all of their heads in, not just Toothpick's.

Toothpick's body was shaking and bucking like he was in his last throes of life, but Red wasn't sure why that was happening. Had she done something when she smashed his head in? Something that set off a final surge of nerve endings in his body?

An incomprehensible amount of blood came out of his mouth. Red hadn't even realized there was that much blood left in him.

"What's happening?" Sam screamed.

Toothpick's stomach and chest tore, like a great mouth opening wide.

And then Red saw it.

The monster.

CHAPTER 15

Supped Full with Horrors

AFTER

It's not what we thought it was.

That was what Adam had said, and because of that Red had thought everything Sirois told her was bullshit (except the part where he said the government was responsible—that part she believed).

She thought that it wasn't really a parasite that grew inside people because Adam's legs were mutilated and whatever it was had to be much, much bigger to do that. And because it didn't make any damned sense. She knew enough about science to know that.

Then she saw its teeth—at first all she saw was teeth—and she realized just how wrong she was.

With that many teeth it can do whatever the hell it wants, Red thought.

Her mind tried to shy away from what she was seeing,

because it wasn't supposed to be. There were things like this in monster movies, but they were robots or puppets or computer-generated inserts. They weren't giant black slugs that uncurled from the remains of a rib cage. They didn't have a head made of teeth.

So many teeth—shaped like a great white shark's serrated triangles and stacked like a whirling buzzsaw in concentric circles, and everything about them defied the biological laws of nature.

It seemed to grow even as Red watched, the uncoiling muscles expanding.

Something like this could only be made in a lab, Red thought, and she almost laughed out loud but it would be a hysterical laughing because her brain was on the verge of breaking. She actually *was* inside one of the horror movies that she loved so much, and there was a flesh-eating monster and a government conspiracy to boot.

And Adam had been right all along—it had been a monster living inside people. *A first in all the history of the world*, she thought, and then tried not to choke on her tears and her fear because this was what had killed him.

The Thing That Should Not Be rose up, not unlike a snake from a basket. But Red was no snake charmer, and there were no eyes on the creature to charm.

"Sam," Red said. "Go inside the house."

Red felt rather than saw Sam shake her head no.

"Sam, you have to listen to me. You have to get away," Red said.

"I don't want to leave you," Sam said in her tiniest voice. "What if it runs after me?" "It can't run. It doesn't have any legs," Red said, and snorted. That crazy laughter was brewing just under the surface. She had to get herself under control. There was a kid present and it wouldn't do for Sam to see her sort-of-guardian completely lose her shit.

"Okay. Here's what we're going to do. We're going to back away slowly."

The Thing That Should Not Be made a kind of hissing noise in their direction. Red realized it wasn't vocalizing. It was just spinning its terrible teeth.

If I ever see Sirois again I am going to shake him until he tells me just what the hell these things are and why anyone thought it was a good idea to create them in the first place.

Red shifted her right foot backward. Sam had a death grip on that pant leg, so the little girl shuffled back too.

"Nice and easy," Red said. "We're just going to leave it here and make our way—"

It leapt with astonishing swiftness. Red saw all those teeth filling her field of vision. She swung the axe purely on instinct, using her leg to push Sam back and away from both the axe and the monster.

The axe caught the creature just behind the buzzing sawteeth. It didn't slice clean, though, because Red hadn't put enough effort into the swing. The axe blade was embedded halfway through but the thing was too

Stupid? Powerful? Magical?

to die just because it had a blade stuck inside it. Red drove her arm toward the ground and the creature bucked and fought, trying to coil its head around to bite her wrist. She slammed the creature onto the ground and pushed the axe all the way through and the end with the teeth popped off.

The other end of the creature lay still but the teeth kept moving, trying to bite. Bright purple fluid leaked out of both ends of the monster, looking like nothing so much as a Secret Lab Solution. Red scrambled away from the corpse and bumped into Sam.

"You killed it," Sam said.

Red eyed the whirring teeth. "I don't know about that."

"Well, it can't chase us," Sam said, and she sounded cheerful for the first time since Red had killed the men who'd kidnapped her.

"Yeah, but when are its batteries going to run down?" Red asked.

She stood up, very slowly, and felt her hands shaking. Adrenaline had gotten her this far and now she was crashing. Pretty soon she would feel an overwhelming desire to sleep. They couldn't sleep out here, though—not even in the brick house with its terrible orange color scheme. There were three bodies in the road and Red didn't have the time or the energy to move them very far.

"Here's the thing," Red said. "These guys were on patrol. That means if they don't return within a certain time frame, then someone from their group will come looking for them. Chances are they won't bother walking, either—they'll come out in a truck."

"So we can't be anywhere near these guys when they do that," Sam said, catching on quickly.

"Exactly," Red said. "Not to mention the fact that Riley and D.J. are waiting for us. I think the best thing to do is to roll their bodies into the ditch so they aren't easy to find, and then we should try going across country diagonally to get back to D.J.'s. There's no need for us to follow the road exactly, right?"

"You were only doing that so you could find out where their patrol was going," Sam said. "And I screwed that up."

"Action now, self-recrimination later," Red said. "I'll roll the bodies into the ditch. You go back and shut that front door. Make sure the house looks like it's sealed up tight, but first double-check that I didn't leave anything in the living room."

"You're sending me away because you think I'm too little for this," Sam said.

"Sam," Red said. "This is disgusting work, and I'm already covered with blood. There's really no need for you to be involved. Besides, the first thing anyone will do when they find the bodies is check nearby houses. Let's not leave any clues for them, right?"

"That guy—the one who had the monster come out of him?" Sam said, pointing at Toothpick. "He said he knew I was around because he'd found my unicorn on D.J.'s lawn."

"Your unicorn?"

"Yeah, I had this dumb plastic unicorn that I carried in my pocket. I've had it since me and Riley left the house. It fell out of my pocket, but I couldn't remember the last time I saw it."

That was what Red had seen Toothpick picking up. It was satisfying to have at least one mystery solved.

Sure, even if you don't know where the monsters came from or why or what caused the Crisis and the Cough, then at least you know why Toothpick was so interested in D.J.'s house.

Red didn't have any idea how long it would take for an alarm to be raised, but she had to assume that Pretty Quickly was the answer.

The men were all stupidly heavy to move—even Toothpick, and he'd had most of his insides blasted out of him by the Thing That Should Not Be.

Despite the chill in the air Red was sweating and out of breath by the time she'd pushed all the men into the ditch. She'd mostly kicked the last one, because it was exhausting to hunch over and try to roll the bodies.

Sam sat on the lawn of the brick house, her arms wrapped

around her knees. Red fell to the ground next to her, legs splayed out. She knew they should move, but she was tired down in her soul. The adrenaline surge and all the physical activity left her head nodding.

"What about the monster?" Sam asked

The thing's head had finally stopped whirring, but Red didn't feel confident that it was no longer a threat just because it seemed to be dead.

"Maybe I better just leave it where it is," Red said. "What if I pick it up and an egg gets implanted in me or something?"

Sam wrinkled her nose. "How is that even possible?"

Red shrugged. "I don't know. It looks like an alien, doesn't it? It seems like the sort of thing that would implant an egg just when you think you're safe."

It wasn't an alien, though, not if Sirois was to be believed. This thing had been created in a lab with government funding. *But why? Biological terrorism?* It didn't seem like an awesome idea to make something that would terrorize friend and foe alike. This creature didn't appear to pick and choose its hosts with any discrimination.

"So you're just going to leave it there?" Sam asked.

"Yup," Red said. "Maybe when the next patrol comes along it will confuse them."

Actually, if they were lucky there would be more of these monsters and they would wreck the whole militia. That would be ideal.

"Um, Red," Sam said. "There's someone coming."

She pointed down the road in the direction of D.J.'s house. There was "someone" coming—there were many someones. A whole line of trucks and jeeps that looked far more official than any militia. They were driving very fast.

"Shit," Red said. "Can't I sit down and rest for a damned minute?"

She struggled to stand again, but her body was worn to pieces and wouldn't cooperate. Not even the fear of getting caught by the military was enough to force her legs to stand and run. The cavalcade would be upon them in a minute. She and Sam had certainly been spotted by now, so even if they did hide in the house the soldiers would just come and drag them out.

Well, there was nothing for it. Red would have to brazen it out. It wasn't as if she hadn't done it before. But she couldn't stand up anymore. Her body was done, at least for the moment.

The head jeep pulled to a halt a short distance from where Red and Sam sat on the lawn, and through some kind of magic all the vehicles behind it managed not to run into one another's bumpers.

Sam huddled close to Red's shoulder. Red expected to be surrounded by barking men with rifles, but only the two men in the jeep got out and walked toward them. One of them was very tall—the tallest person Red had ever seen.

"Sirois," Red said as he and his companion stopped by Red's feet.

"That's Lieutenant Sirois to you," he said, surveying the scene.

"Got a promotion, did you?" Red said, and gestured at the two pieces of the Thing That Should Not Be in the middle of the road. "Found one of your 'tapeworms.'"

He looked at the corpses in the ditch, then at the axe in her hand. "And something else, I see. Does your grandma live around here?"

"Nope," Red said. "I'm still on my way there."

"Not traveling alone any longer, either," Sirois said, smiling at Sam. He turned to the man who hovered at his elbow and gave him a muttered order. The other man dashed away.

"Are you going to tell me what that alien thing is all about now that I've sliced one of them in half?" Red asked.

"It's still classified," Sirois said. "We've had reports that there's another homegrown militia here, one that's been kidnapping women and children. Do you know anything about that, or where they're located?"

Red considered. It went against the grain to help the military, but Sirois had ensured that she escaped that besieged town safely. And if Sirois's group cleared out the Kidnapping Militia, then so much the better. It meant that Red and Sam and Riley could cross through the region without worrying about getting snatched up.

"Deus ex machina again, huh? You're going to sweep in and save the day?" Red said.

"Just like in a movie," Sirois said.

"I'll show you where we think they are if you'll bring a map," Red said. "I'd be happy as hell to have you wipe them off the face of the earth."

Sirois looked from Red to Sam to the corpses and it seemed like he finally jigsawed all the pieces together. He went to the jeep to get the map.

In the meantime, a select group of soldiers had approached the remains of the monster. They all wore gloves and face masks made of thin wire mesh, almost like the kind fencers wore. One of them carried a black box with a hinged top.

Two of the men had their rifles trained on the head. Nobody seemed to care much about the rest of the body.

Sirois returned with the map and handed it to Red. She took it without looking, her eyes fixed on the play before her.

The man with the black box set it carefully on the ground close to the monster's head. He flipped the hinged lid open and Red heard something sloshing inside the box.

Two other men approached the head. They held long sticks that had metal grippers on the end, almost like the kind of thing used to pick up trash. One of them carefully closed the gripper around the back of the monster's head.

As soon as the metal touched it the teeth began to whirr again. Red was very glad that her natural sense of caution had kept her from moving the corpse. Apparently these things were dangerous even when you thought they were dead.

The soldier hurriedly dropped the head into the box. Red heard a splash and then the first man snapped the lid into place.

Red gave Sirois some side-eye. "Classified?"

"Definitely classified," Sirois said firmly.

Red showed him the route she'd plotted on the map based on their observations about the patrols.

"We assume they're in this area somewhere. Although you may not have to go looking for them," Red said. "It's been a while now since I . . . disabled this patrol. I figured that someone would be along any minute now to find them."

"Probably a safe assumption," Sirois said, looking at the places she marked on the map.

He went back to the second man in the jeep. They conferred for a few minutes while Red thought about standing up. A little bit of sun was fighting through the cloud cover and she turned her face up toward it.

She thought about all the days that had passed since the Crisis first started—about the girl she had been and the girl she was now. Red had thought she'd known everything at the start. She thought that knowledge, that preparation would keep her and her family safe. It hadn't. No amount of caution or knowledge or perfectly packed supplies could eliminate danger. That danger had taken her family from her.

Red could never really be at peace with that, but she finally accepted that it wasn't her fault. There were no plans that could have saved Mama or Dad or Adam.

It was only then that she realized she'd been carrying that around with her—the belief that if only she had done something different, better, smarter they would still be with her.

I couldn't have saved them.

She didn't know everything. And she didn't need to know everything. Maybe it was better if she never knew why the Crisis started, where the Cough came from, why there were weird monsters coming out of people's bodies.

You're the one who always said you weren't the Chosen One. Only Chosen Ones worry about all that shit. The rest of us just want to live.

She wondered if Sirois was going to let her and Sam leave.

Red closed her eyes for a minute, enjoying the sun, and Sam leaned into her shoulder.

Red cracked an eye open when Sirois cleared his throat.

"You still have some walking to do?" he asked.

"Yes, I do," Red said.

Sirois gave her a lazy, two-fingered salute. "Good luck to you then, Red Riding Hood."

"You too, Lieutenant," she said, and smiled, and pulled her red hood over her curls.

CHAPTER 16

Tomorrow and Tomorrow and Tomorrow

Red and Sam and Riley had been forced to wait a few extra days before leaving D.J.'s house. It turned out that Riley's sore throat had been regular old strep throat, not a harbinger of the Cough. When Sam and Red returned to the house, D.J. had been frantic with worry.

"His fever is very high and he's been throwing up," he said, after he scolded and hugged Sam in equal measure.

"He always throws up when he has strep," Sam said.

"But what can we do for him?" D.J. said. "If we had antibiotics . . ."

Red laughed then. "This is a problem I can solve."

She pulled the amoxicillin out of her pack like Mary Poppins pulling out a lamp from her carpetbag. "Ta-da."

Riley felt better the next morning, but D.J. was adamant that they not travel until Riley had rested for a few days.

"I'd rather wait until Sirois has cleared the nest of vipers, anyway," Red said.

The day of their leave-taking was a tearful one. D.J. hugged both children tight and then surprised Red by doing the same for her.

"Your grandmother is waiting for you," he said, kissing her forehead.

"And your grandchildren are coming to you," she said.

It sounded like a promise, a wish, a thing made of magic that would come true just because it had been spoken.

And then Red and Sam and Riley had started off again.

25 DAYS LATER

Are we there yet?" Riley said.

He'd been plodding his feet into the ground for the last hour or so. Red and Sam had both scolded him and told him that walking that way would just tire him out more, but he kept doing it anyway.

"Keep it up and I'll stop this car," Red said.

"We're not *in a car*," Riley said. "It would be sooo much easier if we were in a car. Then my legs wouldn't hurt and my feet wouldn't hurt and—"

"And our ears wouldn't hurt from listening to you complain," Sam said.

Red winked at her.

"We're just walking through bushes and trees. There's not even any path," Riley said. "I'm going to get poison ivy."

"You're covered from neck to ankle," Red said. "The only place you could catch it is on your tongue, because you won't stop flapping it."

"Ugggghhhh," Riley said, but he was quiet for a while after that.

Then it was suddenly there, the clearing with the two-story cabin where her grandmother lived. Red and Sam and Riley all paused to gape at it for a minute, because it seemed to have just magically appeared, like a fairy ring.

The chimney puffed a steady stream of smoke, and the smell of bread wafted in the air.

"Something smells *good*!" Riley said. "Race you to the door!"

Red hurried after Sam and Riley, because she didn't know what her grandma would do if two strange little kids banged into her house.

They stopped, though, and waited for her to catch up.

"You'd better go first," Sam said.

"It is your grandma's house," Riley said.

Grandma's house. I'm home, finally home, and there are no wolves in these woods.

Red knocked on the door.

ABOUT THE AUTHOR

Christina Henry is the author of the Chronicles of Alice duology, *Alice* and *Red Queen*, a dark and twisted take on *Alice's Adventures in Wonderland*, as well as *Lost Boy*, an origin story about Captain Hook, and *The Mermaid*, a historical fairy tale about P.T. Barnum's Fiji mermaid. Her dark fantasy novel *Alice* was one of Amazon's Best Books of 2015 in Science Fiction and Fantasy, and came second in the Goodreads Choice awards for Best Horror. Christina enjoys running long distances, reading anything she can get her hands on and watching movies with samurai, zombies and/or subtitles in her spare time. She lives in Chicago with her husband and son.

For more fantastic fiction, author events, competitions,
limited editions and more

VISIT OUR WEBSITE
titanbooks.com

LIKE US ON FACEBOOK
facebook.com/titanbooks

FOLLOW US ON TWITTER
@TitanBooks

EMAIL US
readerfeedback@titanemail.com